11.

Erica Lee

Copyright © 2024 By Erica Lee
All rights reserved. No part of this publication may be reproduced, distributed, or transmitted in any form or by any means, including photocopying, recording, or other electronic or mechanical methods, without prior written permission of the publisher, except in the case of brief quotations embodied in critical reviews and certain other noncommercial uses permitted by copyright law.

Dedication

To the world's best store manager. Janelle - thanks for putting up with me constantly writing on the job. More importantly, thank you for demonstrating just how much heterosexual women like beards. I couldn't have written Candace without your inspiration.

Table of Contents

Chapter 1   *6*

Chapter 2   *15*

Chapter 3   *25*

Chapter 4   *35*

Chapter 5   *47*

Chapter 6   *56*

Chapter 7   *69*

Chapter 8   *79*

Chapter 9   *89*

Chapter 10   *100*

Chapter 11   *110*

Chapter 12   *119*

Chapter 13   *129*

Chapter 14   *139*

Chapter 15   *148*

Chapter 16   *158*

Chapter 17	170
Chapter 18	181
Chapter 19	196
Chapter 20	211
Chapter 21	226
Chapter 22	244
Chapter 23	255
Chapter 24	266
Chapter 25	276
Chapter 26	284
Epilogue	292

Chapter 1
TJ

"So, 11:59, huh?"

TJ Edmonds laughed the same way she always did during interviews. It was a light chuckle with a slight shake of her head that made her long brown hair wave. She made sure to show a lot of teeth as if she was truly happy… because she was… of course. "Exactly."

Giving short answers during interviews was another thing TJ had learned since becoming famous. Don't give too much in the beginning. Keep them asking for more. It shows that *they* need *you*, not the other way around.

The late-night talk show host, Veronica Carlson, smiled, as if she knew exactly what TJ was doing. "You've created a whole brand based around one minute, 11:59 PM. You not only have a best-selling self-help book, but also one of the most popular apps on the market today, which is saying a lot, since it's not made to be used for more than a few minutes a day."

TJ laughed again, a little more lightly this time. "That's right." She flashed the camera a wide grin.

"Please tell us more. Let's start with the book. People are saying you cracked the code on not getting attached and moving on. What gave you this idea? Let us inside your brain, TJ Edmonds, *please*."

TJ smiled again, but this time it was sincere. She had won the game. She was being begged for more. "Well, as most people know, one of the hardest parts of a break-up is at night. You're used to having someone who is either with you at night or just a call or text away. A lot of people get in the habit of always ending their night talking to their significant other whether they are together or apart. That causes an attachment that isn't easy to move on from. We, as humans, then crave that connection. Once things end with this person, we are left with this innate need for more. This is why people don't leave terrible relationships. It's why they get back together with people who don't deserve them. All because they have this sick hold on them." TJ stopped herself there. She couldn't put it all out there at once.

"But, you came up with a solution to that, didn't you?"

"I did." TJ winked at the camera. She was sure the camera man probably zoomed in on her blue eyes and long lashes. Her fans loved them after all.

"Are you going to share it or keep us guessing?"

Another laugh. "Since most people already know, I guess there's no reason to keep it a secret, huh?" Another wink. "The secret is to always end your night talking to someone else, even if it's just one sentence. Just one goodnight text. I've heard some people talk about texting a friend or family member instead of their significant other. I personally don't recommend this. People leave. While, statistically speaking, family and friends are less likely to leave than love interests, they can still leave. So, stick with bots. When I wrote my book, I suggested texting a fake number, like one of those spam political numbers for example, or making a fake email and sending a note to that."

When TJ didn't say anything else, the host smiled knowingly. "But you came up with an even better solution, didn't you?"

"Yes. That's why I created my app, which has the same name as my book—11:59. The app is equipped with a bot that people can text before bed."

"Kind of like *Smarter Child* from back in the instant messenger days?"

TJ laughed a sincere laugh once again. She loved this comparison. "Exactly. You can text our bot about anything. You can even choose to play a game or do trivia with it. It's a great way to end the night."

"What about those who go to bed earlier? Most people don't want to stay up until 11:59 to text a robot."

"That's the beauty of the app. It is open for chatting from 8:30 PM until 2:30 AM and programmed to know which time zone the user is in."

"If I understand correctly, the app has been updated so users can talk to each other rather than just bots?"

"That's right." TJ smiled proudly.

"But I hear that's already stirred up quite the controversy, which you are no stranger to. Your methods have always had mixed reviews. In the past, people have claimed your methods are unhealthy and ruin relationships. Now the claim is that your app promotes cheating. What do you have to say to all of that?"

TJ knew this was coming, so she was prepared. She got questions like this all the time. At first, they bothered her, but now she let them roll right off her shoulders. "My intentions are pure. I want to give people the chance to be independent and move on from their past. The app isn't only for people in a relationship who are trying not to get attached, but also for those who have had their heart broken and want help moving on. If it's used for other things… Well, unfortunately, I can't do anything about that. People will do what they want to do."

"Speaking of which, a few people who have used your app to move on have actually found love on it. How do you feel about that?"

TJ groaned internally but smiled at the camera. "Honestly, I'd rather have them use it to cheat." TJ waved a hand and shook her head to show she was kidding. She didn't need to give people even more of a reason to hate her. She had enough haters already. "I'm only kidding. I think it's great that people have found love on it. I just hope they continue to use the app every night." She winked at the camera one more time.

"And how about you? You've been using this method the longest. Is it still working? If the pictures are anything to go by, it seems to be."

TJ knew what pictures she was talking about. Paparazzi loved to get pictures of TJ with different women.

One gag website had even made a calendar with pictures of TJ with a different woman for each month. "Being able to move on quickly has allowed me to enjoy the company of many different women."

The host laughed. "Oh, yes. We've heard all about that. What do you want to say to people who claim you're nothing but a player who leads women on?"

TJ was a lot of things, but she wouldn't consider herself a player, per se, and she definitely didn't lead people on. Everyone she dated knew exactly where she stood. It was her whole platform. "Listen, I'm like the hokey pokey. I always have one foot in and one foot out. The women I date know that. Some see me as a challenge. They all see me as a good time. It's mutually beneficial."

"So we've heard." The host gave TJ another knowing smile that made TJ wonder what *her* intentions were. If TJ wasn't currently in a monogamous relationship, she would have jumped at this opportunity, but Kara was all about monogamy and TJ respected that. She personally preferred an open relationship, but she liked Kara, so she respected her wishes.

The interview went on for just a few more minutes before they said their formal goodbyes and cut to a commercial break. The host shook TJ's hand once more, this time holding onto it much longer than was necessary. "It was seriously so nice to have you here." As if her flirtatious tone wasn't enough, she also ran her eyes up and down TJ's body. "If you want to stick around, I'm not doing anything after filming. I could show you around La La Land."

"I appreciate the offer, but I have an early flight tomorrow. Gotta get back to the girlfriend." *Not very subtle, but whatever.*

"Girlfriend, huh?" The host ran her eyes over TJ's body once again before reaching into her back pocket, pulling out a business card, and handing it to TJ. "If you ever find yourself back in LA and single, feel free to hit me up."

"I'll keep that in mind," TJ answered flirtatiously. Except, that was a lie. She would *never* date a celebrity, the main reason being that they could very publicly trash her name. Yes, her brand was controversial, but there was a difference between conflicting views on a brand and a celebrity dragging your name through the mud. Even TJ wouldn't dare touch that. Even if the body standing in front of her did seem very touchable… if she was single, of course.

She said a final goodbye then left the studio. She pulled her phone from her pocket as she walked to her rental car and smiled when she saw she had a text from Kara. As soon as she saw what the text said, her smile dropped.

The Hokey Pokey?! Really? Am I nothing but a joke to you?

TJ rolled her eyes. Kara was nice and a lot of fun, but she was much more clingy than TJ preferred. She was one of the women who thought she could change TJ. She thought if she stuck around long enough, TJ's views on love and relationships would change. They were just shy of six months in, and TJ was pretty sure Kara was starting to catch on to the fact that it was never going to happen.

Instead of texting back, TJ called her once she was in the car.

"Hello?"

The tone of Kara's voice told TJ she was in deep shit. *Great. Just what I wanted.* "Hey, baby! Of course you're not a joke to me. You do realize that, right?"

"Oh yeah? Is that why we've been dating for almost half a year and you didn't mention me once in your interview?"

Damn live TV. If this had been taped ahead of time, TJ would have had more time before getting the third degree. "I thought you said you didn't *want* to be mentioned."

Kara was quiet for a moment, and TJ knew she had made a valid point. "Okay. I *did* say that, but I also didn't think you'd talk about all of the women you've banged."

"I didn't talk about the women I've banged." *Was Kara even watching?*

"Oh yeah? When you said you *enjoyed the company of many women*, what exactly did you mean by that?"

"People can take that however they want." TJ kept her voice level and calm. She knew Kara was looking for a fight, but that wasn't her style. She avoided conflict at all costs.

"Well, *I* took it as you bragging about your body count, and I don't appreciate that."

"I'm sorry you feel that way." TJ wasn't really sure what else to say.

Apparently, that answer wasn't good enough because Kara made a sound like a growl on the other end of the phone. "Whatever. That wasn't even a real apology. You can go ahead and take your other foot out, because I'm done. I thought if I loved you enough, you would change, but it's useless. You're never going to change, TJ Edmonds."

TJ knew where this was going. Kara was hurt, so now she was going to try to hurt TJ in return. Little did she know, nothing could hurt TJ, because TJ had heard it all. She'd seen and heard terrible things for as long as she could remember. Of course Kara didn't realize that though, because Kara didn't really know her. Hell, Kara didn't even know her real name. "I'm sorry you feel that way."

"Is that the only fucking thing you can say? You're a fucking robot, just like your stupid fucking app. Have fun texting no one tonight."

TJ wanted to comment about how she texts no one *every* night—since it's kind of her whole brand—but she decided it was for the best to let it go. Kara was already mad enough. No need to add fuel to the fire. "I really am truly sorry I hurt you."

"I'm sure you are, TJ. You sound real fucking sincere right now. Good riddance. You may always have someone in your bed, but you'll never be truly happy."

Tell me something I don't know. "I'm going to hang up now. Not because I'm trying to be rude, but because I don't want you to say even more things you might regret later. Goodbye, Kara. It's been fun. I truly hope you find all the happiness in the world."

Kara scoffed then hung up the phone without another word. TJ turned on her music and hummed along as she drove, a small smile surfacing on her face. *Good riddance to you too, Kara.*

It wasn't that TJ was heartless. Even though she would never admit this out loud, the problem was actually the opposite of that. She had much too big of a heart to handle everything she'd been through in her twenty-eight years of life. She had no choice but to shut down and force herself not to feel anymore. Otherwise, she would feel way too much, and she couldn't handle that.

When she got back to her hotel, she nonchalantly waved to the desk clerk and headed to her room, as if everything was normal. As if she hadn't suddenly been dumped by the woman she dedicated the past six months to. By the time she got ready for bed, it was 11:38 PM. Even though she could have passed right out, she forced herself to stay awake.

As soon as 11:59 hit, she clicked on the number that used to belong to the most important person in her life, but now was just a black hole where all of her random messages from the last five years were stored. It didn't take her long to think of what to say. It never did. Texting the person she wished was on the other side was so much easier than talking to anyone else in her life.

Today was weird. My girlfriend dumped me for something I said during an interview. I'm fine obviously. I would probably feel like a terrible person if I could feel anything at all.

Ps - You're still the last thing I think about each day...

TJ put her phone onto the nightstand then closed her eyes as she prepared for the images that were about to flash in front of them once she was asleep. Every night, she was reminded of her past. Sometimes, it was in the form of dreams, but it was more often as nightmares. Neither one was favorable, because even the dreams made it a nightmare to wake up.

"This is your fault!" her mom screamed as she waved around the bottle of vodka. "This is all your fault, Tiffany Jane."

Tiffany winced. If she had known telling her teacher about her mom's boyfriend would make her come unhinged like this, she might have never done it. She was only eight years old though. She didn't understand much, but she did understand that she was much too young for him to be touching her the way he was. It made her uncomfortable. Especially when he leered at her and told her it could be their little secret. She didn't want any secrets with this man. All she wanted was for him to go away.

When she told her teacher, her wish came true. By the time she got home from school, he was gone. Unfortunately, so was her mom. Not in the physical sense, but Tiffany almost wished she was. She was pretty sure she would rather be home alone than with the woman who was screaming at her right now, blaming Tiffany for all the problems in her life, as if it was Tiffany's choice to be born.

"Why did you do it, Tiffany Jane? Why did you make up those terrible lies about him?"

Tiffany shook her head and looked toward the ground. "They weren't lies, Mama. He did those things."

"I don't believe you." Her mom pointed the bottle of vodka at her, but this time it slipped out of her hand and shattered against the linoleum kitchen floor. Her mom pointed to the mess. "Clean this shit up. It's your fault this happened. You always make such a mess of everything."

When Tiffany didn't move, her mom grabbed her arm to pull her over. Tiffany tripped over her own feet and landed on the floor amidst the shattered bottle, her knee immediately starting to bleed from a piece of glass.

Just like that, her mom's angry demeanor suddenly changed. She began to cry and dropped onto the floor beside Tiffany, pulling her into a tight hug that made Tiffany feel suffocated instead of safe. "I'm so sorry, sweetie. I'm so, so sorry. Mama never meant to hurt you. You'll be okay. I promise you'll be okay. Let's just let this be our little secret, okay? Just our little secret."

Tiffany thought she might throw up. Why did all of the grown-ups in her life insist on keeping secrets?

Chapter 2

TJ woke up in a cold sweat. *Shit. Another nightmare.* She took a deep breath and shook away all of the bad feelings. *In with the good. Out with the bad. In with the good. Out with the bad.*

She picked her phone up off the nightstand and was pleasantly surprised to find that the nightmare woke her early enough for her to shower before heading to the airport. Breathing techniques were great, but nothing helped chase away the bad feelings better than a good orgasm. Since TJ didn't know when she would be getting an orgasm from someone else, she decided to take matters into her own hands. Okay… so it honestly probably wouldn't be very long until she found someone else, but that was no reason to keep herself from pleasure right now.

She started the shower and undressed while it heated up. She smiled when she stepped under the scalding hot water. *Perfect.*

As she closed her eyes and ran one hand down her stomach while the other played with her nipple, auburn hair and hazel eyes flashed in front of her. She forced herself to think about all of the other women she had been with. There were plenty of options. But no matter what, the same face kept coming to her mind. A face she *shouldn't* be thinking of right now.

Fuck it. She needed this. She needed the release so badly, and if picturing *her* was how she was going to get it, she didn't have the power to fight it. As one hand continued to work on her nipple and the other ran through her folds, she let her fantasy take over. She pictured that hair surrounding her, those deep hazel eyes staring down at her, and those perfect hands all over her. She was no longer touching herself. It was someone else entirely. She removed the hand from her breast and used it to hold herself up against the side of the shower while she shoved two fingers deep inside of herself. She moved them in and out quickly, pushing harder each time, imagining that face much more vividly with each thrust against her own hand. And then she came. She came harder than she had in a very long time, and even though she knew exactly why that was, she refused to think about it. The orgasm was supposed to clear her mind, not cloud it even more.

    She used the few minutes of shower time she had left to actually get clean then toweled off and got dressed before throwing her clothes into her carry-on bag and running out the door. The drive to the airport was surprisingly calm for LA, and her flight back to Pennsylvania went smoothly as well. Since she didn't live too far outside of Philadelphia, it only took her about thirty minutes to get from the airport back to her apartment, which she was happy about since she missed Mr. Hobbles after spending a few days away from him.

    Mr. Hobbles was a black miniature lop bunny that she adopted four years ago. Before she rescued him, he had injured his paw, which caused him to hobble every time he tried to hop—hence the name. Luckily, he was in good hands with her roommate, Candace, who loved that little fur ball just as much as TJ did.

    "I'm home," TJ announced as soon as she walked in the door. "Where's my love?"

    Candace walked out of her room and smirked at TJ as she crossed her arms in front of her chest. With her short blonde hair and brown eyes, Candace was the spitting image of her mom, which was something TJ struggled with when they first moved in together three years ago. "Love? Really? You're not my usual type, but fine. I'm down."

    TJ rolled her eyes at her *very straight* friend. "Ew. You were almost my sister by adoption. That's weird."

    Candace's smile grew, and TJ was pretty sure she knew what was coming. "Didn't stop you before."

    TJ glared at Candace. "We don't talk about her."

Even if I did think about her while I was getting myself off in the shower this morning. "Remember?" TJ pointed toward her bedroom. "Plus, I was obviously talking to Mr. Hobbles."

"Ah, yes, the only one in TJ Edmonds' life who is worthy of her love."

"Can you really blame me?" TJ tried to keep a joking tone, but there was a bite to her voice.

Knowing she struck a nerve, Candace's smile dropped as she looked toward the ground. "No, I can't. I'm sorry. I was only kidding."

TJ waved a hand and forced a laugh. "No, I'm sorry. I'm just tired and grumpy. I know you're only joking."

Candace was the only person in TJ's life who knew a little bit about what TJ had been through. At least, she knew the parts that she'd witnessed firsthand, which was everything that happened with *her* family. TJ swore she would never have anything to do with anyone from the Baker family. That was until Candace Baker showed up three years ago and told her she had cut off her own family and needed a place to stay. Who was TJ to say no when she was part of the reason Candace had cut them off? Being three years younger than TJ, she was only twenty-two at the time and fresh out of college. TJ may come across as cold to most people, but she wasn't completely heartless. And although she would never admit it, she actually enjoyed living with Candace. They had a very surface-level relationship most of the time, for which TJ was very appreciative.

"Here he is."

TJ was so lost in her own thoughts she didn't even realize that Candace had left the room to get Mr. Hobbles, but now she was standing right in front of her, holding him. TJ gasped when she noticed him and pulled him right into her arms, nuzzling her face up against his. She held him away from her so she could take a good look at him. She had missed that fluffy body and those little patches of white fur around his nose and belly. She held him close again and kissed his nose.

Candace laughed. "If you treated your girlfriends this way, maybe one of them would actually stick around."

"Speaking of which, another one bites the dust."

"Aw, really? I actually kind of liked Kara. It was totally the hokey pokey comment, wasn't it?"

TJ looked up from Mr. Hobbles to roll her eyes at Candace. "Seriously? I don't see what was so bad about that."

Candace smiled proudly. "So, I'm right, aren't I?"

"I don't think you have room to judge."

Candace threw a hand over her chest as if she was offended. "Excuse me. I am still recovering from growing up in an overly religious household."

"Is this a twelve dick…" TJ brought a hand to her forehead as if she accidentally misspoke. "I'm sorry, I mean twelve *step*, program?"

"You know, you should really be nicer to your only friend."

TJ scratched Mr. Hobbles in his favorite spot, right behind his ear. "I'm very nice to Mr. Hobbles."

"Asshole."

"Church kid."

"Too far." Cadence pointed a finger at TJ and appeared to be trying to keep a straight face, but ended up cracking a smile.

"You brought up you know who. Consider us even."

"Fine. Want an early dinner? I figure you probably haven't eaten much since it was breakfast time when you left LA and now it's almost dinner time here."

TJ lifted an eyebrow. "Is this your way of offering to make us something?"

"Yep. I'm going to *make* a call to Dominick's to get us some pizza and wings."

Dominick's. Hell yeah. The tiny hole-in-the-wall Italian restaurant was, by far, TJ's favorite place to eat. "Mm. You sure do know the way to my heart. Keep this up and maybe I would be down for converting you to my team."

"Ew, sisters, remember?"

"Whatever. You wish. I'm going to get a shower to get the stench of the plane off me."

As TJ started to walk away, Candace shouted after her. "No masturbating in there!"

"Already did that today," TJ shouted back, laughing as she made her way down the hall to their shared bathroom.

By the time she freshened up, the food had arrived and Candace already had it arranged on their coffee table with a plate for each of them. TJ inhaled deeply through her nose as she walked over to the table. "God, that smells good. I think I could get off from that smell alone."

"Please don't. It's one thing when I have to hear it coming from your bedroom or the bathroom. It doesn't need to happen right in front of me in the living room, too."

TJ grabbed a slice of pizza and moaned as she took a bite. "Don't act like you don't love it."

Candace fake gagged before taking a bite of her own pizza. "It's not an act. You're a disgusting horn ball."

"Oh yeah? And what are you?"

Candace stuck her nose in the air, as if even being asked a question like this was below her. "I am a distinguished woman who is enjoying the pleasures of having full control of her body after years of being shackled by her faith."

TJ spit out the piece of pizza she had just taken a bite of and cackled at Candace's response. "I love how you can make a bunch of one-night stands sound so poetic. Maybe you should be a writer."

"*You're* the writer. I'll stick to working random jobs until I figure out what to do with this Bible and Theology degree."

TJ laughed once again. With how Candace was now, she almost forgot that's what she went to college for. "I have no clue *why* you ever thought that was a good idea."

Candace threw a piece of her pizza crust at TJ. "Hey! You know my parents were in complete control of *everything*. Just think of how long you stayed in the closet because of them."

"Touché." Only, TJ really *didn't* want to think about that right now. She would be happy to never think about Mr. and Mrs. Baker ever again. Just like so many other parts of her life, it was one she wanted to forget. "Want to watch a movie or something?"

Candace shrugged. "Sure. What are you in the mood for?"

"*Scream*?" Nothing like watching people get stabbed to death to take her mind off things.

Candace groaned. "Seriously? It's June. It's nowhere close to Halloween."

"Scary movies aren't like Christmas movies. There's no rule about when you can and can't watch them."

"Fine, but can we do something that's a little more dark comedy, like *Happy Death Day*?"

"Deal." People were still getting tortured and killed, and that's really all TJ needed right now.

As soon as the movie ended, Candace announced that she was going to head to bed early. Since TJ was still on West Coast time, she wasn't tired at all, so she made the dumb mistake of scrolling through new reviews for her book. Most were good, but of course, it was the bad ones that caught her attention.

☆ **Not even worthy of a star**
I would give this book zero stars if I could. First of all, Miss Edmonds is not a writer and that is very obvious to anyone reading this book who has more than a fifth grade education. Second of all, this is the worst advice I've ever heard. Essentially, her big revelation is that being a stone cold bitch keeps you from getting hurt. This girl is in serious need of therapy.

Tell me something I don't know. TJ laughed to herself. *Do these people really think they can hurt me with the truth?*

☆☆**Pity Review**

I'm honestly only giving this book two stars because I feel bad for the writer. Clearly she's f'ed in the head. Someone must have done a real number on her. She can claim to not get attached, but I think we all know the truth. This chick had her heart broken BAD. Take your money and move on.

Okay. I stand corrected. TJ threw her phone to the other side of the couch as if it was on fire. If she didn't look at it, she didn't have to think about that review, which was clearly wrong. She had moved on, at least in her own way. She was happy. That's all that mattered. She was... happy. *Maybe if I tell myself that enough, I'll actually start to believe it.*

TJ shook her head. Nope. She refused to think like that. Instead, she just wouldn't think at all. She turned on *Happy Death Day 2* and followed it up with *Scream*. She was partway through *Scream 2* when her alarm went off, telling her it was almost midnight. For a moment, she considered not sending the text. She didn't *have* to. She could put her phone away and go to bed. Except... she couldn't.

She grabbed the phone and pulled up the one-way text thread, filled with her innermost thoughts, dreams, and fears (things she would never actually share with anyone).

It was another weird day. I'm not really sure what else to say, except that you're still the last thing I think about each day...

It wasn't a lie. At least, not completely. It was more of a half truth, since she thought about the old owner of that number multiple times throughout the day. TJ groaned as she stood from the couch and walked to her bedroom. It was going to be another long night.

"Hey! I'm Brooke."

Tiffany stared at the outstretched hand in front of her as if it might burn her, but after much consideration, accepted the handshake. "I'm Tiffany."

The girl kept their hands connected then leaned in as if she had a secret to tell. "You're going to love the Finnegans," she whispered. "I've been with them for almost a year now. They're great."

Tiffany nodded. She was just shy of twelve years old, but she already understood how this worked. This was her third time being taken from her mom. At this point, you'd think the state would learn that maybe her mom just wasn't fit to be a parent, but Tiffany was sure that just like the previous two times, her mom would prove herself, then go back to doing the same shit right when Tiffany was back with her.

She honestly wasn't sure why her mom still tried to get her back. She didn't even seem to like Tiffany that much. All she ever did was get drunk or high and then yell about how Tiffany ruined her life. Yet, when she didn't have her, she suddenly wanted her back.

Anyway, this other girl was talking. Tiffany smiled at Brooke then finally took the time to actually look at her. When she did, her breath caught in her throat. Tiffany had never had this type of reaction to another person. Maybe it was the red hair that fell just below her shoulders. Maybe it was the eyes, with a color she hadn't quite identified yet, that sparkled as if they held a bunch of secrets. Maybe it was that this girl was treating her like a person, which was more than she could say for most people, especially kids their age. Most of them just looked at Tiffany as if she was some strange code they had yet to crack, and maybe she was. She wasn't like the rest of them. She had seen things in her life that some of them would never see. Maybe Brooke had too. Maybe that was why Tiffany felt connected to her and had a sudden longing to be her friend. She normally kept to herself in situations like this, but she trusted Brooke. Even without really knowing her, she was willing to take a chance on a friendship for once.

"What grade are you in?" Brooke asked. The way she tilted her head and stared at Tiffany with unblinking eyes made it appear like she was actually interested in the answer. "I'm in seventh. I'm a little old for my grade though."

"I'm in sixth," Tiffany answered when she finally found her voice.

"Really?" Brooke's face lit up. "We'll be at the same school then. That's amazing. I can introduce you to my friends. They're great. You're going to love Woodbury Middle School. I know how scary it is to start at a new school. I was new last year."

Tiffany shrugged. "I've been new a couple of times." That's what happened when you were in and out of foster care.

"I get it." The look in Brooke's eyes told Tiffany she actually did. "I think this is going to be my forever home though. Maybe it will be yours too."

"Yeah. I'm not really sure about that." This time was different with her mom. When Tiffany called 911, she actually thought she was dead. She had no idea what she had taken to get her to that point, but it scared the hell out of Tiffany. Her mom wasn't wonderful, and Tiffany didn't think she ever wanted to go back with her, but it was still her mom. She still loved her.

"Well, no matter how long you're here, I'm going to make sure it feels like home to you."

Tiffany didn't actually know what home felt like, but when Brooke took her hand and guided her inside on her first day at Woodbury Middle School, she was pretty sure she had found her home.

Chapter 3

TJ sat in front of her blank computer screen and stared at the blinking cursor that was teasing her. According to Candace, every good advice book had a sequel. Since TJ was self-published and therefore didn't have a publisher to confirm that information, she had no choice but to listen to her. She was doing well right now, but there would come a point when her book sales would fall, the app would lose popularity, and the media frenzy would die down. She would be forgotten. Because that's how life worked. People forgot you. They moved on, and it was as if you never existed to them in the first place.

TJ pushed these depressing thoughts from her mind and focused on the task in front of her instead. She just needed to stay relevant, and she could do that by writing a second book. *But how do I follow up from my first one?*

She smiled to herself when an idea popped into her head. Her smile grew as she typed out, *Never Say Good Morning: The Eye Opening Sequel to Best-Selling Novel, 11:59.*

Oh, yeah. She could definitely work with this. TJ never said good morning to her significant others. There was something way too intimate about it. She even refused to say good morning to… *nope. Not thinking about her right now.* It was bad enough that TJ had dreamed about *her* every night since getting back from LA a week ago. She refused to dedicate her waking hours to her as well. Except, of course, at the end of the night. Maybe if TJ stopped the texts, she would also stop the dreams, except she knew she wasn't going to stop them. She couldn't. No matter how many lies she told in her book and during interviews, those texts were her security blanket. Sometimes, it felt like that was all she had. Well, that, and a bunch of women in and out of her bed. She smirked to herself. Definitely not the worst thing in the world.

TJ cracked her knuckles and began writing. With her help, no one would ever have to get their heart broken again. People could say what they wanted about her methods, but no attachment meant no heartbreak. It was her duty to save those poor, pathetic, hopeless romantic souls who actually believed the right person *wouldn't* break your heart.

When TJ finally leaned away from her computer to take a break, she was surprised to find how late it had gotten. She closed her laptop then stood from her desk and walked over to her bed. She lay down and pulled her phone out of her pocket. 11:59 PM. Just in time.

I'm working on a new book. You'd totally roll your eyes if you knew what it was about. I miss those eyes. I miss you…

TJ put her phone onto the nightstand then slipped a hand into her pants. Her hand might have been all she had since ruining things with Kara, but, hey, at least *she* wasn't one of those pathetic hopeless romantics. These thoughts, along with the orgasm she gave herself, provided her comfort as she drifted off to sleep.

"Happy adoption day to you, happy adoption day to you, happy adoption day, dear Brooke, happy adoption day to you," Tiffany sang as she carried a cupcake with a "zero" candle into Brooke's room.

She woke up extra early so they could share this moment before anyone else in the house woke up. In the past year since the Finnegans had started fostering Tiffany, Brooke had become her person. Calling Brooke her best friend didn't seem to do their relationship justice. Calling Brooke her sister was too optimistic, even if they were in the process of trying to get Tiffany's mom to agree to terminate her parental rights. Tiffany didn't know why that would be an issue when her mom hadn't made any effort to see or speak to her in the past year, but she had also learned not to have expectations.

"Aw, you made me a cupcake?" Brooke sat up in bed, the sweetest smile ever on her face. "What's the zero for?"

"They say being adopted is kind of like being re-born into a new family, so that makes you zero today." Tiffany knew that was lame, but the only other candle that could have worked said "it's a girl," and that was even more strange. "Also, I didn't make it. I bought it."

"So, if I'm just a baby, does that mean you're going to feed me?" Brooke asked with a laugh.

Tiffany had no idea why, but her ears heated up in response to Brooke's question. Even weirder was the fact that it sounded oddly satisfying. She could picture herself bringing the cupcake up to Brooke's mouth and holding it there while she took a bite, her lips lightly brushing Tiffany's fingers. She had no idea why she was having those thoughts, but she chalked it up to the fact that it was just because of the connection they shared, nothing else. Nothing to harp on. That was for sure. She forced out a laugh and shook her head. "Not a chance."

"Fine." Brooke pushed out her bottom lip in a fake pout. "Will you at least share it with me?"

"That I can do. Halfsies?"

"Always." Brooke patted the spot beside her on the bed and smiled when Tiffany sat down. "Just think, this will be you soon, and then we'll officially be sisters."

Tiffany stared down at the bed and ran her fingers over the extra soft comforter. "I'm not so sure about that. Good things like that normally don't happen to me."

Brooke playfully nudged Tiffany in the side. "Not with that attitude."

"How do you always stay so positive?"

"Things are going to happen whether I'm positive or negative, so I figure I might as well be happy."

"You're like sunshine and I'm rain. I honestly don't understand why you spend so much time with me." Sure, they lived in the same house, but Brooke chose to hang out with Tiffany even when she didn't have to. In fact, she had stayed home from multiple school dances, even though she was a social butterfly, just because Tiffany didn't want to go.

"Flowers need both the sunshine and the rain."

Tiffany laughed. "I didn't know we were trying to grow flowers."

"It's a metaphor, dork."

"A metaphor for what?"

"I've got no clue. All I'm saying is you're important to me, okay? No matter what happens, you'll always be the most important part of my life."

Tiffany laid her head on Brooke's shoulder. She always tried not to get attached to her foster families, but Brooke was different. She couldn't help but get attached to Brooke. "Promise?"

Brooke stuck out her pinky for Tiffany to take. "Promise."

"Shit!" TJ looked beside her at the empty bed. *Shit. Why? Why are the happy dreams always the ones that get interrupted?*

TJ pulled her phone off the nightstand and blinked at it until the time came into view, 2:54 AM. *Perfect.* She could go back to sleep. Maybe if she closed her eyes quick enough, she would get transported right back to that very same dream. Maybe she could watch the way Brooke's eyes lit up when they said the adoption was official. Maybe she could feel the warmth of Brooke running right over to her and jumping into her arms. She could hear the way they both laughed as TJ twirled her around in a circle. She could hear the soft gasp Brooke let out when the Finnegans gave her a cell phone to celebrate.

TJ squeezed her eyes shut and tried her best to conjure up dreams of that time, but as she slipped into darkness, she knew that wasn't what she was going to get.

"Home sweet home," Tiffany's mom announced as they walked into a house that was much smaller than the one she had lived in with the Finnegans. "It's small, but nice. I promise."

As she led Tiffany down the short hallway of the one-story house, Tiffany couldn't help but judge what she saw. Paint was chipping from the walls. The carpet was worn with stains that had probably been there longer than she'd been alive. There was a stale smell throughout the house and Tiffany wondered if it was mold. She had no idea how the State could possibly believe this was a better situation for her than staying with the Finnegans, all because the woman she barely knew at this point was the one to give birth to her.

It was all so fucked up. It was the summer before high school, and she had been taken from the only people she ever let herself care about and transported two hours away.

"Can I have a phone?" she asked, thinking about how much easier it would make things if she could at least call Brooke.

Her mom pointed back down the hall. "We have one right in the kitchen."

"I meant a cell phone."

"We can certainly think about it." Her mom smiled, but it was clearly forced. "Buck has one, but he's two years older than you." Her mom's smile suddenly became genuine. "You're going to love living with Buck and Hank."

Honestly, Buck and Hank both kind of creeped her out, but especially Buck, her soon-to-be stepbrother, if her mom and Hank ever actually got married. Given her mom's track record, that seemed unlikely, but time would tell.

At that moment, the front door opened and Hank shouted, "Honey, we're home."

What is this—the 1950s? *Tiffany thought to herself.*

"Just showing Tiffany her room," her mom shouted back excitedly.

The room was nothing to be excited about, but it was a room with a bed and she appreciated that. The Finnegans had spoiled her the last two and a half years, but she also knew what it was like to have much less, so she appreciated anything she could get.

"You ladies ready to get some dinner?"

When Tiffany turned around, Hank and Buck were standing at her open bedroom door. Buck looked her up and down and licked his lips in such a predatory way that all of her instincts were telling her to run away. "I'm pretty tired," she lied. "I think I'd rather just stay in tonight."

"Well, we want to celebrate so we're going to go." Hank raised his eyebrows as he stared at Tiffany's mom. "Right, sweetheart?"

"That's right." Her mom looked at her with that fake smile once again. "We're just so happy to have you home that we wanted to get out, but if you don't feel up to it, we can bring something back for you."

"That sounds great."

The truth was, it sounded ridiculous. They were really about to celebrate Tiffany being back with them by going out without her?

She made conversation with them for a few minutes but was honestly relieved when they left. She could tell her mom was trying in her own way, but Tiffany felt like she was surrounded by strangers.

Tiffany went to the kitchen, found the phone, and dialed the number she had made sure to memorize. After just two rings, Brooke picked up. "Hey! How's it going?"

Tiffany sat down at the wobbly kitchen table and sighed. "It's going."

"Come on. You have to give me more than that. What's it like being home?"

"This isn't home." Tiffany's voice cracked as she tried to stop herself from crying. "You know home will always be sitting next to you in your bed and watching a movie together."

"I know." Brooke's voice sounded just as sad as Tiffany felt. "I really miss you."

"I miss you, too."

Don't cry, Tiffany. Don't you dare cry, *she thought to herself.*

"Maybe I can get Mom and Dad to drive me to see you sometime soon."

"I would really like that, actually."

"Then we'll definitely make it happen."

"Do you have anything going on tonight? It's really nice to hear your voice, and I'm not ready to say goodbye."

"You know I'd cancel every plan for you, Tiff. We can talk for as long as you want. Also, you know it's never really goodbye with us. I'll always be with you."

I'll always be with you.

I'll always be with you.

I'll always be with you.

The words seemed to echo within Tiffany's brain, getting quieter each time until they faded out completely.

"No," TJ said to herself as she tossed and turned in bed. "Please no. Come back. Please come back."

As she slept, this scene slipped into another scene. It was a scene she knew way too well and didn't want to see right now.

There was a light tap on her door and before she could even say anything, Buck walked through the door into her room. Even though it was dark, she could see his white teeth as he leered at her.

"What are you doing here?" she whispered.

Buck took a few steps toward her bed and ran his tongue across his top teeth. "I think you know exactly what I'm doing here."

"Interrupting my sleep?"

In the year since moving back in with her mom, Tiffany had grown a big distaste for Buck. He was lewd and classless and was beginning to creep her out more and more with each passing day. He reminded her of a certain man from her past that she had no interest in thinking about. Just the thought alone made her sick.

"I think we both know that's not it." A few more steps. "Come on, Tiffany Jane. I see the way you look at me."

"With disgust? You're right."

"I know you like what you see." Buck laughed as he took a few more steps. "Why fight it anymore?"

Tiffany was seething. "Buck, I'm telling you, get the fuck out of my room right now."

"I like when you talk dirty to me." Buck was now standing right beside her bed, hovering over her like the predator he clearly was.

"Buck, this is your last warning. If you don't get out of my room right now, you're going to regret ever coming in here."

"Is that a threat?"

"It's a promise."

His face came closer. That goddamn ugly ass face. Closer. Closer. Closer.

  TJ sat straight up in bed. Her breathing was ragged and her heart was beating at a mile a minute. She took one big breath in then blew it out. *In with the good. Out with the bad. In with the good. Out with the bad.*
  What was good though? She hadn't even hooked up with anyone since getting back to Pennsylvania. Maybe that was exactly the problem. That could explain why the nightmares had gotten even worse lately. She just needed a little loving, and as soon as the sun came up, she was going to go out and find it.

Chapter 4

"I still can't believe I'm actually out on a date with TJ Edmonds. It's so crazy. You've, like, written a whole book. How weird is that?"

TJ laughed politely. "Totally weird."

Avalon Grayson wasn't the brightest crayon in the box, but she was certainly nice to look at. At seven years TJ's junior, she didn't have as much worldly experience, but she was old enough to meet out at a bar, and that's really all that mattered to TJ right now. Between her long blonde hair, dashing blue eyes, and big boobs, she was exactly what TJ needed to keep her mind off of things.

Avalon giggled and twirled a piece of hair around her finger. "My friends just aren't going to believe this. I bet you're totally rich, aren't you? You probably live in this big mansion all by yourself. I bet it gets lonely there." Avalon bit her bottom lip as if she had to seduce TJ into sleeping with her tonight. The girl didn't have to do anything. It was already a done deal.

"Something like that." *A small apartment with a roommate who won't leave me alone, but close enough.*

"So, what do you say we get out of here and check it out?"

Shit, think fast. "I have a better idea. Do you have roommates?"

Avalon pushed her bottom lip out in an exaggerated pout. "I do. Three of them."

"Want to really make them jealous?" TJ lifted an eyebrow. "We could go back to your place."

A sly grin surfaced on Avalon's face. "I like the way you think."

And I like the way you look. "Soon that won't be the only thing you like about me."

"I'm sure it won't."

Luckily, Avalon's apartment wasn't far from the bar where they met, so after a ten-minute walk, they reached their destination.

"All three of my roommates are home tonight. How fucking perfect is that?" Avalon asked with a giggle as she worked to unlock her apartment door. "Only one of my roommates is queer, but all of us have agreed we would definitely bang you if we had the chance." Avalon stopped fumbling with the door and looked at TJ with wide eyes. "Not that I'm using you or anything."

TJ licked her lips and leaned against the wall. "Honestly, I hope you use me a lot tonight."

"Okay, shit. That was so sexy. You don't mind if we don't stop to chat, right?"

"I would prefer we didn't." TJ nodded her head toward the door. *Why the hell hasn't she opened it yet?* "Need any help with that?"

Avalon giggled once again. "No, sorry. I'm good." Finally, she pushed it open and led TJ into the apartment that was exactly what she expected of someone in their early twenties.

Three girls, who TJ assumed must be Avalon's roommates, were sprawled out across the old furniture. On the walls hung a mishmash of posters and motivational quotes. Shoes, socks, and other random clothes were scattered across the floor.

"Hey, guys! This is TJ Edmonds. I'm sure you all know that though. We'll be in my room." Avalon turned to the girl lying on the couch. "You'll have to stay out here tonight. Sorry, babes."

"Ladies." TJ nodded at all three of them. "I'd like to apologize in advance for any noises you may hear tonight." She winked then followed Avalon back toward her room, satisfied at the whispers and giggles they were leaving behind them.

"They seemed nice," TJ said once they were inside Avalon's room that looked very similar to the parts of the apartment TJ had just walked through.

"I don't want to talk about them." Avalon put her hand on TJ's chest and pushed her onto the bed.

Hell yes. Tonight's going to be fun. "What do you want to talk about?" TJ teased.

"I don't want to talk."

This girl was a fireball and that's *exactly* what TJ needed tonight. "Good. I have much better uses for my mouth. Speaking of which…" TJ scooted up the bed and lay her head on the pillow. "Take your clothes off. I'm ready for you."

"Do you mean…?" Avalon giggled instead of finishing her sentence.

"Yes. I want you to ride my face… right now." Foreplay could wait. TJ was ready to get the night started, and Avalon was the perfect appetizer.

Luckily, Avalon wasted no time stripping out of her clothes and revealing the perfect body. *Those curves.* TJ was ready to eat her up. *Literally.*

Avalon positioned her legs on either side of TJ's head and her center right above her mouth. She let it drift above her like a carrot on a string, just out of reach. The perfect tease.

"Come on, baby. I'm ready for you."

"I'm not going to hurt you, right?"

"Trust me, babe, I've been the operator of this ride quite a few times. I know exactly what I'm doing." Then a thought hit TJ. Avalon was young and seemed nervous. Was this new for her? "Are… are you okay with this? Because if you need to slow down, we can."

"Did TJ Edmonds just ask permission to eat me out? That's so sexy." Another giggle. "And, no, I don't want to slow down."

Avalon finally lowered herself onto TJ, and TJ wasted no time getting started. She ran her tongue across the length of Avalon's center and moaned. This girl even tasted perfect.

Any reservations Avalon may have been having before seemed to go away as she moved her body against TJ's mouth. TJ took advantage of this by licking and sucking every spot she came in contact with. Avalon moved even closer to TJ and made the greatest mixture of noises TJ had ever heard. As if that wasn't enough, she rested her hands against the wall then began pounding it with the rhythm of TJ's tongue. TJ had no idea how much of this was real and how much of it was a show for her friends, but she didn't care. She was so turned on that she was pretty sure she was just as wet as Avalon at this point. Well, maybe. If the taste of Avalon's pleasure on her tongue was anything to go by, her noises weren't completely fake.

When TJ knew she was close, she brought her hands to Avalon's ass and pulled her even closer. It only took a few more strokes of her tongue before Avalon came in her mouth. *Sexy. As. Hell.*

Avalon fell onto the bed beside her and struggled to catch her breath. "I'll… be… good… in… just… a minute. Just… need… to… catch… my breath."

"Take your time. I'm enjoying the view." What a view it was. With each deep breath, that perfect chest moved up and down, making TJ's mouth water. She was ready for more but knew it would be worth the wait.

And it certainly was. After three more rounds, TJ was exhausted. Technically, she could have gone for more with just a little break, but it was now 11:47. To make sure she wasn't in the middle of anything at 11:59, she had to cut it off now. "It's been fun, but I better get home."

"So soon?" Avalon asked, that exaggerated pout coming out once again.

TJ stood from the bed but leaned down to place one more kiss on those pouty lips. "Sorry. Big day tomorrow." *Doing absolutely nothing.*

"I understand, Miss Best-Selling Author."

You don't, but it's really cute that you think you do. "Thanks, babe. You have my number. If you ever want to use me again, just give me a call."

"I'll text you. For sure."

Of course you will. "I look forward to it."

TJ smiled as she slipped back into her clothes and left Avalon's room. Avalon wasn't the type of girl you spent forever with, at least not at the point she was at in her life right now, but she was sweet and sexy, and that's all TJ needed. It was the perfect transaction. TJ got no-strings-attached sex, and Avalon could forever brag about how she hooked up with TJ Edmonds. Even though the whole thing seemed crazy to her since she was nothing special at all, she was sure Avalon and her friends would be talking about this for a long time.

When she walked into the living room, she noticed that Avalon's roommate who had been banished to the couch was still awake. TJ pointed her thumb down the hall. "You can have it back now."

The girl stared as if she couldn't believe TJ was talking to her, mouth agape and eyes wide. "Th-thanks."

TJ nodded her head then walked out of the apartment. She removed her phone from her pocket and began to type.

Today was a better day. Not great, but none of them are. Is life ever really great for anyone or are we all just trying to survive? Sometimes I think that's all this is. A bunch of people walking around trying to prove that they are happy, when no one really is.

I sound like such a pessimist right now. You would HATE that, ha. I miss the motivational speeches you used to give me. I miss making fun of you every time you got really caught up in whatever you were talking about. I miss you.

No matter what, you'll always be the last thing I think about at night...

TJ smiled a sad smile as she looked at the number that would never respond then shoved her phone back into her pocket. She hoped the sex was enough to keep her from having nightmares tonight, but only time would tell.

"You better start explaining, young lady. And you better have a damn good reason for why I was woken up in the middle of the night to the sounds of my boy screaming and found him in your room holding onto his balls while his nose bled all over your carpet."

Instead of looking at Hank, Tiffany smirked at Buck, who now had a tissue shoved up his nostril and an ice pack on his crotch. She was proud of herself. After the sudden shock, and terror, of him showing up in her room, she snapped into self-defense mode and gave him what he deserved. He got what every man who ever thought he could touch a woman without her consent deserved. She wouldn't apologize for that. No way.

After a few minutes, she looked up at Hank and smiled. "I'll tell you exactly what happened. Your son came into my room and tried to touch me, even after I told him no multiple times. Since words weren't working, I had to use actions instead."

A scoff across the room brought Tiffany's attention to her mom just in time to see her roll her eyes. "Not again." She gave Hank an apologetic look. "She's done this before. I thought she was over it."

Tiffany practically leaped from her seat. Her mom couldn't be serious right now. "Done what before? Been touched inappropriately? You're right. I am over it. That's why I gave Buck exactly what he deserved."

"She's obviously lying. I wouldn't touch her with a ten-foot pole, no matter how much she begged for it, and trust me, this girl's asking for it."

"You do walk around the house in those booty shorts. I believe my boy if he said he didn't do anything, but he is a man. He has wants and needs. You can't just parade your body around and not expect to have any consequences."

"Are you fucking kidding me right now?" Tiffany looked around the room in disbelief. *"I'm the victim here and you're all just going to act like nothing happened? You're going to somehow try to put this back on me? What a fucking joke."*

"You better clean up that mouth of yours right now, young lady," her mother warned.

Tiffany couldn't believe it. The woman claiming to be a whole new person the past year hadn't changed at all. She was still the same mother who wasn't there for her at the scariest time in her life. She had never really been there for her.

Tiffany threw her hands up in the air. "That's it. I'm out of here. I don't have to stay here and take this." Before leaving, she turned around and pointed a finger at her mom as if she was the adult. "You better think long and hard about the decisions you make tonight. I can make sure I'm taken out of your life just as quickly as I was put back in it." Tiffany didn't actually know if she had that kind of power. Honestly, it didn't feel like she had any control over her life at all, but at least the threat did appear to have some effect on her mom, who swallowed hard before looking to the ground.

Tiffany walked out of the house, making sure to slam the door on the way out to really make her point. She walked through town until she got to the one pay phone that still existed there. She dialed the one number she had memorized and started to cry as soon as she heard Brooke's tired voice.

"I'm really sorry. I know it's the middle of the night. I just didn't know who else to call. Can you just talk to me for a few minutes? Please."

"Where are you?"

"Some 24-hour mart by my house."

"Is it safe there? If not, go somewhere that is and give me the address. I'm coming to get you."

"Brooke. You can't. It's the middle of the night. The Finnegans would never let you. You don't even have your senior license yet."

"You know they sleep through everything. They'll never even know."

"Yeah, until they wake up and find me in their house."

"We'll figure it out. I don't really care. Something clearly happened and you need me. I'm your person. You're mine. I'm going to be there for you." Brooke was silent for a moment before she spoke again, this time more quietly. "What did happen, Tiff?"

"It was Buck. He… he…" Tiffany couldn't even get the words out before she started to sob again. Luckily, Brooke knew her well enough that she didn't have to.

"I'm going to kill him. I swear to God, if you tell me it's okay, I'll kill that little shit."

It wasn't like Brooke to talk like that, so Tiffany couldn't help but smile. "I don't need you to kill him. I just need you. I'll be fine at the 24-hour mart. It's only two blocks from my house. I know the owner."

"Okay. Stay safe and I'll get there as quickly as I possibly can. And Tiff?"

"Yeah?"

"I love you more than anything in the world."

Tiffany's body warmed all over in the same way it always did whenever Brooke said sweet things to her. "I love you too, Brooke."

After hanging up, Tiffany went into the 24-hour mart where the owner, Mr. Blake, sat by the cash register on his phone. Instead of saying anything, he gave her a knowing smile and threw her a bag of chips. The two of them sat in silence like this for the next two hours until Brooke's car pulled up out front. When Tiffany said goodbye to Mr. Blake, he stared at her for a long time like he wanted to say something but just waved goodbye to her instead.

As soon as Tiffany saw Brooke's face, she could feel the weight of the night being lifted from her shoulders. Once she was in the car, Brooke reached across the middle console and pulled Tiffany into her arms.

"How do you always do that?" Tiffany asked as she melted into Brooke's hug.

"Do what?"

"Make me feel safe with just one touch."

Brooke pulled back and put her hands on Tiffany's cheeks. "I hope I never stop being your safe space."

Looking into Brooke's eyes at that very moment and seeing all of the sincerity in them, Tiffany knew she never would. They spent most of the car ride relatively quiet. Brooke had one hand on the wheel and the other gently gripping Tiffany's. They listened to the music that Brooke knew Tiffany loved and every so often the two of them sang along to it together. It was truly the first time in months that Tiffany had felt like herself.

When they pulled up at the house, Tiffany saw a light on inside and could tell it was coming from the kitchen. Brooke lifted her phone and whispered a barely audible, "Shit."

"Busted, huh?" Tiffany asked quietly.

Brooke squeezed Tiffany's hand and gave her a reassuring smile. "It will be okay. I promise."

They walked into the house, still hand-in-hand, and were greeted by both Mr. and Mrs. Finnegan sitting at the kitchen table. Their eyes were tired but wide. They didn't necessarily look mad, but they also didn't look happy.

Mrs. Finnegan smiled sweetly at Tiffany. "First of all, it's really wonderful to see you, honey. I don't want you to think it's not." She stood from the table and pulled Tiffany into a tight embrace. "I want you to know that you're always welcome here." She pulled out of the hug and switched to her stern face. "With that being said, you girls need to tell us what's going on here."

Brooke took a step toward Mrs. Finnegan. "Tiff was in a really bad situation, so I went to help her. I know I shouldn't have snuck out, but it was an emergency."

Mr. Finnegan looked at Tiffany, concern now written all over his face. "Are you okay?"

Tiffany nodded. "I am now. Thank you, sir."

"Could we save the interrogation for later, though?" Brooke asked. "Tiff is exhausted. She needs rest. Please let her sleep for a little before you attack her with questions."

Mr. Finnegan sighed and rubbed his face then looked toward his wife. The two of them stared at each other for a long time, as if they were having a silent conversation.

When they finally broke eye contact, Mrs. Finnegan sighed and nodded. "I guess that's okay. You do look exhausted. I need to tell someone you're here though."

"Could you just call my mom?" *Tiffany pleaded with her eyes.* "I don't want to bring anyone else into this."

Everyone in the room understood what she was asking much too well, so Tiffany was happy when Mrs. Finnegan nodded in agreement. "Okay. Just give me her number." *She looked over at Brooke.* "Take care of her, okay?"

"Of course, Mom."

After Tiffany wrote down the number for Mrs. Finnegan, Brooke took her hand and led her upstairs to her room. The room across the hall, that used to be Tiffany's, now had a sign that said, "Mateo's room: enter at your own risk."

"Still like your foster brother?" *Tiffany asked as they walked into Brooke's room.*

"Mateo is a little stinker, but he's wonderful." *She looked at Tiffany with apologetic eyes, as if she was afraid she had said the wrong thing.* "He's not you, of course."

"No one could be, right?" *Tiffany tried to keep her voice light.*

"No. No they couldn't." *In contrast, Brooke's tone wasn't light. Her words were heavy with meaning.* "Go ahead and lay down. Is there anything else I can get for you?"

Tiffany shook her head. "Do you think you could just… hold me?" She and Brooke had shared a bed before, but something about it felt different this time. She felt like she was somehow asking for more.

"Of course I can."

They both crawled into bed and Brooke offered her arm to Tiffany, wrapping it around her when Tiffany snuggled in close to her. Tiffany rested her head in the crook of Brooke's neck and breathed her in. How was it possible to feel this safe with someone? How could someone's touch make her forget about everything else in her life? Part of her worried what it all meant—the fact that she felt different around Brooke than anyone else in her life—but the bigger part of her didn't want to overthink it. They were together. Brooke made everything better. That's really all that mattered.

As she drifted off to sleep, she wished she could stay right there in Brooke's arms for the rest of her life.

When TJ opened her eyes, she was no longer in those arms. She was back in her bed, all alone. Alone, just as she had been for years now. Even with the multiple women who made their way in and out of her bed, she was still alone. As her eyes stung with the tears that threatened to fall, she almost wished tonight had been another nightmare.

Chapter 5

TJ stared down at the phone she had been avoiding all day for reasons even she didn't quite understand. She had two emails asking about interviews, a bunch more pertaining to her book and the app, ten new messages on the dating app she used, and three texts.

She clicked on the text from Avalon and smiled as she read it. *Free tonight? I came up with a few new positions for us to try.*

In the month since they first hooked up, TJ and Avalon had gotten together six more times. At this point, they didn't even waste time on petty things like drinks. TJ would go right to Avalon's apartment and they would head straight to her room, where they would have sex that somehow became hotter every single time.

Even though the prospect of sex, especially with new positions, was tempting, TJ wasn't feeling up to it. Her mental health was at an all-time low, and no one should have to deal with that. Especially not a hook-up buddy. *Not tonight. Sorry. I have other plans. Raincheck?*

Avalon didn't need to know that her plans were to sleep as much as possible. The next text was from Candace. This one made her laugh.

Ey, shithead! Are you going to stay locked in your room all day? I'm bored to tears!

To this, TJ simply responded, *Yep.*

She knew Candace wouldn't let her off that easily, so she wasn't surprised when another text came through right away. *Dinner at least? Isn't that podcast interview going up tonight? We could order pizza and listen.*

Speaking of which... that was the other unread text on TJ's phone. Instead of responding to Candace, she pulled up the text from Elon Drumheiser, the operator of the podcast "Elon's Elites," which TJ had been interviewed for last week. *Podcast is going live at 9pm tonight! Tweet,* email, send out your gay bat signal. Do whatever it is you do to make sure your groupies get my listens nice and high.*

Elon was a complete douchebag. There was no other way to put it. For the longest time, she vowed she would never do his podcast for that very reason, but she somehow let him convince her she needed this podcast to stay relevant. The questions he'd asked her were weird and overly intrusive, so she couldn't even imagine what it was going to sound like.

TJ ignored his text and went back into her text thread with Candace. **The podcast doesn't go up until 9.**

Okay, grandma. I didn't realize you would be in bed that early.

I won't be. It's just a little late for dinner.
I'll have a snack.
Dick?
I was thinking more like chips, but that doesn't sound like such a bad idea. Maybe I'll go on Tinder.
Have fun. I'll see you at 9.
Cool. Meet you in the living room.

TJ looked at the time and was happy to see that it was only five. That meant she could wrap herself up in her comforter and hide from the world for a few more hours. She wasn't sure if she actually wanted to take a nap or not, but she didn't think she had much of a choice. She was exhausted from being stuck inside her own brain all day. She crawled into bed, set an alarm, and didn't fight it as her eyes shut and she drifted off to sleep.

"This is all your fault, Tiffany Jane," Tiffany's mom said as she stared down at the bills on the table. "I wouldn't be having trouble paying these if you hadn't scared away another boyfriend of mine."

Scared away was certainly an interesting way of putting it. Tiffany guessed in a way it was true. After showing up at the Finnegans in the middle of the night six months prior, Mrs.

Finnegan insisted on being the one to drive Tiffany home. Tiffany and Brooke sat in Tiffany's room while Mrs. Finnegan talked to Tiffany's mom. They couldn't hear everything that was being said, but it was pretty clear Mrs. Finnegan was making some big threats.

After Brooke and Mrs. Finnegan left, Tiffany was banished to her room once again so her mom and Hank could have a conversation. She couldn't hear this one at all, until the end when Hank raised his voice so loud she was sure everyone in the neighborhood could hear him.

"Fuck this shit. I'm not staying in a place where my son gets threatened by some resident saint from your goddamn past. He's a football star. He can't have false accusations being thrown around about him. Fuck it. You're not worth it. Good luck with that slut of a daughter of yours."

When he slammed the door, Tiffany squeezed her eyes shut, hoping that would somehow transport her out of this time and place. Unfortunately, it didn't. She laid there all day listening to Hank and Buck come in and out of the house, both of them yelling as they removed their items one by one. At least, that's what Tiffany assumed was happening, given the noises she was hearing.

Her suspicions were confirmed later that night, when she finally came out of her room and found over half of the small house emptied out. There was no furniture, no TV, and only a few sets of dishes, bowls, and silverware.

Tiffany's mom was locked in her room and remained there for the next four days. When she came back out, she was completely different. The new woman she had been pretending to be since Tiffany moved back in with her was completely gone. The monster Tiffany remembered from her past was back.

That's how it had been the past six months. Terrible. Absolutely terrible. "I can get a job," Tiffany said quietly. "I've been meaning to anyway." The reason she wanted a job was so she could finally pay to get a cell phone, but if she had to get a job to keep their electricity from being shut off, she would do it.

"I think you should." Tiffany's mom stood from the table and walked toward her until they were toe-to-toe, clearly trying to intimidate Tiffany. "You know what else I think you should do?"

"Wh-what?" Tiffany hated to admit it, but the intimidation tactic was actually working.

"You should ditch that bitch of a friend of yours. The one whose mom got us into this mess. I never liked that lady, and she has programmed that girl to be just like her."

Tiffany shook her head. "No." Her mom scared her, but she couldn't ever scare her enough to get her to agree to something so asinine.

"Excuse me?" Her mom furrowed her eyebrows and showed Tiffany her teeth, as if she was an animal getting ready to fight. "Maybe I should have worded that differently. You will ditch Brooke Finnegan. I don't ever want to hear about you going to see her, and I certainly don't ever want to see her around here."

Normally, Tiffany wasn't the type to talk back to a grown-up, but she put her foot down when it came to Brooke. She didn't care who she was talking to. She would always fight for Brooke. She refused to back down. Especially because Brooke just happened to be on her way right now, and there was no way Tiffany was going to tell her to turn back around.

She had been looking forward to this for weeks. "Maybe I didn't make myself clear. Brooke is my best friend, and nothing you do or say will ever change that."

Before Tiffany knew what was happening, a hand slapped her face. "Don't you dare speak back to me like that."

Tiffany brought a hand to her cheek, which was now screaming in pain. In the times she had lived with her mom, she had heard her yell, curse, and make degrading remarks multiple times. But never before had her mom laid a hand on her. This was all new, and the scariest part was, she didn't look like she regretted it at all. Tiffany ran past her and out the back door because she was afraid of what she might do next. As she rounded the corner to the front of the house, she ran right into someone.

"Tiffany?" a soft voice said, as warm arms wrapped around her. "Oh my God, Tiff. What happened? Are you okay?"

Tiffany shook her head. "Could we please get out of here?"

The blaring of her alarm startled TJ awake. *Shit.* It was already 8:45. Hopefully, Candace ordered the pizza because she obviously hadn't.

When TJ walked into the living room, she found Candace sitting on the couch with her legs propped up on the coffee table and a slice of pizza just inches from her mouth.

"I was getting worried you weren't going to show." Candace nodded toward the TV. "I connected my computer to the TV so we can hear you nice and clear."

"Great." TJ took a seat next to Candace and grabbed a slice of pizza.

"Come on, it can't be that bad."
"This guy is a grade A douche."
"Then why'd you do the interview?"

TJ shrugged. "Exposure."

Before Candace had the chance to respond, the podcast started to play through the TV speakers. TJ let herself zone out through the introduction and preliminary normal interview questions. All she was really worried about was how she sounded when he started digging. She wanted to make sure her voice didn't quiver when he brought up things from her past that she'd rather forget.

"You must know a lot about moving on since my sources tell me you were in and out of multiple foster homes growing up."

TJ didn't know who Elon's sources were, but she wanted to kill them. "That's right," her voice answered on the podcast.

That's right. Short and sweet. In this case, she wasn't using the *leave them wanting more* tactic. Instead, it was about Elon minding his own goddamn business.

"Is that really all I'm going to get?" Elon asked with a chuckle. TJ remembered what came next, so she braced herself. "At least tell us this much. Did you ever end up finding a family for yourself?"

TJ cringed as she waited to hear her answer. The question had shocked and upset her so much she had practically blacked out during her answer. All of her focus was on not letting this asshole know how much he had upset her.

"Some people are born into a family. Some people find them. Others, like me, buy their family." *Oh yeah. Now TJ remembered.* She smirked to herself.

"How does someone *buy* a family?" Elon chuckled once again, but this time it sounded more strained.

"Easy. I went on critterrescue.com and paid the adoption fee for Mr. Hobbles—my miniature lop bunny. Also, just for the record, critter rescue is not sponsoring this video, but if you want a little furry friend, they're great."

"How adorable." Elon's voice was dripping with sarcasm. "You couldn't get adopted, so you did the adopting."

"Mr. Hobbles is the perfect baby. He doesn't complain, he doesn't talk back, he's a great snuggler."

"And an added benefit is that he can't leave you like everyone else in your life has."

There was a beat of silence, and TJ knew that was because Elon had edited out her comeback. Instead of her reply, *"Yeah. I guess you wouldn't know anything about that. People have to come into your life in the first place to leave, but no one ever chooses to be around you,"* the next sound was another question from Elon.

"Speaking of people leaving, there's a theory out that you are all about moving on because you had your heart broken in the past. Some people believe you used this experience to help develop your brand. I believe something terrible happened and you never actually moved on from it."

There was another beat of silence, before TJ's voice responded. "I didn't hear a question there."

"Avoidance. Great tactic. You know what I'm asking. What's the truth?"

"The truth is, I've been lucky to have a lot of great women in my life. My tactics have allowed me to have *many* wonderful experiences."

"More avoidance. Interesting. So, you're saying there's never been someone in your life that stood out above all the rest? Someone who actually made you want to stick around?"

This was another question TJ had essentially blacked out for. This question immediately made her mind go to the one person she actually wanted to stick around. The person it had killed her to lose. TJ listened to her answer and hoped her voice didn't give anything away.

"I'm TJ Edmonds. I love women. *Women.* That's plural. While I truly cherish the time I've spent with each woman from my past, no one could ever make me want to settle down. I don't need anyone. Just myself. I'm all I ever needed and all I ever will need. And that's that."

Her voice didn't give anything away, but her answer still made her sick. It minimized certain people in her life that didn't deserve to be minimized. One of those people was the woman she couldn't ever truly get off her mind, but the other one was sitting right next to her on the couch.

Speaking of which… Candace blew out a long breath. "Can I be honest with you, dude? I get why you answered that way. That guy was baiting you during this whole podcast. He's a jerk, and I honestly don't understand how anyone listens to him. I know you well enough and understand enough about your past to realize most of your answers were complete and utter bullshit. Not going to lie though, hearing everything you had to say here still kind of hurt. I know we've never really talked about it, mostly because I'm afraid I'll scare you away, but you're the only family I have. I guess I just kind of wish you felt the same way."

Shit. TJ had really done it now. "Candace, I…."

Candace shook her head and stood from the couch. "You don't have to explain yourself. Seriously. I think I'm getting my period, because I've been an emotional bitch lately. It's really no big deal." She took a few steps then turned back around, a smile that didn't quite reach her eyes now on her face. "You seriously killed it though. That guy was trying to break you, and you didn't let him." Candace turned back around and was out of the room before TJ could say anything else.

TJ sat on the couch for a long time, frozen by her own feelings. Of course she didn't let him break her, because how could you break something that was already broken?

When TJ was finally able to get herself off the couch, she moped back to her room and threw herself onto her bed. She took her phone out and began mindlessly scrolling. At least, she thought it was mindless until she went into Instagram and typed, "Brooke Finnegan" into the search bar. Brooke was still just as beautiful as she had always been. Her eyes were still full of so much light. She was everything good about this world, yet to everyone else, TJ acted like she didn't even exist. TJ was pretty sure Brooke was the only reason she had even made it to twenty-eight, but no one would ever know that. It was such a damn shame too, because someone like Brooke Finnegan deserved to have her name screamed from a mountain top, something TJ had never been brave enough to do.

It wasn't 11:59 yet, but she still went into the text chat that had become one-sided so many years ago after Brooke changed her number so TJ couldn't contact her any more. It still felt like a punch to her gut every time she thought about that night.

I'm a fraud, she typed out, not even hesitating before hitting send. Clearly, this number didn't belong to anyone. If it did, the person would have either texted her telling her to shut up years ago or would have sold the texts to the tabloids in order to expose TJ Edmonds.

When her phone vibrated from a text a few minutes later, TJ assumed it was either from Candace or Avalon. Her eyes practically shot out of her head when she saw the number it had actually come from.

Who's a fraud? TJ Edmonds or Tiffany Jane Edminston?

What the actual fuck...?

Chapter 6
Brooke Finnegan

What did I just do?
    For five years, Brooke had kept it a secret that she never actually changed her number. She'd let over fifteen hundred texts go unanswered. It wasn't an easy feat, sometimes much harder than others. It had all become too much though. Maybe it was the build-up after all these years. More likely, it had to do with the podcast she had listened to earlier. She wasn't sure who she wanted to kill more—Elon Drumheiser or Tiffany. Okay, that wasn't actually a comparison. She wanted to jump through her computer and strangle Elon when she heard the questions he was asking Tiffany. They were so unfair. So heartless. He was trying to toy with her emotions, doing anything he could to get a reaction. Tiffany didn't give in. In all of the interviews Brooke had ever read or listened to, she never did.
    She was also completely fake. She never once let on about everything she *actually* went through growing up. On one hand, Brooke couldn't blame her. Tiffany had been through so much, and Brooke was there to witness a lot of it firsthand. She didn't blame her for wanting to move on and pretend it never happened. She also knew how terrible it was to do that. Brooke had made it a point to face all of her demons from the past so she could move on and live a normal life. Well, most of the demons from her past. Although, her texting thumb seemed to have decided to have her face the only demon she hadn't been willing to.
    Even though Brooke hadn't had an actual conversation with Tiffany for five years, the woman she still kept tabs on over social media wasn't the same woman she knew from before. She often wondered which part of it was real—the person she saw on the internet or the one sending her texts at the same time every night.

Apparently, she couldn't take it anymore. She had finally broken down and asked. She could only imagine what must be going through Tiffany's head right now. Did she realize it was Brooke answering her or was she trying to figure out who was messing with her?

Brooke was sure she would find out soon enough, except the longer she waited for an answer, the more unlikely that seemed to be. An hour passed, but no matter how hard Brooke stared at her phone, it didn't force a reply to come through. Part of her worried this was it. That maybe her reply would cause the texts to stop. Part of her hoped it was. Maybe then she could finally move on. Maybe she would be able to meet someone, settle down, and finally start the family she always dreamed of having.

Memory after memory flashed through her mind, but one kept coming to the forefront. Hearing Elon question Tiffany about family made her think of the decision she made behind Tiffany's back that led to a series of events that put her where she was today—no family, except a bunny, apparently. If she could go back, she's sure she would make the same decision all over again, but it was hard knowing everything she knew now. Tiffany's biological mom had physically hurt her though. What other choice did Brooke have?

Brooke had been whistling to herself as she got out of her car and walked toward Tiffany's house. It had been way too long since they had seen each other, and Brooke was excited just to feel her close once again. Apparently, that was going to come sooner than expected since Tiffany came around the corner from the back of her house and ran right into Brooke.

It didn't take Brooke long to realize that Tiffany was shaking. Brooke instinctively pulled her into a tight hug. "Oh my God, Tiff. What happened? Are you okay?"

Tiffany shook her head, and Brooke could feel tears on her neck where Tiffany had her head resting. "Could we please get out of here?"

"Of course." But as soon as Brooke pulled away from the hug, she saw it. There was a big red mark on Tiffany's right cheek that was quickly turning into a bruise.

"Tiff... did... did she do this to you?" Brooke asked the question even though she already knew the answer, and it made her physically sick.

"I don't want to talk about this here. Please? Let's just drive somewhere."

"Of course."

Brooke took Tiffany's hand and led her to the car. Once in the safety of the car, Tiffany quickly opened up to her and told her what happened.

Brooke felt awful that the fight started because of her. "Tiff, if you can't... if we can't..." She couldn't even get the words out since she couldn't imagine her life without Tiffany in it.

"No, don't even think about saying whatever you were about to say. You're my home. You're the only thing that matters to me. I can't lose you."

"Of course. You'll never lose me." Brooke squeezed Tiffany's hand. "We need to tell someone about this though. I can't let you go back there. I won't let you get hurt again."

Tiffany shook her head. "No. Please don't. My mom is awful, but something is better than nothing, right?"

"But, what if...?"

Tiffany shook her head once again. "No, please. Just drop it."

"At least spend the night at my house. I don't want you to go home when your mom is so worked up. Give her some time to cool down."

For the first time since getting in the car, Tiffany smiled at her. "I would love that."

Once back at the house, Brooke lied to her parents and told them that Tiffany's mom knew she was spending the night. They spent the whole day locked in Brooke's room, doing everything but talking about what had happened. When they were too tired to keep their eyes open anymore, Brooke pulled Tiffany into her arms and relished how good it felt to have her best friend back. She wished the circumstances were different, but she was just happy to be together.

As Tiffany slept soundly beside her, Brooke spent most of the night awake, trying to figure out what she should do. She didn't want Tiffany to get hurt, but she also didn't want to shake up her world again. When she finally was able to doze off, she had a nightmare that Tiffany was seriously hurt at the hands of her mom. Her eyes shot open, and she focused on the beautiful girl lying in her arms. She wasn't going to let that happen. Tiffany might not like what Brooke was about to do, but she didn't think she had much of a choice.

She snuck out of the bed and was happy to find that Tiffany didn't wake up. It was early in the morning, but she knew her mom would be up any minute, so she went downstairs and put coffee on for both of them.

"I keep telling you you're too young for that," her mom said when she joined Brooke in the kitchen.

"Whatever." Brooke took a sip of her coffee that sat down at the kitchen table. "I need to talk to you about something."

Her mom poured herself a cup of coffee then sat down across from her. "Sounds serious. What's up?"

"It's about Tiff." Brooke took a deep breath. "Her mom hit her. She slapped her and left a bruise. I told her I wouldn't say anything, but—"

Her mom lifted a hand and shook her head. "No. I'm glad you did. We need to report this."

"Do you think they'll take her from her mom?"

Brooke's mom shrugged. "I honestly don't know what they'll do, sweetheart."

"Well, if they do, she can come here, right? You guys can take her in again?"

"Oh, sweetie. We're not fostering anymore. You know that. We have you and Mateo. We don't have the space or money to take in anyone else."

"But…"

A choked sound almost like a sob from outside the kitchen caught Brooke's attention. When she turned toward the sound, she saw Tiffany. Her face was red and her eyes were bloodshot. "This is why I told you not to say anything. No one wants me."

Before Brooke could even respond, Tiffany ran away from the kitchen and out the front door.

***

Almost 24 hours passed and there was still no response from Tiffany. As Brooke stared at her phone that now read 11:56 PM, she wondered if this would be the first night she didn't get a text at 11:59. Then, like clockwork, her response came. Brooke cringed at the irony of the contact name she had Tiffany's number stored under.

No Matter What DON'T RESPOND (11:59pm): Who the hell is this?

Brooke really hadn't thought this through. She didn't want to lie, but she also wasn't sure if she was ready to tell the truth. **You didn't answer my question.**

Perfect. Simple and to the point. She would put the ball back in Tiffany's court.

No Matter What DON'T RESPOND (12:01am): How do you know my name?

For God's sake, this woman was still just as stubborn as she always was.

How about this? You answer one of my questions and I'll answer one of yours.

No Matter What DON'T RESPOND (12:05am): Depends on the question.

Brooke groaned. What the hell was she thinking sending that stupid text? How did she let her emotions get the best of her after all this time?

I already asked the question. Who is the fraud: Tiffany Jane Edminston or TJ Edmonds?

No Matter What DON'T RESPOND (12:08am): That's too personal. Start with something else.

Brooke thought long and hard. She could stop texting right now. That could be the end of it. Maybe Tiffany would stop texting too. She could finally be out of this never-ending cycle. But, why did that thought make her stomach hurt? Why did the idea of Tiffany never texting again leave her feeling empty?

Fine. When was your first kiss?

Brooke was really opening a can of worms here. She had no idea why she was doing this. She wondered after all this time, and after all the women she'd been with, if Tiffany even remembered her first kiss.

No Matter What DON'T RESPOND (12:11am): Middle of tenth grade.

No Matter What DON'T RESPOND (12:12am): If you need more—It was January 17 at approximately 5:57am.

No Matter What DON'T RESPOND (12:14am): My turn. Who are you?

Brooke typed the words then contemplated whether or not to actually send them. She stared at the phone for a long time before taking a deep breath and blowing it out. Then she did it. She hit send on what could end up being one of the dumbest texts she'd ever written.

I'm the one who kissed you…

Even though these memories were the last she wanted to relive given how things had ended between them, her mind went back to that same morning once again.

"Tiff, wait. Please," Brooke begged as she ran after her.

Brooke caught up to her on the sidewalk and reached out to grab her arm, but Tiffany jerked it away as if the touch had burned her. "I told you not to say anything," she said softly.

Tiffany had stopped running, but Brooke didn't dare touch her again. "I know, but I'm scared, Tiff. I'm so scared that you're going to get really hurt, and I could never forgive myself if that happened."

Tiffany turned around and shook her head. Her arms were wrapped tightly around her waist, and she looked so weak and delicate that Brooke thought she might break at any moment. "You don't understand."

"Of course I do."

Brooke and Tiffany had met for the same reason. They had both been thrown into the foster care system after being born into families that couldn't take care of them. Of course, Brooke hadn't been through any of the trauma that Tiffany had, but if anyone could understand what foster care was like, it was her.

Tiffany shook her head once again. "No, you don't." *She waved her hand toward the house.* "You have a whole family in there who wants you. No one wants me. My mom doesn't want me. The Finnegans don't want me. I—"

Brooke couldn't take it anymore. Tiffany could try to push her away all she wanted, but she wasn't going to let that happen. She took a step closer and wrapped her arms tightly around her. "That's not true."

Tiffany was shaking now, and Brooke knew it was because she was trying to hold in a sob. "But it is. My mom doesn't want me. Not really. She just doesn't want to live with the fact that she failed, and she thinks if she keeps me around, she didn't. No matter how terribly she treats me. The Finnegans don't want me now that they have their perfect family. No one—"

Brooke wasn't sure what came over her at that moment, but when she pulled back to look into Tiffany's eyes, she couldn't take it anymore. Feelings that she had pushed down for years finally came to the surface, and there was no denying them anymore. She couldn't stop herself if she tried. She put her hands on both of Tiffany's cheeks and pulled her close so their lips were just inches apart. "I want you."

She looked down at Tiffany's lips so there was no question what she wanted. She couldn't speak the words out loud, but she also wasn't going to be another person in Tiffany's life who did something like this without her permission. Tiffany appeared terrified as she looked from Brooke's lips up to her eyes, but then she gave Brooke the slightest nod, and that was all she needed. Without thinking about it any further, she brought her lips to Tiffany's in the softest kiss.

It didn't last long. It didn't get further than the one little peck. But, at that moment, Brooke felt her whole world stop. For a few seconds, she was frozen in time, and everything in her life suddenly made sense.

When she removed her lips from Tiffany's, she leaned her forehead against hers so they could still be connected in some way. "I want you. Okay? I always have and I always will."

The sound of the front door opening caused the two of them to jump apart. "Can we please talk about this inside?" Brooke's mom asked. "It's freezing out here."

Brooke hadn't even noticed the cold air. She would forever be warmed by the memory of Tiffany's lips on hers.

The sound of another text coming through brought Tiffany back to the current moment.
No Matter What DON'T RESPOND (12:25am): Listen... I don't know who the hell you think you are, but you need to stop fucking with me
I'm not messing with you. It's Brooke.
No Matter What DON'T RESPOND (12:28am): This isn't funny. I'll call the cops. I'll report you for harassment.
Brooke knew Tiffany wouldn't actually do that. She might not know much about the woman she was today (aside from what she saw on TV and online), but Tiffany had

always had a very strong distaste for authority figures, and Brooke assumed these last few years definitely wouldn't have changed that.

I'm not trying to be funny. It's really me. She wasn't sure if she should add the next part, but she did anyway. **I never actually changed my number, Tiff. I've been here the whole time.**

No Matter What DON'T RESPOND (12:32am): Prove it.

Brooke groaned. What had she been thinking? Why the hell had she brought herself back into this mess? It was like walking back into the storm after escaping into safety. She was out there now though, so she might as well just enjoy the thrill.

The kiss. It happened outside of my parents' house. The house where we first met. The house where I first fell in love with you, even if I didn't know that's what it was at the time.

No Matter What DON'T RESPOND (12:42am): You're really pissing me off now. I don't know why you think you know so much about me, but you're not Brooke. The Brooke I used to know wouldn't lie, disappear for years, then suddenly show back up on a random Sunday night.

No Matter What DON'T RESPOND (12:43am): Trust me. I was the one who pushed her to her breaking point. I was the one who ruined my own life. I would know.

Brooke had no idea what to say to that. What the hell was there to say at this point? She had brought herself into this mess, but now she had no idea how to take herself back out. The worst part was, she didn't know if she wanted to. Tiffany had always had this hold over her. It was exactly why she cut her off in the first place. Before she could think of what to type, another text came through.

No Matter What DON'T RESPOND (12:46am): Call me.

Without thinking, she clicked on Tiffany's contact name and hovered over the Call button. Luckily, she was able to stop herself before she did something stupid. She shook her head and went back into the text thread instead. *I can't.*

No Matter What DON'T RESPOND (12:49am): Then leave me the fuck alone!!

That was it. There was nothing else Brooke could say. The only way she could convince Tiffany it was her was by letting her hear her voice, but she couldn't do that. Texting was one thing. A stupid thing she shouldn't have done, but she could still come back from it. She could never come back from hearing Tiffany's voice speaking to her once again. There was no way. It would completely break her. Everything she had worked so hard for these past few years would be gone from that one sound.

So, she had no choice but to do exactly what Tiffany said. She was sure this was the end. The texts would stop, and she would be free of Tiffany once and for all. That didn't cause her relief though. It did the complete opposite. Her stomach tied up in knots and her head spun. She needed to force herself to go to sleep before she threw up.

***

The next night, Brooke was still awake as the clock clicked down to midnight. She didn't know why she was doing this to herself. It was pure torture to subject herself to the silence that was about to come. Except, it wasn't silence. Just like before, at 11:59 a text came through. Not only did they come through that night, but they continued the whole week.

Matter What DON'T RESPOND (Monday 11:59pm): *I don't actually believe that you are who you say you are, but if you are, I want you to know that I've meant what I said—You're still the last thing I think about every night.*

No Matter What DON'T RESPOND (Tuesday 11:59pm): *I have no idea how you knew about that kiss,*

but just for the record, it was the best damn kiss of my entire life.

No Matter What DON'T RESPOND (Wednesday 12:00am): Okay, that's a lie. It was the best first kiss a person could ever have, but I had a lot of really amazing kisses after that. All from the same person...

No Matter What DON'T RESPOND (Wednesday 12:01am): I realize I said "Just for the record," but everything I sent is OFF RECORD. If you share this (or anything I've said in these texts), I'll track you down and make sure you're arrested for harassment.

No Matter What DON'T RESPOND (Wednesday 11:59pm): If this really is you, I'm sorry about the harsh texts. I hope you sleep tight tonight. I still see your face in my dreams...

No Matter What DON'T RESPOND (Thursday 11:59pm): I just want to hear your voice, even if it's just one more time...

No Matter What DON'T RESPOND (Friday 11:59pm): I know this isn't *you* but pretending it is makes me feel better. You always made me feel better.

No Matter What DON'T RESPOND (Saturday 11:59pm): On the off chance that this is you, I want you to know that I'm really freaked out by the fact that it could be a random stranger responding to me. I'm going to stop texting this number. I'll use my app and text a bot instead. I want you to know, in my heart, I'll still be texting you though. You'll still be the last thing on my mind at the end of the night. You were my whole world. In a lot of ways, you still are. I can't risk this though. If it is you, I hope you understand...

Brooke stared at that final text for a long time. All of these years, Tiffany texted this number with no expectation of anything in return. Brooke couldn't help but worry she really messed things up for her by responding. But if she called her now, she could really be messing things up for herself. It was too late though. She couldn't stop herself. She hit the call button and took a deep breath. *Buckle up, Brooke.*

Chapter 7
TJ

"Hello?" TJ was sure that within a few seconds she would hear a stranger laughing on the other end of the phone. She was positive someone was getting their jollies at her expense.

The last thing she expected was the soft voice on the other end. A voice she thought she would only hear in her dreams. "Hey, Tiff. It's me."

TJ didn't know what to say. It had been years. *Years.* She had accepted the fact that Brooke was out of her life, at least this real version of her. After everything TJ had put her through, she didn't blame her. She never had. "I go by TJ now."

What the hell? You get the chance to talk to the girl of your dreams again, and those are the words you choose? "You... You can call me Tiff though. It's just that no one else does anymore."

"If you want me to call you TJ, that's fine."

You can call me "asshole" if you promise to never ever end this call. "Why did you call me, Brooke?"

Still striking out. Where was the smooth TJ that all the women loved? Oh, that's right. She was gone. Replaced with early-twenties *Tiffany*, who was confused and lost and so very in love with the girl currently on the phone with her.

"You told me to."

TJ shook her head and groaned. In all the times she dreamed about Brooke reaching back out to her, this isn't how she imagined it would go. "Okay, then why did you text me?"

"I don't know." Brooke giggled, but it wasn't lighthearted. It was forced and strained. "A moment of weakness?"

"After all these years?" TJ was still trying to wrap her head around this. Did Brooke seriously see every single text

TJ sent since she cut her off? "Why didn't you say anything before? I thought you changed your number. That's what you said you were going to do."

There was a moment of silence before Brooke spoke again. "I was going to, but then you started sending those texts, and I don't know. I guess I liked getting them. I liked the fact that I still felt connected to you and didn't have to lose you completely."

TJ's initial reaction was to be pissed off, but she couldn't. She had hurt Brooke so badly over the last few years they still spoke that she couldn't blame her for anything she had to do to take care of herself. It still didn't make sense though. "I don't get it. You cut me off because you said you needed a clean break. Why continue to read my texts?"

"I... I don't know, Tiff... ah, TJ, sorry. I didn't want to lose you, but I couldn't keep doing what we were doing. I figured if you didn't know I was actually there, you couldn't keep luring me into your bed, and it would make things easier."

Okay, so maybe there was something Brooke could say that would piss her off. "Lure you into my bed?" She was seething now. "You make me sound like a predator."

"Oh God, no. That's not how I meant it. Shit, Tiff... TJ, sorry. I didn't mean for it to come out like that at all. I know how triggering that is for you. Shit. I'm really sorry. Seriously. Both of us were very much involved in the decision to continue to jump back into bed together. You know I just always wanted more than that. I wanted late-night texts. I wanted the good mornings."

TJ looked at the *Never Say Good Morning* document that was up on her computer, and her demeanor softened. She could tell Brooke was truly sorry about the way she had worded that. Brooke knew her better than anyone else in the world. She knew everything TJ had been through. She was there for everything TJ had put her through.

"I'm truly sorry I couldn't give that to you."

"In a weird way, without realizing it, these past few years, you kind of did. Since you didn't know I was on the other end, you shared a part of yourself with me that you hadn't in years."

"So, why didn't you ever say anything? After all the things I told you…." TJ thought back on all the texts she had sent over the years. All of the things she had opened up about. *How could Brooke just ignore that?*

"I was afraid if I ever said anything… if you knew I was still there… the texts would stop."

TJ couldn't blame Brooke for assuming that. Hell, she was probably right. Except, she hadn't stopped. This past week, even though she was sure Brooke was someone messing with her, she couldn't stop. On the off chance that it was Brooke, she couldn't let go. She couldn't lose her again. But then she got into her own head and started to worry what would happen if all of this came out. If it wasn't Brooke, she would literally have nothing if the person decided to expose her. She reminded herself that wasn't true. She still had Candace, even if things had been a little rocky between them since the podcast. Candace and Brooke… the only two people who actually gave a shit about her, and she still hurt them. *Maybe I'm more like my mom than I want to admit.*

"Tiff? Sorry. TJ? Are you still there?"

The sound of Brooke's voice brought TJ back to the present moment. "Yeah, sorry. I got lost inside my own head."

Brooke giggled again, but this time it was real. "You used to do that a lot."

"Turns out I still do." TJ wracked her brain for something else to say. "What's new with you? Where are you living now?"

"I actually, um," Brooke cleared her throat. "I live in the city."

"New York?" TJ couldn't picture Brooke as a city girl, but then again, she didn't know much about the person Brooke was now. Correction: she didn't know anything about her.

"No, not New York." She hesitated once again. "Philly."

No way! "How long have you been in Philly?"

"About three years."

TJ couldn't believe it. Brooke had been living so close to her for three years and she had no idea. When she didn't say anything right away, Brooke spoke up again. "I didn't move there for you. Just for the record. I wasn't, like, weirdly following you. It's just a coincidence. I, um, moved there because my fiancé, Priscilla, got a job there."

TJ's stomach dropped. "Oh, you're engaged. Or I guess maybe married at this point? Congratulations. That's great." TJ tried to make her voice sound convincing, but she was pretty sure she failed.

Another long pause. "No, I'm not actually. It didn't work out."

"What happened?" TJ shook her head as if Brooke could actually see her. "Never mind. You don't have to tell me that. It's none of my business. Sorry."

"It's okay." That's where Brooke left it though. She obviously didn't want to share, and why would she? TJ was nothing but a stranger to her now.

Again, TJ was left with silence and the looming threat that Brooke could hang up any second. "Want to get together sometime?"

Silence. Again. These long pauses might kill TJ. "I don't think that's the best idea."

TJ felt the same hurt she did when she thought Brooke was married. "Why not?"

"I think you know why."

"I know I hurt you, but it's been a long time. I've grown. I've changed." *Have I, though?*

"You've developed a whole brand based around not letting people in. I'm happy that you're doing well, but it seems like the root of all our problems is still very present."

"We didn't have problems when we were friends, though. They all started once we were more than that since we weren't on the same page." *Since I was stupid.*

"Do you really think we could ever be friends again?"

TJ felt desperate to find a way to change Brooke's mind. She had to take advantage of the miracle she had been handed. She couldn't let it slip away. She couldn't let *Brooke* slip away. "Of course we could. It's been years. You've had plenty of time to move on." TJ couldn't say the same for herself, but she wasn't going to mention it. Although, all of her messages probably made it pretty obvious.

"TJ...." Brooke let her voice drift off after that one stern word.

"What?"

"Don't make me say it."

"Brooke, I truly don't know what it is you think I'm making you say."

"I can't see you again."

TJ groaned. They were talking in circles, and she couldn't take it. "Why not?"

"Because even after all these years, I haven't moved on. At least, not fully. I'm afraid if we see each other, I'll fall all over again."

"What if I'm there to catch you this time?" *Also, when did I get so poetic?*

"What does that even mean?"

"I... Well, I don't know, but I won't hurt you."

"I'll think about it, okay? I don't want to make a decision on the spot and regret it later. Let me sleep on it."

"Of course. Yeah. Definitely." TJ couldn't have hidden the excitement from her voice if she tried. It wasn't exactly a yes, but it also wasn't a no, and that was much more than she ever expected.

"Speaking of which..." Brooke let out an exaggerated yawn. "I need to go to bed."

"Can I talk to you tomorrow?" TJ didn't care if she sounded desperate because that's exactly what she was.

"Text me at the usual time."

TJ didn't know how she could possibly wait that long, but she agreed anyway. She would wait forever if she had to.

***

TJ spent the whole next day trying to get writing done, but it was no use. All she could think about was getting to talk to Brooke again. She wanted to respect her space, so she waited until 11:59 just like she requested.
Hello there!
TJ rolled her eyes at herself. How could she be so smooth with all other women but such a dork with the only one who ever mattered? Luckily, TJ didn't have to overthink it for long since Brooke's response came through less than a minute later.
***Her* (11:59pm): Hey! How was your day?**
Weird. How was yours?
***Her* (12:02am): Same.**
TJ didn't want to push things, but she also couldn't handle not knowing. **Did you give any thought to getting together?**
***Her* (12:05am): Most of my thoughts today were about that...**
***Her* (12:06am): Can I call you?**
Instead of texting back, TJ hit the Call button.
"I guess I'll take that as a yes?" Brooke asked as soon as she picked up.
"Did you even have to ask?"
Brooke laughed, and it was the greatest sound in the entire world. Her laugh slowly died down and silence followed. "I'm not ready to get together."
TJ's heart dropped. "So, what now? Do you want me to leave you alone? Just say the word, and I will." *I don't want to, but I will.*
"Is that what you want?"
"Of course not. I never wanted that."

"I never wanted it either. I just didn't think I had any other choice. You couldn't give me everything I needed, and I couldn't give you what you wanted."

TJ's heart was practically beating out of her chest. "What did you think I wanted?"

"A fling. Fun. A friend with benefits. I don't know. Take your pick."

The truth was, TJ wanted forever with Brooke, but she didn't have it within herself to give it to her. In her experience, everyone left. How was TJ supposed to give her whole heart to Brooke knowing she could walk away just like everyone else did? In the end, that's exactly what happened. Of course, TJ had pushed her to that point, but she still left—further proving TJ's point that anyone and everyone would leave her eventually.

"I want to try to be friends."

Brooke's voice brought TJ back to the present, and her words made TJ's heart skip a beat. "How does that work if we don't see each other?"

"Can we start with texts and calls, then go from there? I'm not going to lie, I never planned on texting you. I don't know what came over me. I guess listening to that stupid asshole's podcast sent me over the edge. Everything you were saying on there was so different from the things you texted me, and I couldn't take it anymore. I suddenly had to know the truth. I didn't even think it through before sending it. So, yeah, I'm rambling now, but what I'm trying to say is that, even though I brought this on, I never expected it. I'm not ready to just jump right back in as if nothing ever happened between us."

"I get that. I'll honestly take whatever you're willing to give me. I've missed you so much." TJ figured there was no use to holding back since she had unknowingly shared so much with Brooke the past few years.

"I've missed you, too. There were so many times I thought about actually changing my number so I could fully move on, but I just couldn't do it. I couldn't lose you completely."

"I feel the same way. It's why I kept texting even when I thought you weren't there any more." TJ paused. "So, texts and calls? Is there a rule for how many?"

Brooke laughed. "I doubt I have to worry about you overdoing it. That was never your style. But since 11:59 has been our time, why don't we stick to that for now?"

"That's not too late for you? I happen to remember you always passing out early." TJ's mind flashed back to all of the times spent in Brooke's bedroom then her dorm room and how she always passed out a few minutes into every show or movie. TJ never minded since Brooke would fall asleep with her head on TJ's chest or her shoulder. She actually loved those times. It was one of the things she missed the most about Brooke.

"I'll have you know, I've actually gotten much better at staying awake. I can make it through at least half of a movie now. How 'bout this? I'll text you when I start to get tired and if you're free, we can talk."

"And if I'm not, will you still update me on your day?" TJ didn't care if she sounded pathetic. She never felt the need to play it cool around Brooke. Why start now?

"I can do that."

TJ couldn't help the wide grin that spread across her face. "Perfect."

"Perfect."

TJ pinched herself to make sure this was real life and not another one of her dreams. She couldn't imagine waking up and finding out that none of this had really happened. Even though she could very clearly feel the pinch, she still had to ask. "Am I really talking to you right now?"

Brooke laughed. "Who else would you be talking to?"

"I don't know. This just doesn't seem real. I'm still having a lot of trouble believing it."

"It's real. I promise." Brooke's voice was a little quieter now, almost like a breathless whisper.

"I'll let you go." It's not what TJ wanted, but she also didn't want to overdo it. She didn't want to ask for too much and lose Brooke all over again.

"Talk to you tomorrow?" Brooke asked, her voice still soft.

"I'll be waiting by the phone." TJ wasn't kidding. There was no way she was going to make plans when she had the possibility of talking to Brooke again.

"Goodnight, Tiff."

TJ didn't bother to correct Brooke, since the name sounded so good coming from her lips. "Night, Brooke."

TJ smiled as she fell back onto her bed. She didn't know whether her night would be filled with dreams or nightmares, but she did know it wouldn't be quite so bad to wake up tomorrow.

"I did it! I got into Bellman!" Tiffany knew she was screaming, but she didn't care. She had never been so excited about anything in her entire life.

Brooke squealed on the other end of the phone. "Ah! I knew you would do it, but oh my God, I'm so excited that it's official."

"I know! We'll finally be back together again."

After the incident with her mom, social services had been called. Tiffany was sure they wouldn't have done much about it if her mom hadn't taken matters into her own hands. She decided once and for all that she was done. Her exact words were ones that Tiffany would never forget.

"You, Tiffany Jane, are a lost cause. I give up. No one will ever want you."

Sure, her mom was drunk when she said it, but she didn't change her mind once she sobered up. The next few months were filled with her mom officially rescinding her parental rights once and for all and Tiffany moving into a group home for teens.

The group home was even further from Brooke, so they had barely seen each other the past two years. Even though she didn't say it, Tiffany was pretty sure Brooke had chosen Bellman for college because it was a little closer to her. It wasn't close enough though. Between the distance and Brooke's already busy class schedule, they hadn't gotten the chance to see each other since she started.

But now they had the promise of seeing each other all the time next year. Tiffany just had to get through the rest of her senior year and then she would finally be back with Brooke.

Brooke… the girl who kissed her two years ago then never said another word about it. Sure, Tiffany's world had kind of imploded after that day, but she still wished that hadn't been where it ended. She had no idea whether she was gay, bi, or something else, but all she knew was she had really strong feelings for Brooke.

She had no idea if Brooke felt the same way about her, or girls at all for that matter, but she had vowed to herself that once they were at the same school, she would find that out. She just hoped Brooke didn't fall madly in love with someone else before she got there.

Less than a year… she could do it.

Chapter 8

Brooke

"Good morning," Brooke said as she walked into the kitchen to have breakfast.

Priscilla leaned on the counter and sighed as she smiled at Brooke. "Good morning, sweetie."

"You can't call me that anymore, remember? We broke up. *You* broke up with *me*."

"Hasn't stopped you from falling into my bed every night."

Brooke cringed. *How do I always end up the fuck-buddy?* It's not that she didn't like sex with Priscilla. That had always been a part of their relationship that was really good. She was looking for forever, though, and having sex with the ex she still lived with wasn't the way to find that.

Priscilla poured coffee into a mug and walked it over to Brooke. "Speaking of which. I missed you last night."

Brooke's initial reaction was to apologize, but she shouldn't have to apologize for not having sex, especially with someone she's not even dating anymore. "Yeah. I was on the phone and then passed out."

"So I heard." Priscilla lifted both eyebrows and smirked. "Wanna share who you were talking to for so long?"

Not particularly. Brooke was sure the last thing Priscilla wanted to hear was that she was talking to the person that ultimately led to their demise. Priscilla had broken off their engagement six months ago because she was tired of trying to compete with a ghost from Brooke's past. Brooke didn't want it to be that way, and she tried to convince herself it wasn't, but all of the points Priscilla made were true. If Brooke had truly moved on, why didn't she just block Tiff's number? Why did she still read every article about her?

Still, Brooke didn't want to lie, and she definitely didn't want to keep secrets. If she was going to keep talking to Tiff, or TJ as she went by now, she was going to have to tell Priscilla eventually. "If I tell you, do you promise not to kill me."

"It was *her*, wasn't it?" To Priscilla's credit, her smile only faltered slightly.

Brooke didn't have to ask who the *her* was that Priscilla was talking about, because they both knew exactly who it was. "Yeah. It was her."

Priscilla's eyebrows lifted up once again, but this time it was clearly more out of shock. She stood from the table and blew out a long breath. "You need to explain exactly how this happened, but first, I need another cup of coffee."

Brooke waited for Priscilla to finish refilling her coffee then recounted the events from the past week. When she was done explaining, Priscilla stared at her and didn't say a word. Brooke had no idea how long this lasted, but it was long enough to make her start to sweat.

"So, how do you feel about all of this?"

Brooke couldn't help but laugh at Priscilla's question. "Am I talking to my ex-fiancé or my therapist right now?"

Brooke was happy when Priscilla started to laugh along with her before reaching across the table to playfully push her shoulder. "I'm serious, Brooke. This is a big deal. Are you okay? What do you want from this?"

Brooke really wanted someone to talk to about all of this, but she was pretty sure Priscilla probably wasn't the right person. "Isn't this weird for us to talk about? I just feel like it's one of those things that is kind of off limits."

Priscilla waved her hand. "Nah. If you can't talk to me about it, who can you talk to? It's not like I don't already know the story." She waved her hand once again as if to say *let's go.* "Come on. Let it out."

Brooke's resolve broke from Priscilla's insistence. She couldn't really get upset if she asked to hear about it. Plus, she was right. Brooke didn't know who else she could talk to. There was no one else who knew all the details of what happened between her and Tiffany. *TJ... whatever.*

"I honestly don't know how I feel. You know I've never really...." Brooke trailed off. She still wasn't sure how honest she should be. This was the woman who had planned to marry her at one point.

"Moved on from your ex? Honey, I'm well aware. Remember?"

"Yeah. Sorry. I don't know. I could never be anything other than friends with TJ at this point, but I also really don't know if I can be her friend. As much as I don't want to admit this out loud, my feelings for her will always go beyond friendship. But after hearing her voice again..." *Just say it.* "I don't want there to ever be a day that I don't hear it."

Much to Brooke's surprise, Priscilla cackled. "Aw man, girl, you've got it even worse than I ever imagined."

Brooke sat down at their kitchen table and put her face in her hands. "I know. I have no idea why I did this to myself."

Priscilla sat down with her and pulled her hands away. Her face was much more serious now than it had been just a moment before. "I think it's good that you did. I don't mean this in a bitter way, but this is part of your past that's been holding you back. I think the only way to truly move on is to move forward with what you're doing."

"What if I can't move on, though? What if this makes it even harder to move on?"

"Then doesn't that tell you something?"

Brooke looked up from her coffee to study Priscilla's face. She couldn't possibly mean... "What does it tell me exactly?"

Priscilla gave her the type of sweet smile you would give a little kid who just asked a stupid question. "That maybe this is something worth exploring again. If you can go years without seeing someone and still fall right back into them, that says something."

"It says that I'm pathetic."

Priscilla put her hand on Brooke's and squeezed. "No, it says that you're a human with a heart that you just so happened to give away a long time ago and never got back."

Brooke groaned. "I'm screwed, aren't I?"

Priscilla laughed. "Oh, you're definitely getting screwed. And if what I read is true, it's going to be very good."

Brooke didn't doubt that if she actually did have sex with TJ (which she obviously wasn't going to) that it would be amazing. She didn't have to go off of what the internet said because she had experienced it for herself. TJ had probably gotten even better since they were together, since Brooke was her first, but that was hard to imagine. Brooke would never admit this to Priscilla, but sex with anyone else had never compared to sex with TJ. But, then again, no one ever really compared to TJ in any way.

When Brooke remembered what had sent her mind down that rabbit hole, she crossed her arms in front of her chest. "No one here is getting screwed, okay? Nope. Not happening."

Priscilla held a hand in the air. "Whoa. Back up. Let's not say that. If you hang out with this girl and need a way to get out all of that pent-up sexual energy, but don't want to do it with her, I am *happy* to assist you."

"Do you really think that's a good idea?" Nothing about this situation seemed like a good idea to Brooke.

Priscilla scoffed, as if Brooke had just asked her a stupid question. "I think it's a great idea. Really. Honestly, I think it's completely necessary." She put her hand on her chest. "As your ex-fiancé, I think it's my civic duty to do this for you."

Brooke shook her head but had to laugh. "I still don't understand how you're being so cool about this."

Priscilla shrugged. "I think from the time I met you, even before I heard the whole story of you and your first love, I could tell I would never really have you. Our intense sexual chemistry and how well we get along was enough to allow me to ignore it for a long time. I've been dealing with this for much more than six months. We were over long before I ended things. I just finally realized I wanted the fairy tale, and we were never going to have that."

Great. Now Brooke felt awful. "I never meant to hurt you."

Priscilla smiled a sad smile. "I know that. I never wanted to hurt you either. And if I could go back and change things, knowing that it didn't work out in the end, I wouldn't. I loved the time we had together. Hell, I love the time we're *still* having together."

"You're never going to find the fairy tale if you keep holding onto me though, you know." It was sweet of Priscilla to let Brooke live with her even after breaking up, but Brooke still felt like she was somehow dragging Priscilla along because she didn't move out yet. The truth was, she just didn't know where to go next. She always wanted to move back to her hometown, but she wasn't sure if she wanted to move back in with her parents, no matter how much she loved them.

Priscilla threw her head back in laughter. "Don't take this offensively because I do still love you as a friend, but I'm not holding onto you. I'm holding onto the amazing sex we have. Is that so bad?"

Brooke laughed once again. "No. I guess not."

"Perfect. In that case, wanna meet in my room before bed tonight?" When Brooke hesitated a moment too long, Priscilla shook her head. "Let me rephrase that. Want to meet in my room before you call your star-crossed lover tonight?"

"That I can do." Brooke smiled in spite of fearing the possible mess she was getting herself into. *Might as well enjoy the ride.*

***

After two rounds of sex with Priscilla, Brooke fell into bed and hit the contact that was still labeled as "No Matter What Don't Respond." *Hm, maybe I should change that.*

She was happy to find that TJ picked up after just two rings. "Hello?" TJ asked sleepily.

"I'm sorry. Did I wake you? I didn't think you'd be in bed already." Brooke was surprised when she looked at the clock that only read 10 PM at this point. TJ was normally much more of a night owl than her. At least, she used to be.

"You're fine. I was just napping. It's one of *those days*."

Even after all this time, Brooke knew exactly what she meant. TJ was always pretty good at masking her struggles (even from Brooke), but there were days when her depression and anxiety got the best of her, and she had trouble doing anything other than sleeping.

It always scared Brooke to see her that way. The girl who was normally so full of life shut down completely. It was hard since all Brooke wanted was to fix it, and she knew that wasn't possible. She did what she could though. She held TJ tight and let her know that Brooke would never let anything or anyone hurt her. It was a promise she sadly couldn't always keep, but she tried her best. It made her wonder if TJ had anyone to do that for her now. She couldn't think about that though. It wasn't her place.

"I'm really sorry," she said softly.

"Eh, you know how it is. No big deal."

Yep. That's the girl she knew. It was just like her to blow it off as if it was nothing. Brooke wanted to tell her that she didn't have to act so strong, especially not around her, but it was best to keep things light. This was already a lot. No need to make it even more.

Before Brooke could figure out how to change the subject, TJ spoke again. "But enough about me. How was your day? Do anything fun?"

"Not unless you consider work fun."

"Depends. Do you still teach? I know you always loved it."

"I do. For now. I'm doing online classes right now to get my master's so I can hopefully become a principal." Brooke couldn't help the bit of pride in her voice. She had always talked to TJ about her dreams to work in school administration so she could be there for kids like them, and it felt good to tell her that she was actually on her way to doing it.

"No way!" TJ's voice went up two octaves, the same way it always did when she was extra excited about something. "Brooke, that's amazing. I'm so happy for you! All of your dreams came true."

Not all of them. "Thanks. That means a lot coming from you. Truly."

"Well, I'm seriously so pumped. I wish I could throw a party for you or something."

Brooke laughed like she hadn't in a long time. TJ had always been so extra about everything and it appeared that hadn't changed. "Maybe we should wait until I actually get a job for that."

There was a silence that held a little longer than Brooke was comfortable with before TJ spoke softly. "Really? We can do it?"

Shit. Did Brooke just agree to hanging out with TJ? Sure, what they were talking about wasn't anywhere in her near future, but she still wasn't willing to commit to seeing the woman who broke her heart. "Um, I'm not sure. Sorry. We'll see what happens."

"Good enough for me! Just the chance of seeing you is more than I ever thought could happen. I really never thought you would ever talk to me again." TJ quickly stopped her excited ramble and cleared her throat. "So, you moved to Philly for your ex-fiancé, but you're still there now. Is that where you want to stay?"

"No. Not really. I'd love to go back to Woodbury. The ultimate dream would be to be principal at Woodbury Middle School, since that's the place where I first felt at home. We'll see, though."

"If that's what you want, I have no doubt that you'll get it."

Brooke sighed. "We'll see. I'd probably have to teach there for a few years first before they would consider me, and I think the current principal is close to retiring, so it doesn't seem likely."

"Aw, come on. You're my... You're Brooke. You can do anything."

Brooke had to close her eyes and take a deep breath. Even before she and TJ got together (probably more so before they got together since all that seemed to do was mess everything up), TJ always called her *My Brooke*. Hearing TJ say that was always like cuddling up by the fire after being outside on a cold night. What killed Brooke was that it still felt that way. *Don't do it. Don't fall back into this.*

"So, do you have your own place in Philly, or do you live with other people?"

For once, Brooke was thankful for TJ's total avoidance of anything important. Except, now she was embarrassed over what she had to admit. "I actually still live with my ex. We broke up six months ago, which was only two months after signing a year lease, so we figured it was easier to just keep living together."

TJ let out a low whistle. "How is that? Is it awkward when one of you brings someone back?"

Brooke rolled her eyes. Of course that's where TJ's mind would go. From what she heard, TJ couldn't go more than a few days without someone in her bed. "Neither one of us have hooked up with anyone else since the break-up. We're still just trying to get used to the new normal."

"Wow, you're stronger than me. Six months without..." TJ's voice trailed off, and Brooke knew she had been caught. "You're totally still having sex with her, aren't you?"

TJ's question wasn't accusatory. It was actually light and fun. It was as if she was talking to an old friend. It was as if she didn't find it strange at all, which Brooke definitely did. *Why are my exes so comfortable hearing about each other?* "Busted."

TJ cackled on the other end of the phone. "Knew it."

"Am I that predictable?"

"Nah. I just know you." TJ's laugh trailed off. "I know it's hypocritical for me to ask this, but you're okay with it, right? She's not just stringing you along?"

Brooke shook her head even though TJ couldn't see her. "No, she's not. I know we're done. She's been very honest with me about that. We just weren't meant to be, but we get along well."

"I hope you find whoever it is you are meant to be with. I wish it was me, but I know I ruined that. I ruined a lot, and it will always be my biggest regret."

"It's never too late to turn things around, you know." Brooke wasn't in the mood to give a lecture, so she hoped TJ could read between the lines. She deserved more than jumping from girl to girl and making a brand Brooke wasn't even sure she actually believed in.

"It's too late for some things, though, isn't it?" TJ's voice was soft and sincere, and there was no doubt she was talking about Brooke.

Brooke had no idea what to say. She wished she could be honest and tell TJ the real reason Priscilla broke up with her. She wanted to tell her that she was pretty sure she had found the person she was meant to be with and it *was* TJ, but the pain of the end of their relationship was too much for her to bear. She couldn't ever go down that road again.

"No matter what happens, you know I'll always care about you." There. Safe, but true.

"I never doubted that once, Brooke. You did what you had to do, and I'll never blame you for that."

Brooke yawned dramatically. Even though she didn't want to stop talking to TJ, she was also worried about the direction the conversation was headed. "I'm really tired. I better get to sleep."

"Oh... of course."

Brooke could tell TJ was trying, and failing, to mask the disappointment in her voice. For a second, she thought about saying never mind, but she knew it was for the best. "Goodnight. I hope tomorrow is a better day for you."

"Thanks. Talk to you soon."

Brooke hung up the phone, got ready for bed, then placed the phone on her nightstand. Unable to sleep, she lay there for the longest time, staring up at her ceiling. That was, until her phone dinged from a text. She couldn't help the wide smile that spread across her face as she read the words.

No Matter What Don't Respond (11:59pm): *I want you to know that no matter what happens from here, you'll always be the last thing I think about at night. That has never been a lie, and it never will be. Sleep tight, Brooke.*

Chapter 9
TJ

TJ took a deep breath before knocking on Candace's bedroom door. She wasn't normally one to get nervous, but she didn't usually have serious conversations.

When Candace opened her door, she raised her eyebrows as if she was surprised to see TJ standing there. "What's up?"

"Sorry." TJ pointed her thumb behind her. "I ordered us pizza and was hoping we could talk."

"You really didn't have to do that." Instead of looking at TJ, Candace looked down at the floor. When she finally looked up at her, after much too long, a wide grin was on her face. "But I'm really glad you did. Pizza sounds banging."

TJ blew out the breath she'd been holding. "So, that's a yes?"

Candace playfully pushed TJ as she walked past her out of her bedroom. "That's a hell yes."

After filling their plates with pizza and taking seats next to each other on the couch, Candace stared over at TJ in a way that made her feel nervous all over again. When TJ didn't say anything, Candace waved her hand in a *go on* motion. "So... what's up?"

"I just wanted to apologize for that podcast interview."

"You already did. At least, I think you tried the night it was on. I don't know." Candace took a big bite of her pizza and spoke as she chewed. "I'm really not worried about it."

Candace was giving her an out, which TJ would normally take full advantage of, but she wasn't going to do that this time. Candace deserved to hear what she had to say. "No, seriously. I need to let you know how sorry I am. Not just for the podcast, but for everything. I've always kept you at arm's length even though you've done so much for me."

Candace waved her slice of pizza around. "It's seriously fine, dude. It's what you do. I've always known that. Honestly, it's one of the things I like about you. It's kind of nice being around someone who doesn't give a shit most of the time."

TJ laughed as she playfully slapped Candace on her shoulder. "Could you shut up and just let me talk? I'm trying to have a sincere conversation here." TJ was satisfied when Candace dropped her slice of pizza back onto her plate and placed it on the coffee table then looked at her once again, this time her face much more serious. Since she finally seemed to have her full attention, she continued. "Listen, this isn't easy for me to say since I've never actually had a family that stuck by me, but you're like a little sister to me. An annoying little sister who won't ever leave me alone. But I love the shit out of you, dude. Seriously. I'm sorry I haven't done a good job of showing that."

Candace blinked a few times, and for a second, TJ thought she might cry, but then a wide smile spread across her face. "That's the sweetest thing anyone's ever said to me. Which makes it extra surprising that it came from you." She nudged TJ in the side and laughed. "I almost even cried, which you know I don't do. I love the shit out of you, too."

TJ laughed along with Candace. "Good. Now that that's over, can we hug it out and pretend this conversation never happened?"

Candace opened her arms to TJ. "There's nothing I want more."

After sharing a hug, they both went back to their ends of the couch and ate their pizza as if nothing had happened. At least ten minutes must have passed by the time Candace spoke again. "So, now that things are done being weird between us, what's new with you?"

"Nothing," TJ answered as nonchalantly as possible. Even though she wanted to talk about what was going on with Brooke, she didn't want it to seem like that was the only reason she had apologized.

"Lies," Candace said with a laugh. "There's clearly something new. You take smaller bites of pizza when you're lying, and that's exactly what you're doing right now."

Seriously? "Okay. There is something new, but I don't want you to think I apologized just so I could talk to you about it. I've wanted to talk to you since the night of the podcast, but couldn't figure out the right thing to say."

"Well, your speech was perfect, so you're okay to share whatever it is that has you so flustered right now."

"So…" TJ hesitated for just a moment. Candace was definitely going to think she was completely insane. *Oh well.* "I've been talking to Brooke for the past two weeks."

Candace spit out the piece of pizza she had just taken a bite of. "*Brooke* Brooke? As in the one that got away? The love of your life? The reason you're so fucked up in the head now?"

TJ laughed once again. Leave it to Candace to be completely honest. "First of all, there are many reasons I'm fucked up in the head. You can't put that all on her."

Candace put both hands in the air and nodded. "Fair enough. But that is who you're talking about, right?"

TJ nodded slowly. "It is."

"Okay. You're going to need to tell me everything, because you literally just blew my mind."

TJ explained exactly what happened as Candace took in the whole thing, her mouth slightly agape through the whole story. She shook her head as soon as TJ finished. "*She's* the number you've been texting this whole time? Miss Don't-Get-Attached still texts her ex every night to tell her she misses her?"

"Technically, I didn't know she was seeing all of them."

"You still sent them. I can't believe you never told me that. I knew you texted *a* number at 11:59, but not hers. Shit." Candace shook her head once again. "Also, she was reading them the whole time? That's like some *Notebook* shit or something."

"Technically, I think that's kind of the opposite of *The Notebook*."

"Whatever. Not important. The important part is what comes next. Are you going to let her thaw your cold, dead heart?"

TJ shrugged. "I don't think she's willing to let that happen."

"This girl let you text her for years just so she knew what was going on in your life. She's clearly still in love with you."

TJ shrugged once again. She refused to let herself believe that could be the case. She couldn't let herself get excited about something that had no possibility of being the case. And even if it was, it didn't matter. "No matter how she feels, that ship has sailed. I hurt her too much to ever make things right again."

Candace studied her, a look of sincerity in her eyes that TJ had never seen before. "If you could, though, would you be willing to try?"

TJ considered the question. It's not that she didn't know her answer. It was that she was too scared to say it out loud. If she couldn't talk to Candace though, who could she talk to? Maybe it was time she stopped holding everything inside. "I'd go to the ends of the earth until my very last day of life to make things right with her."

Candace was quiet for a minute then let out a soft chuckle. "Shit. You're a fucking poet. I had no idea. Maybe your next book should be a poetry book."

TJ laughed but shook her head. "Hell no. That's the complete opposite of my brand."

Candace considered her words once again, which made TJ a bit uncomfortable. This was the most honest conversation the two of them had ever had. "Have you ever thought that maybe it's time you change your brand?"

Every day. TJ couldn't do that though. "My brand is the only thing that's never let me down." TJ shook her head. She needed to correct that. "Aside from you, of course."

"Hm, I happen to remember a foster sister turned best friend turned lover turned friend-with-benefits that never let you down. That is, until you pushed her away so much that she had no choice."

Candace was exactly right. Well, almost. "Even when Brooke cut me off, she didn't let me down. That was all on me."

Candace laughed and waved her slice of pizza at TJ. "Oh, trust me, I'm not saying it wasn't. I don't know everything that happened in the end since I only know about the parts I was there for and what I could force out of you, but I know you had to do some real bad shit to make Brooke walk away. That girl worshiped the ground you walked on."

TJ groaned. "Thanks for the reminder, sis. Really nice to be told just how much I messed up."

Candace smirked and shrugged, clearly not feeling an ounce of guilt over what she said. "That's what I'm here for." They both silently took a few more bites of pizza before Candace spoke again. "For what it's worth though, I'm really sorry for how much my family contributed to fucking you up in the head."

"Hey, you had twenty-two years of being fucked up by them."

Candace laughed as if TJ had said a joke rather than speaking the absolute truth. "Look at us now though—getting fucked all over the place."

"Ay-yo!" TJ put her hand in the air for a high five then nodded toward the coffee table. "Speaking of which, be careful where you sit that pizza."

Candace cringed as she picked her plate up off the table. "The coffee table? Seriously? Is nothing sacred?"

"That coffee table was sacred to me and Kara. And me and Jessica. And Harley and Ethel. Trying to do two of them on there at once. Woo. That was a feat. I think that's it. Wait. There was also Kinsley. That girl was an animal. I wish she hadn't gotten married." TJ smiled as she thought back on all of her amazing hookups. Life hadn't been *all* bad. Still, none of those hookups would ever be as fulfilling as a life with Brooke.

TJ shook her head at herself. She couldn't start thinking like that now just because Brooke was back in her life. She had done a good job of pushing those feelings away and refused to harp on them.

"Wanna watch a movie or something?" Candace asked, bringing TJ back to reality.

She wished she could say yes, because she didn't want to disappoint Candace, but this conversation had been too much for her. She needed some time alone to center herself. She was obviously going to do that the healthy way by masturbating then taking a nap. Who needed meditation when you had masturbation? "Raincheck? I'm sorry. I just need some time right now."

Candace nodded knowingly. "I get it. I'm going to scroll through Tinder and watch some trashy reality TV, so feel free to come back out and join me if you want."

"Thanks." TJ stood up and walked a few steps but turned back around before leaving the room. "Thanks for everything. Seriously. Everything you've done and everything I'm sure you'll do in the future that I won't show enough appreciation for."

"Always," Candace answered with a wink before looking down at her phone, most likely already logging on to Tinder.

Once TJ was in her room, she lay down on her bed and wasted no time slipping her hand into her pants. Even though she didn't mean to, her mind immediately went to Brooke's auburn hair and hazel eyes once again. She thought about stopping herself from imagining her, but she also wanted to come quickly, and this was a sure way to make that happen.

So, she let herself daydream. She closed her eyes and let Brooke's auburn hair fall all around her. She pictured those hazel eyes looking intently into hers and pretended it was Brooke's slender fingers that were sliding inside of her instead of her own. She thought of the way Brooke constantly asked "Is this okay?" and "Do you like that?"

She nodded her head the way she would if Brooke was actually there with her, because the truth was, she always liked everything Brooke did to her. If Brooke was there right now, it wouldn't be any different. TJ moaned as she moved her fingers in and out of herself more quickly. "Yes. Oh God, yes, Brooke. Yeah, baby. Right there. Oh baby, you've always been so good to me. Don't stop."

She normally wasn't vocal when she masturbated but she was a bit delirious and also very turned on at the thought of Brooke, so she couldn't help it. She came hard and fast and passed out without another thought. She had wanted to set her alarm to make sure she didn't oversleep, but she was too exhausted from one of the world's greatest orgasms to do it. Her last thought as she drifted off to sleep was that she hoped her talk with Candace didn't influence her dreams. She had a sinking feeling they might.

Tiffany looked out the window at the February snow that she hoped would be the last of the season and sighed. It was a month until her 18th birthday, and she was equal parts excited about it and dreading it. Turning 18 meant she was legally an adult, which meant even though she could still get help if she wanted it, she was no longer a child of the state. While that was extremely exciting, it was also heartbreaking. Tiffany had come to the conclusion a long time ago that she wasn't going to be adopted since no one wanted a teenager, but there was still the slightest chance. Even though it was technically legal to adopt someone over eighteen, she knew that would never happen to her. As rare as it was for a teenager to get adopted, it was almost unheard of that a legal adult would be adopted.

"Tiffany? There's someone here who would like to speak to you," Mrs. Grimes, the director of the child and youth center, said from behind her.

Since Tiffany wasn't expecting anyone, the sound of her voice made her jump. She turned around to face Mrs. Grimes then pointed to herself. "They want to speak to me? Who is it?"

Mrs. Grimes waved a hand. She was nice but also always straight to the point. "You ask too many questions. Follow me."

Tiffany followed her through the long hallway and down the stairs. When she got to the bottom, a woman with blonde hair, blue eyes, and a bright smile was staring at her as if they knew each other.

Tiffany gave Mrs. Grimes a questioning look, but she only responded by squeezing Tiffany's shoulder, as if to reassure her she had nothing to worry about.

The blonde stranger took a step closer to Tiffany and reached out her hand. "Hello, Tiffany! It's so nice to finally meet you."

Tiffany looked at the hand in front of her, which appeared to have a fresh French manicure. Much different than Tiffany's short, somewhat dirty, fingernails. She stared at the hand a moment longer before looking up at the woman it belonged to. "I really hate to be rude, but do I know you?"

The woman's smile didn't falter as she quickly shook her head back and forth. "You don't, but I know a lot about you."

Tiffany swallowed hard. That was creepy. "Oh, okay."

The woman shook her head once again, but this time chuckled. "I'm sorry. I'm getting ahead of myself. Let me start with an introduction. My name is Bernice Baker."

Tiffany swallowed hard once again. She had no idea what the hell was happening. Still, she took the woman's hand and gave it a solid handshake. "It's very nice to meet you, ma'am."

Another chuckle. "No need for formalities, dear. I'm hoping we are going to be very close." Mrs. Baker looked at Mrs. Grimes as if she was asking her if she had permission to go on. Once Mrs. Grimes nodded, Mrs. Baker focused her attention back on Tiffany. "A few months back, God put it on my heart to adopt a child who was about to age out of the system. That is when I learned about you. I'm very impressed with what a fine young lady you are, and I'm hoping you will give my family a chance to take you in and, if all things go as planned, adopt you someday."

Tiffany's head was spinning. There was no way any of this was actually happening. "You want to adopt me?"

"Yes. Well, only if that is what you would like, of course."

"But, I'm almost eighteen."

Mrs. Baker nodded emphatically. "Which is the perfect age to fit right in with our family. My husband and I have two sons, Cyrus and Cain, who are twenty-four and twenty-two and a daughter, Candace, who is fourteen."

"I'm going to college an hour away in the fall." Tiffany didn't know why she was fighting this when it was all she ever wanted. A big, loving family was a complete pipe dream just ten minutes ago.

Mrs. Baker put another hand on top of Tiffany's hand that she was still holding. "I know, dear. Bellman University. I hear you have an academic scholarship and everything. We'd love to help you with whatever else we can though. I thought a car would be nice to get you there and back. Maybe we could get you one as soon as this summer, in case you wanted to visit any friends before you go."

A car meant she could visit Brooke this summer and spend more than just a weekend together. Even though they would have plenty of time together next fall, Tiffany didn't want to wait that long. "Wow. That's very nice of you, ma'am."

"Well, we're very serious about making you part of the family. God's will is mighty and his voice is strong. He made it loud and clear that you are meant to be with us."

Tiffany had no idea how she felt about God, but if the guy was going to get her a family and a car, maybe she should give Him a chance. "What now?" Tiffany asked as she looked between Mrs. Baker and Mrs. Grimes.

Mrs. Baker pulled a card out of her purse and handed it to Tiffany. "For now, you think all of this through, and once you feel comfortable, give me a call. You can come stay with us if you'd like or we could start by picking you up to go to dinner or church or anything you would like. Next month, or any time after that, if you decide we are a good fit and you'd like to move in with us, we have a room waiting for you."

Before Tiffany could respond, Mrs. Baker gave her a bone-crushing hug, then walked right back out the door. Tiffany watched her leave, then looked down at the card in her hand.

Jesus saves. Ask me how I know.
Mrs. Bernice Baker
Daughter of The Most Holy
Mother, Guider, and CEO of God's Army
Phone number: 555-786-2929

She honestly wasn't sure if this was what dreams or nightmares were made of, but she was willing to give it a try.

    TJ startled awake and immediately searched her nightstand for her phone. She had five texts and a missed call. Her eyes scanned to the time next. 11:53 PM. *Shit.* She didn't mean to sleep this long. She just hoped Brooke was still awake. One look at her texts shattered that hope.

    ***Her* (9:03pm): Hey! I hope you had a good day. I'm already getting tired, but I'll try to stay up until at least ten so we can talk if you're around.**

    ***Her* (10:02pm): Just called to say goodnight! Sorry I missed you. Hope you're having a good night. I'll talk to you tomorrow.**

    TJ thought about what to say in reply while also chastising herself for sleeping through Brooke's text and call. As she tossed all of this around in her head, she opened her other texts.

    Candace (9:33pm): Do you think this profile picture says big penis or small penis?

    Candace (9:34pm): (Picture attachment)

    Avalon :-p (11:24pm): I'm bored. Down for some fun tonight?

    TJ closed out of each of those text threads and went back into the one with Brooke, typing quickly so she didn't miss the chance to send the text at 11:59. ***I'm so upset at myself for missing you. I was taking a nap (I know... normal people don't nap after 9... you've told me... ha). Anyway, I hope today was a great day for you. I'm going to make sure I'm around tomorrow so I don't miss you. Thinking of you now and always...***

    TJ sighed as she sat her phone down on the nightstand. What a sucky end to her night. After wallowing in self-pity for approximately thirty seconds, she picked her phone back up and opened up her text from Avalon, quickly sending one back. ***I'll be right over. Have the big one ready. You know which one I mean ;)***

Chapter 10

TJ

"Happy birthday to you. Happy birthday to you. Happy birthday, Dear Tiffany. Happy birthday to you."

Tiffany smiled down at the Triple Chocolate Meltdown sitting in front of her. She stared down at the candle and thought long and hard about what to wish for. It almost felt like all of her wishes were starting to come true. She had spent time with the Bakers on a few different occasions now, but couldn't believe it when they offered to take her out to eat for her birthday. The youngest daughter, Candace, was the only one who did a slight eye roll when Tiffany suggested Applebee's. Everyone else smiled kindly and told her they couldn't wait.

The only thing that would make this whole night better would be if Brooke was there. So, even though it was pretty much impossible that it would come true at this point since she was busy studying, Tiffany wished Brooke could be there with her.

As soon as she blew out the candle, cheers erupted all around her. Then, suddenly, there was a new voice joining in with the cheers. Tiffany looked up and she couldn't believe it. Her wish had actually come true. Brooke was there. In front of her. Tiffany had to blink a few times to convince herself she wasn't just imagining it. Nope... she was really there.

Without thinking, she jumped from her seat and ran around the table, pulling Brooke into her arms as soon as they were side by side. "Oh my god. I can't believe you're here," Tiffany whispered as she continued to hold onto Brooke as if she was going to disappear if she let go. "But... I thought you had to study."

Brooke pulled back slightly, but kept her hands resting on Tiffany's arms. Her smile was bigger than Tiffany had ever seen it before as they stared into each other's eyes as if no one else was in the room with them. "I did… I do… it doesn't matter. This is a huge day for you. You're officially an adult. I would have been here for dinner if I didn't have a night class. I practically sprinted out of there."

"I'm just glad you're here now." Tiffany pulled Brooke in for another hug. "How long can you stay?"

"Well, I don't have class until three tomorrow. I know they have strict rules against overnight visitors at the center, but I could at least stay until they kick me out. Or you could come back to school with me for the night. We could—"

"Or the two of you could just stay at our house. Then you don't have to drive far. We do have a room all ready for you, Tiffany."

Tiffany looked to Brooke for confirmation that it was okay and Brooke nodded approvingly. Knowing Brooke was okay with it, Tiffany focused her attention back on Mrs. Baker. "That would be great, ma'am. Thank you so much."

When they left the restaurant, Tiffany turned to follow Brooke to her car.

"The car is over here, sweetie," Mrs. Baker said from the opposite direction.

"I figured I would ride with Brooke."

Mrs. Baker sighed, but kept her polite smile. "I would really prefer it if you rode with us. It's safer." She turned toward Brooke. "No offense, dear. You're just young. You haven't been driving as long as my husband. Plus, as we all know, men are just naturally better at some things." Mrs. Baker giggled as if this wasn't a complete 1950s attitude.

Tiffany looked to Brooke for reassurance, and this time Brooke just shrugged in response. "I'll text you the address. It's not far." Tiffany smiled apologetically at Brooke and silently let her know that she would rather be with her.

Once back at the house, Tiffany waited for Brooke to park and get out of her car before heading into the house. Tiffany had visited the Baker's house before, but she had never seen the room they apparently had prepared for her. She was happy Brooke would be with her the first time she saw it.

"Follow me," Mrs. Baker said in a singsong voice. "I'm so excited for you to see your room."

Luckily, Tiffany had packed an overnight bag just in case the Bakers asked her to stay, so she was prepared. Brooke had brought a bag of her own on the off chance the youth center bent the rules and let her stay. They both hoisted their bags higher on their backs and followed Mrs. Baker up the long staircase. The Baker house was bigger than any single-family home Tiffany had ever been in, and with walls filled with family pictures and Bible quotes, it had a nice homey feeling to it. At least, what Tiffany figured a home should feel like. She hadn't experienced anything close to that since living with the Finnegans.

The room that would be Tiffany's if she chose to move in was at the end of a long hallway. When Mrs. Baker opened the door, the first things to catch Tiffany's eye were the blue comforter and all the blue accents around the room. Not only had Mrs. Baker asked what her favorite color was, but she had actually taken Tiffany's answer into consideration. Sure, *all of the Bible quotes hanging on the wall weren't necessarily her, but she could respect the Bakers' beliefs. She actually thought it was cool that they believed in something so strongly.*

Mrs. Baker stood by the doorway while Tiffany and Brooke walked inside. "I'll let you two catch up. I'm going to make some cookies, so come down if you'd like any."

Tiffany smiled kindly at Mrs. Baker. She really hoped she could tell how appreciative she was. "Thank you so much." She motioned around the room. "This means more to me than you'll ever know."

Mrs. Baker squeezed her arm before leaving the room and closing the door behind her. Both Brooke and Tiffany were quiet as they looked around the room, taking in everything from the queen-size bed to the pictures on the wall.

"They seem… nice," Brooke said quietly after a few minutes.

Her voice sounded unsure, which was strange. Normally, Brooke was overly positive and Tiffany was the one to be skeptical.

"Why did you say it like that?" Tiffany sat on the bed and pulled Brooke down beside her.

"It's just…" Brooke hesitated, then shook her head. "Nothing. I'm sure they're great. I'm really happy for you."

"If you have something to say, just say it." Tiffany tried not to sound annoyed, but she could tell Brooke was keeping something to herself, and that wasn't like her.

"I'm just being weird because I care about you." Brooke grabbed Tiffany's hand and squeezed it, causing a warmth to spread through Tiffany's whole body. *"Just remember that you do have family. It's me, and I'll always be here."*

Was Brooke jealous? Was she afraid Tiffany was going to replace her? She had to know that would never happen.

"No, idiot. She knows something you don't."

Brooke morphed into an older version of Tiffany. "Don't be stupid. She knows something you don't."

"She knows something you don't. She knows something you don't. She knows something you don't."

TJ thrashed back and forth in her bed as she repeated those words under her breath. She shot straight up and put her hand over her heart that was now beating a million miles per hour. Whenever TJ dreamt about the *good times* with the Bakers, she was able to pick up on the red flags and would spend the whole next day berating herself for not realizing it before they made her even more of a mess than she already was. All she wanted was to pick up her phone and talk to Brooke about it, but she knew Brooke wanted to take this slowly, so she was going to respect that. She could wait until tonight to dissect it with her. That is, if it was still weighing on her mind. At that point, she might just want to forget about it again. That was her usual way of dealing with things—push them way down until she didn't have to think about them again.

***

TJ jumped from her desk chair as soon as she heard her phone go off. It was earlier than Brooke normally texted, so the chances of it being her were low, but she didn't care. It's not like she was having any luck writing anyway.

A huge smile spread across her face when she picked her phone up off her bed and saw that it was actually Brooke texting. That smile quickly evaporated as soon as she read the text though. *I'm going out with some co-workers tonight, so I won't be able to call! Just letting you know.*

TJ was honestly heartbroken, but she obviously wasn't going to tell Brooke that, so she texted her back and acted like it was no big deal. It was a huge deal though. Since missing her last night, TJ had been looking forward to their call all day. Now what was she supposed to do?

As if reading her mind, Avalon texted at that very moment. *I have a proposition for you...*

I'm intrigued. What's up?

Soooo my roommate, Eliza, thinks you're hot and keeps bothering me about getting you to hook up with her. I'm not giving you up to her, so I thought, why not all of us? What do you say?

TJ smiled. If the best way to get over someone is to get under someone else, the chances must double with two people. It was basic math. *Are you two free tonight?*

For you—we're free any time.

I'll be over in an hour.

***

TJ couldn't believe this was her life. It's not like she had never had a threesome before, but two younger, hot girls? She had literally hit the jackpot. Even though Avalon and Eliza didn't actually look alike, their matching blonde hair was enough for TJ to be able to imagine she was fulfilling her twin fantasy.

"So, we were thinking," Avalon said once the three of them were in the bedroom. "We don't want things to get weird between the two of us, so for tonight we just want to do things to you and vice versa. We don't wanna do anything together. At least not now. Maybe in the future. We'll see."

TJ's mouth watered at the thought of this being a regular occurrence. And obviously, she wasn't going to complain about all the attention being on her. This night just kept getting better and better. TJ stretched her arms out to the sides. "Ladies, whatever you want from me, I'm all yours."

Avalon licked her lips as she ran her eyes along TJ's whole body. "You can start by getting naked."

TJ stared at the two women she was desperate to ravage. "Why waste time with formalities? Let's all get naked."

Avalon and Eliza looked at each other and giggled then promptly began stripping out of their clothes. TJ paused before removing hers because she refused to miss out on this view. While Avalon was well-endowed up top, Eliza had small breasts and a large bottom. *Absolute perfection.*

Avalon pointed toward her bed. "Sit on the edge so we can get you prepared."

TJ lifted an eyebrow as she sat down as directed. "Prepared for what?"

Avalon and Eliza smiled at each other then Avalon looked at TJ and bit her bottom lip while lifting one eyebrow. "For me to fuck you with the dildo from behind while Eliza pleasures you with her hands and mouth from the front. Then Avalon is going to ride your face while I go down on you."

So fucking hot. "You already have this all figured out, huh?"

"Just the first two rounds," Avalon said while sitting on one of TJ's legs and rubbing her already wet center against TJ's knee.

"The rest of the night is up in the air," Eliza added before straddling TJ's other leg.

TJ looked between the two women rocking on her lap, but it was Eliza who grabbed her face and directed it toward hers. "Avalon has had you plenty of times. It's my turn."

Without hesitating, she put her lips on TJ's in a searing kiss. It was only a matter of seconds before her tongue was slipping inside TJ's mouth while Avalon fondled her breast. The kiss was cut off way too quickly but only so Avalon could kiss her now. As if they had choreographed this, Eliza's hands took over. Back and forth they went like this, the two women fighting over possession of TJ's mouth while running their hands over her body at the same time. When Avalon's hand touched TJ's already-very-wet center for the first time, they both purred in delight.

"I wanna know what's so exciting down here," Eliza said before running her fingers through TJ's folds. "Wow, so wet. That means it won't be any problem for me to do this." Eliza pushed a finger deep inside of TJ.

TJ groaned as she moved against Eliza's hand.

"Whoa. Calm down, you two. We already made a rule that we wouldn't let you come until the next part." Much to TJ's dismay, Avalon pushed Eliza's hand away then stood up and pulled Eliza with her.

The disappointment only lasted a few seconds, since Avalon soon went to her nightstand and pulled out her dildo, which she expertly put on in no time. She pulled TJ to her feet, and as promised, stood behind her, while Eliza stood in front. Eliza kissed a path from TJ's chest down her stomach. When she reached TJ's center, she ran her tongue over it while Avalon wrapped her arms around her to play with her boobs from behind. This continued for a few more minutes before Avalon and Eliza decided TJ was ready to handle what came next. Eliza continued to lick and suck TJ while Avalon entered her from behind. The sensations pulsated throughout TJ's whole body were too much to handle, so she knew she wouldn't last much longer. With one especially good lick from Eliza and a hard thrust from Avalon, TJ was sent toppling over the edge.

She barely had any time to recover before Eliza and Avalon were pushing her toward the bed. "So, I was thinking," Eliza said as she positioned herself over TJ's face. "Have you ever taken it in the butt before?"

TJ scoffed. *Who does this girl think she's talking to?* "Obviously."

"After this, I think one of us should fill you from behind while the other fills you from the front."

Admittedly, that was something TJ had never done before, which meant she wanted it more than anything in the world. "I think that can be arranged."

"Perfect."

Eliza brought her center even closer to TJ's face while Avalon spread her legs apart to prepare to eat her out. TJ was more than ready for round two. At least she thought she was until she heard her phone start to ring. *Shit. Why didn't I put that on silent?*

She tried to ignore it, but the ringing continued. When TJ didn't immediately go to work on Eliza's center, Eliza pointed to the phone. "Do you need to get that?"

Maybe I should say yes. Maybe it's Brooke. She shook these thoughts from her head. Of course it wasn't Brooke. Brooke wouldn't call her when she was out with friends. It was probably just Candace messing with her since she knew what her plans were for the night. That was definitely some shit she would pull. As TJ contemplated this, the ringing stopped, then about a minute later, her phone dinged from having a new voicemail. *Okay. Candace definitely wouldn't leave a message. No one I know would...*

TJ practically pushed Eliza off her. Even though she still wasn't convinced it was Brooke, she had to know. She said a quick apology to Eliza before springing from the bed and felt her mouth go dry when the missed call and voicemail were both from ***Her***. She put up a finger to signal for Eliza and Avalon to give her a minute then listened to the voicemail.

"Tiffany Jane! Why didn't you pick up? I miss you so much. I just want to talk to you. Shit. I'm also so so drunk. I totally shouldn't be calling you right now, should I? This is a very bad idea, isn't it? Oh God, what am I doing? You don't have to call me back. I probably shouldn't pick up. That'd be the smart thing to do. You know, not talk to you after I've had a bunch of shots. Oh shit. I need to go. Please ignore this. Pretend it didn't happen. But also, call me back if you can!"

TJ had no idea if Brooke would actually pick up if she called back, but the possibility was enough for her. Enough to give up a fantastic night of guaranteed pleasure with two amazing women. "I'm really sorry, ladies, but that was my friend. She's super drunk and needs me, so I have to go. Can we pick this up some other time?" TJ was already rushing around the room, gathering her clothes, and tossing them back on. Nothing was going to stop her from leaving.

"Are you sure someone else can't take care of her? Our other roommates won't be back for hours. You could have us in every room of the apartment, on each piece of furniture." Avalon brought her hands up in a praying motion.

Damn her for knowing TJ's weakness. Except, what she didn't know was having sex on multiple surfaces wasn't TJ's biggest weakness. Her biggest weakness always was and always would be Brooke Finnegan.

Chapter 11

Brooke

What the hell was Brooke thinking? In what world was it a good idea to call TJ when she was super drunk and had very little control over what she was saying or doing? Thank God TJ didn't pick up. Now, if TJ called back, Brooke could do the smart thing and just ignore it.

One ring. That's all it took before Brooke picked up TJ's call. *So much for being smart.* "Hello?"

"Brooke! Hey. I wasn't sure if you'd pick up."

"I tried not to." *Briefly. Hardly.*

TJ chuckled, and it was like music to Brooke's ears. "Well, I have to say, this is one instance where I'm happy you failed. I really wanted to talk to you."

The way TJ's voice became softer and deeper when she said the last part sent a chill through Brooke's body. "I really wanted to talk to you too," Brooke said just above a whisper. She leaned against the cold brick wall of the bar she had left her coworkers inside.

Why was she doing this to herself? Why was she letting herself be pulled back into TJ's orbit? It took her years to get to the point she was at today, and now, it was like none of that time had happened. She was back in her early twenties, basing her life around someone who only gave half of herself in return. Except, was that really this TJ? This TJ called Brooke right back. This TJ respected her boundaries. This TJ created a whole app based on not getting attached to people... no, Brooke didn't want to think about that part right now. She liked this drunken dreamland she was in where she actually believed TJ could change.

One thing didn't change though. Brooke still had no control around her, even when she wasn't actually in her presence. But... she could be. "I wanna come over."

"Wh-what?" TJ sounded just as surprised by the words Brooke said as she was.

What the hell am I doing right now? Why don't I want to stop? "For one night. Let's just forget the rules I made. Let's forget all the rules. I just want to be spontaneous for once. I want to do something stupid. I deserve to do something stupid." *Stop rambling.*

"If you want to do something stupid, find a girl in the bar to go home with. Convince one of your straight coworkers to experiment for the night."

"Is that really what you want?" Brooke was whining, but with all of the alcohol in her system, she didn't care.

"Of course that's not what I want. Even though I have no right, it breaks my heart to think of you with anyone else. But any of those are better ideas than getting twisted up with me. Sober Brooke wouldn't want that."

Brooke pushed out her bottom lip. "Sober Brooke is boring."

"That's not true. Sober Brooke is funny and sweet and smart and... beautiful."

The way TJ said the last word in a breathy whisper made Brooke's legs wobbly and her heart race. "If I came over, I could—"

"Please don't finish that sentence. I'm trying to be respectful, but shit, Brooke, I'm still human."

"And I'm—" *Horny. Nope. That's not what this feeling is. It's something else completely.* "I'm gonna be sick."

"Are you okay?"

Brooke giggled. Why do people always ask that when they clearly know you're not? Oh shit. Giggling was bad. Giggling made the world spin even more.

"Brooke?" TJ's voice was laced with concern now, making Brooke feel guilty for worrying her.

"I'm fine. I just don't know if the sky is spinning or I am."

"Where are your coworkers?"

"Oh. I don't know."

"I'm going to call you a rideshare. What bar are you at?"

"A gay one." Brooke giggled once again. She couldn't believe she actually convinced her coworkers to go to a gay bar tonight.

"Can you share your location with me?"

Brooke fumbled with her phone, taking deep breaths to keep herself from throwing up just from looking at the screen that was going in and out of being a complete blur. Somehow, she was able to find the button to share her location with TJ.

"Perfect," TJ said a few seconds later. "Your ride will be there in two minutes. I put in a random address though, so you'll have to give him your actual address. And just stay on the phone with me until you get home, okay? I want to make sure you're safe."

Soon, a car pulled up beside the curb. The window went down and the driver stared out at Brooke as if he was confused. "TJ?"

Huh? Oh right. TJ's account. "That's me."

The guy, who appeared to be around her age, pointed to the backseat. "Get in."

Luckily, Brooke remembered that TJ told her she needed to give him her address, so she did that right away. The guy typed something into his phone then started to drive.

As promised, TJ talked to Brooke for the whole ten-minute drive. Brooke wasn't even sure what they talked about, but she knew TJ kept her word, which stupidly made Brooke swoon. Even drunk, she could rationalize that she needed her standards to be higher.

"I'm gonna let you go so you don't say anything else you regret."

Shit. What did I say?

As if reading her mind, TJ laughed. "I can hear you thinking. You didn't say anything you need to be embarrassed about. Don't worry." TJ's laughter tapered off and her voice became serious. "It's 11:59, by the way. I guess I don't have to text you tonight. Thanks for thinking of me tonight. I know you're drunk and when you wake up, you'll probably regret calling, but it really means a lot to me that I got to talk to you. There's nothing I'd rather do, and I'm still so sorry there was ever a time that I made you feel otherwise."

This serious turn in conversation was a total buzz killer, but not in a bad way. For the first time since having those shots, Brooke felt like she could form a reasonable thought. "The past is the past, TJ. Let's just focus on moving forward as friends." She paused for a moment, wondering if she should say the next part. "For what it's worth though, I don't regret anything that happened between us."

Of course, Brooke wasn't happy about the fallout, but all of her best memories since she was in middle school were with TJ. Nothing could ruin that.

"Sleep tight, Brooke."

Brooke wasn't sure what it was, but there was something different to TJ's voice. If she didn't know any better, she'd think maybe she was crying. She did know better though. She hung up the phone without another word because she knew if she stayed on any longer, she'd confess even more. TJ was right. She probably *would* regret this conversation in the morning, but she couldn't go back now. *Shit.*

"Have something you need to share?"

Brooke jumped at the sound of Priscilla's voice and brought a hand up to her chest. "Shit. You scared me. I didn't see you there."

Priscilla smiled and lifted an eyebrow from where she was sitting on the couch with her feet propped up on their coffee table. "I know. You were busy mumbling something to yourself as you walked in the door. I heard you talking out in the hall. Who was out there?"

"Oh, um…" Brooke looked toward her feet. At least the ground was only slightly moving now. "I actually… ah… called TJ."

Priscilla's eyes went wide and she started to laugh. "Oh shit. You didn't say anything stupid, did you?"

"No. No. Of course not. Just totally invited myself to her apartment. No big deal."

"You went to her apartment?" Priscilla's eyes were so wide, Brooke thought they might honestly pop out of her head.

"No. She turned me down."

"Huh." Priscilla stared up at the ceiling and tapped her chin as if she was contemplating this. "Wanna take your sexual frustration out on me?"

"Seriously?"

Priscilla shrugged as if it was no big deal.

How is she always so chill?

"Why not?"

Brooke could think of about a million different reasons *why not*, but she was drunk and turned on and it was easy with Priscilla. It was almost too easy at times, but she liked that. After her past, she appreciated the ease of their relationship. It's what made her fall for Priscilla.

"So, is that a yes?"

Priscilla smirked and raised one eyebrow, and if Brooke hadn't already been convinced, that would have done it. "Let's do it."

In no time at all, they were in the room that they used to share but was now Priscilla's. Brooke's back was up against the closed bedroom door while Priscilla kissed her as if it was the last time she'd have the chance. Guilt coursed through Brooke's body at the fact that it was TJ's lips she was picturing on her own. It was TJ's hands on her body. When they stumbled over to the bed, it was *TJ's* clothing she removed and TJ's naked body she stared at, mapping out how she was going to devour it. It wasn't Priscilla who was on top of her. It wasn't Priscilla who made her moan at the first touch of her fingers. And it certainly wasn't Priscilla who made her scream out as she came. It wasn't Priscilla that she made sure to make come at the exact same time because she wanted them to topple over the edge together.

It was, however, Priscilla who had to wrap Brooke up in her arms when she embarrassingly started to sob right after they finished. Priscilla rubbed her back as Brooke cried against her chest. "Wow. I knew I was good, but I can't say I've ever had *this* type of effect on someone."

Brooke laughed through her tears. There was Priscilla, making things light and easy as usual. Why couldn't Brooke just love her the way she used to love TJ? It wasn't fair. "I'm so sorry. I really am."

"Sh. Don't worry about it, sweetie. I was the one who suggested sex when your emotions were high. I had this coming."

Brooke laughed once again. "You don't deserve this. You don't deserve any of it. I'm leading you on. I'm dragging both of us along."

"In your defense, *I'm* the one who keeps asking for you, even though I broke off our engagement."

This made Brooke cry even harder. Even though she rationally knew this was completely different from what had happened between her and TJ, in her drunken state she wasn't able to be rational at all. "Is this all I'm good for?"

"Wait. What?" Priscilla pulled back and stared at Brooke. Her eyebrows were furrowed and lips curved slightly downward, as if she had just realized how serious Brooke was.

"No one wants to be with me. They just want to get with me." *Completely irrational. Pull yourself together, Brooke.*

"You don't actually think that, do you? Brooke, sweetie, I would have spent my whole life with you if you had been able to give your whole heart to me."

Now the tears came out even faster. Brooke was such a bitch. "I'm sorry. I'm so sorry." She wiped her eyes and shook her head. "We can't do this anymore. I… I can't be this person again. I need to figure some things out."

"Like whether or not you're willing to open your whole heart back up to the only person who ever really had it?"

Priscilla's words were soft and sweet. There was nothing accusatory to them. No hint of resentment or annoyance. Nothing but care and understanding.

"I can't give my whole heart to TJ. Not again."

"What if you don't have a choice? What if you already have?"

***

When Brooke woke up the next morning, she was still naked in Priscilla's bed, but Priscilla wasn't there anymore. It was just Brooke, one massive pounding headache, and the memories of the night before. Crying in her ex's bed after having sex with her definitely wasn't her finest moment, but that wasn't the worst part. Not only had she called TJ, but it was essentially a booty call. *Shit.*

She searched the room for her phone, but it wasn't in there. She slipped on a pair of Priscilla's sweatpants and a T-shirt and headed into the living room of their apartment, where Priscilla was back in the exact position she had been when Brooke got back from the bar.

"I mean this in the most loving way, but you look like shit," Priscilla said with a laugh.

Brooke grabbed her phone from where she had apparently tossed it on the floor when Priscilla suggested sex. She took a seat next to Priscilla on the couch and let herself sink into the cushions, half hoping it would just swallow her up. "I feel like shit."

Even though it broke the rules that Brooke herself had established, she opened her text thread with TJ and sent her one. ***I'm so, so sorry about last night. I really hope I didn't say or do anything stupid.***

Brooke obviously knew she had, but she hoped if she pretended she couldn't remember, TJ would never bring it up again.

She didn't have to wait for her answer since TJ texted her back almost immediately. ***You didn't. Don't worry. I was just happy to get to talk to you.***

Why does she always say the right thing? Brooke contemplated how to respond to this before sending out another text. **Let me know how much I owe you for the ride. It was super sweet for you to do that.**

Again, almost no time passed before TJ texted once again. **You don't owe me anything. It's the least I could do. I know you'd do the same for me. I just wanted you to be safe.**

Thank you. I really appreciate it. Brooke knew she should just let the conversation stop right there, but she couldn't stop her fingers from typing out another text. **I hope I didn't interrupt anything.**

Nothing important.

That's good. What were you up to? Just realized I was rude and didn't ask last night.

This time, it took much longer for TJ's reply to come through. **Honestly? Nothing you want to hear about. Trust me.**

What could she have been doing that Brooke wouldn't want... *oh shit. She was having sex. Did she stop for Brooke? No. No way. She couldn't have. She wouldn't. Right?*

TJ must have taken her non-response as anger or annoyance because she texted back a minute later apologizing.

You have nothing to apologize for. It's your life.

Much to her surprise, instead of getting another text back, a call came through from TJ instead. Brooke picked up the phone and walked back to her room. "Hello?"

"Sorry. I know it's not my usual time to call, but I don't know. I just don't want you to think..." TJ sighed as if she was frustrated with herself. "Actually, I don't know... anything you think about me is probably true. So, I don't know what I'm getting at right now."

"That's okay." Brooke wasn't sure what else to say since she honestly had no idea what TJ was trying to say or why she sounded so upset.

"I just want to make sure I'm always honest with you, but it feels weird to be honest sometimes too, you know?"

"I get it." *Kind of.*

"I'd always choose you. If… if I could."

"TJ, you're fine. I'm not jealous or anything. You don't need to explain yourself." Okay. So maybe Brooke was a *little* jealous, but she wasn't going to tell her that. They were going for friendship and friends talked about hook-ups. No big deal. Sure, Brooke wasn't going to ask her for details or share how she cried to Priscilla after having sex with her last night, but she was fine with knowing TJ had a life outside of this little bubble they found themselves in.

"Cool. So, is your favorite color still magenta?"

Brooke laughed. This was the strangest conversation ever. "Super random, but yes, it is."

"Sorry. I just realized there's so much I don't know about you now, and I want to know it all."

This launched Brooke and TJ into a conversation about all of their favorite things. The previous awkwardness was forgotten as they noted what was different and what had stayed the same, laughing as they discussed some things that would never change, like TJ's weird obsession with eating hot peppers straight out of the jar and her insistence that this was a very normal snack.

Maybe friendship is possible after all.

Chapter 12

TJ

"When was the last time you had sex?"

TJ laughed at Candace's question. "Keeping tabs on me? What are you? The orgasm police?"

Candace rolled her eyes. "No, I'm just curious, especially since I don't think you've even left this apartment in like a month."

"First of all, I'm busy working on my book. Second of all, I just left yesterday."

Candace rolled her eyes once again. "To go to the store and buy more energy drinks."

TJ shrugged. "You know how I get when I'm caught up in my work."

"Except *your work* has never kept you from having sex."

TJ groaned. "Could you just make whatever point you're trying to make so we can move on?"

It was Thanksgiving. All TJ wanted to do was what they did for every holiday, which was watch a movie and eat the ungodly amounts of food Candace had picked up from the twenty-four-hour diner by them. *Thank God that place doesn't close for any occasion.* "I'm just saying. I haven't heard you talk about having sex since you had that threesome that you walked out on so you could talk to Brooke."

TJ really regretted telling Candace about that. It had been a whole month, and she still hadn't let her live it down. "Maybe I just don't feel like sharing my sex life with you."

Candace snorted. "That would be a first."

"Fine. I haven't had sex since that threesome. Are you happy?"

Just as TJ expected, Candace's eyes went wide and her jaw dropped. "Whoa. I knew it was bad, but not this bad."

"What's that supposed to mean?" TJ asked, starting to get defensive.

"You're just in so fucking deep. You spend all day with your face buried in your phone texting Brooke, and then stay up half the night talking to her."

TJ wanted to argue that what Candace was saying wasn't true, but it completely was. Ever since Brooke had broken her own rule and texted TJ the morning after her drunk call, texting throughout the day had become a normal thing. They didn't talk about anything specific. Just mentioned small things here and there about their days. Brooke would tell her about something stupid one of her students did. TJ would explain how she spent her whole morning fighting with herself over how to spell the word *"the"* since she was convinced it didn't look right in her Word document.

Simple things like that. Simple things that made her whole fucking day, but she didn't need to admit that to Candace. "Do you have a problem with my friendship with Brooke?"

Candace shook her head. "Of course not. I just don't want you to get hurt again. You've had enough trauma in your life. You don't need any more."

"Brooke wouldn't hurt me."

"I'm not saying she would. From what I remember, that girl is cool as shit. I'm worried about you finding a way to hurt yourself."

"Brooke thinks you're cool, too." TJ had no interest in talking about all the different ways she could mess this up, so she went with her favorite tactic of *avoidance*. "When I told her that you're my roommate, she was obviously very confused at first, but then she said that you were the only Baker she ever actually liked."

Candace smiled smugly. "Of course I was. Every single person in my family is a manipulative monster. Thank God I was enough of a disappointment to keep my parents from making me another one of their clones. You know they took someone else in after you? Tried to shape her the way they couldn't shape you."

This actually surprised TJ. Not that they would do that, but the fact that she didn't know until now. "You never told me that."

"I don't like wasting my breath on those people."

"So, why are we talking about them now?"

"Don't know. Maybe this shit fascist holiday has me feeling nostalgic."

"Those assholes don't deserve for you to feel nostalgic." TJ pointed toward the TV. "What are we starting with? *Christmas Vacation* or *Bad Moms Christmas*?"

Candace closed her eyes and scrunched up her nose, as if this was the world's most important question. "What if we do all four *Vacation* movies today, then both *Bad Moms* movies tomorrow. After Black Friday shopping, of course."

"I love the way you think."

After over six hours of movie-watching, TJ finally tore herself off the couch from where Candace was snoring beside her. **Happy Thanksgiving! How was your day?** TJ typed out to Brooke before walking to her room and throwing herself down on the bed.

Normally, they would have already started texting long before this, but TJ didn't want to bother Brooke when she was busy with family. *Family that TJ would never have.* She tried not to let this sting so badly. She didn't want it to. She was happy for Brooke. It wasn't her fault that things had turned out this way. When she was being rational, TJ could also admit that it wasn't the Finnegans' fault either, but she was still a little bitter over the fact that they didn't end up taking her back in. Okay… a lot bitter, but no one needed to know that.

Luckily, TJ was saved from going down that mental spiral by Brooke texting her back. **Happy Thanksgiving! My day was really good! We went to Gram and Gramp's house. I ate way too much food and passed out on the** *floor for like three hours while everyone else watched football. How was your day?*

TJ smiled at the thought of Thanksgiving at Grandma and Grandpa Finnegan's house. The Thanksgivings she spent there while living with the Finnegans were still some of her favorite memories. Even her bitterness couldn't taint those sweet memories. *It was good. Same old, same old. Ate a bunch of food from our local diner and spent the whole day watching movies with Candace.*

While TJ waited for Brooke to text back, she went into Instagram and typed in her name. As expected, Brooke had posted a picture of herself and all of her extended relatives sitting at a long table, eating what could only be described as a Thanksgiving feast. Her hazel eyes and big grin shined like she didn't have a care in the world. She was wearing a brown sweater, which looked like the epitome of fall with her loosely curled auburn hair falling down her back. TJ wouldn't have ever stopped staring at that picture if it wasn't for the fact that Brooke texted her back. As much as she loved looking at her, talking to her would always win out.

I'm really happy you have Candace. It seems like you guys have really created your own little family.

Ew. Stop. You know I hate the F word. TJ smiled as she pictured Brooke rolling her eyes when she read this text.

Are you free to talk right now?

Hm. Let me check my extensive social calendar. TJ waited a moment before sending another text. *It looks like I can pencil you in.*

A few seconds later, TJ's phone rang. "You're a dork," Brooke teased as soon as she picked up.

Instead of addressing Brooke's comment, TJ jumped right back into the *favorites* game they had become so fond of playing together. "Favorite Thanksgiving memory."

Brooke giggled. "Wow, not wasting any time, huh? Definitely Thanksgiving my freshman year of college."

"But, you didn't even go home that year." TJ should know since she was there.

"I realize that, dweeb. Are you really so surprised that I would choose the Thanksgiving the two of us spent together?"

"After everything that happened between us? Honestly, yes. Plus, you have these great big Thanksgivings every year. We ate microwaved ramen in your dorm room that year."

Brooke laughed once again. "Trust me, I remember. I remember everything about that day. You were being stubborn and wouldn't come home with me, even though my parents said it was fine, so I picked you up on Thanksgiving Eve and drove you back to Bellman with me. You were such a brat. I practically had to drag you from the group home kicking and screaming."

Now, TJ laughed along with Brooke. "That's because I didn't think you should give up Thanksgiving with your family for me."

"I was trying to be a good friend."

"By kidnapping me and forcing me to sleep on that small-ass, twin-size bed with you?" TJ joked.

"Obviously." Brooke sighed. "God, I wanted to kiss you so bad that whole night." Brooke was silent for a minute, and TJ swore she could *hear* her internal freak-out. "Shit. I shouldn't have said that. I don't know why I did. I didn't even drink any of Aunt Jackie's special juice today."

Normally, TJ would change the subject so Brooke didn't feel uncomfortable, but she wanted to talk about this. She loved the chills that ran through her body just at the thought of that innocent night. "I thought you were going to. I was waiting for it, honestly. Every time you snuggled closer to me, I thought it was going to happen, then it didn't."

"That's because I had no clue how you felt. You never said anything about our first kiss. I was sure I must have freaked you out. There was no way I was going to initiate it again."

"Thank God for that frat party then." Much to TJ's surprise, and disappointment, Brooke didn't laugh along with her this time.

"I think we're kind of crossing a line into things we probably shouldn't talk about. I'm sorry. I know I started it. Can we talk about something else though?"

"Of course. That's my favorite Thanksgiving memory too, obviously. Your turn." This was one of the first times in her life TJ was actually disappointed to change the subject. Normally, she was the one initiating it, but she liked the way it felt to rehash her memories with Brooke. It was like she was being zapped back to life for the first time in years. Still, she wanted to respect Brooke's wishes. It was the least she could do.

"Favorite holiday movie."

"Still *Christmas Vacation*. That will never change. It's a classic and nothing can ever beat it. How 'bout you?"

"*Lez Bomb.*"

"What the hell is that?"

"Seriously? It's great. It's kind of like a very low-budget lesbian Thanksgiving version of *Christmas Vacation*."

"Hm. Not doing a great job of selling it."

"The actress who plays Meredith Blake in *The Parent Trap* is in it."

"Sold." Brooke still knew her so well. "I'll make Candace watch it with me tomorrow."

"How is Candace doing? I still can't believe you two live together."

"Candace is crazy, as always. A girl in her early-twenties getting away from her overly controlling religious family is like unleashing a wild beast after keeping it caged for years. She literally can't be tamed."

"In that case, I'm sure you two get along great."

"Ha. Very funny. True though. Okay. Favorite Hallmark Christmas Movie."

Brooke hummed as if she was actually considering TJ's joke of a question. "Definitely the one where the girl leaves the big city and her terrible fiancé to move to a small town where she falls in love with the single dad struggling to keep his business afloat."

"Hm. Don't think I've seen that one."

Brooke laughed, and it was so contagious, TJ laughed along with her. She couldn't remember the last time she laughed like this. It was almost unnatural to have a smile on her face that she didn't force. Her face actually hurt from using those muscles so much lately. They continued to laugh and talk for another two hours before Brooke finally cut it off by saying she needed to go to bed. TJ could have stayed on all night, but now that she didn't have Brooke to talk to anymore, she closed her eyes to force herself to get some sleep. She just hoped the sound of Brooke's voice was enough to keep the bad dreams away for one night.

"You're here!" Brooke squealed as she skipped down the sidewalk in front of the dorm Tiffany would be living in for her first year of college.

Brooke wrapped her in a hug so tight, Tiffany dropped the bag she had been holding. When she let go, Tiffany turned toward Mrs. Baker, who was looking around with a strained smile on her face. "So, this is Bellman, huh?" Her smile became a little more convincing when she focused on Tiffany. "You'll find out about the Christian clubs they offer here during orientation, right?"

"Of course." Tiffany had started going to church with the Bakers every week since she moved in with them after her birthday. She wasn't sure how much she believed in everything that was being preached, but at least the people who attended were nice. At least, to her they were. She often heard Mrs. Baker gossip with her church friends, which seemed a bit strange given what they stood for, but who was Tiffany to judge? The whole Baker family had done a lot for her already.

"And you'll find a church in the area to attend?" Mr. Baker added.

"Uh, yeah, sure." If that was important to them, Tiffany would do it.

Brooke lifted an eyebrow at her as if to ask why she had just agreed to that, but Tiffany simply shrugged in return. "Let's head inside. I can't wait to see my room."

"Where did you guys park?" Brooke asked in her sweet voice she always used to impress adults. "I can help grab some stuff."

Mrs. Baker waved her hand. "Don't worry, the men will take care of that. The job of us ladies is to get the room nicely decorated." As Mr. Baker and Cyrus turned to go back to the car, Mrs. Baker wrapped her arm around Tiffany. "Let's go see where my little girl is going to live this year."

"I thought I was your little girl," Candace pouted. She was the only Baker who hadn't warmed up to Tiffany yet.

"I have two little girls now. I'm a very lucky mom."

Whenever Mrs. Baker said things like that, it gave Tiffany a warm and fuzzy feeling inside, like a blanket was being wrapped around her heart. Even her biological mother never really wanted to claim her as her own. Tiffany hadn't become comfortable referring to Mrs. and Mr. Baker as Mom and Dad, but they insisted she could whenever she was ready. They hadn't talked about a formal adoption at all, but Tiffany was happy with what she had right now. She didn't need a piece of paper to make it official.

When Tiffany opened the door to her dorm room, her smile grew even bigger. It wasn't much. A small empty room with two twin-size beds, two worn-out desks, and two closets that she was pretty sure could fit about five of her shirts. But it was hers. All hers. Well, all hers to share with the roommate she hadn't met yet.

After unloading and decorating the room, the Bakers took Tiffany and Brooke out to dinner before leaving.

Brooke walked Tiffany back to her dorm then gave her a hug that Tiffany wished she could stay wrapped up in forever. "I'm going to head to my place, so you can spend some time with your roommate. Call me later?"

"Of course." Tiffany felt a bit nervous now that her security blanket was leaving, but at least Brooke wouldn't be far.

Brooke took a few steps then turned back around. "Hey, Tiffany? You know you don't have to do any clubs you're not interested in. I know the Bakers want you to join the Christian clubs, but that's really not your thing."

This wasn't the first time Brooke had argued about something the Bakers said. Tiffany still suspected it was jealousy, which kind of pissed her off. Brooke had no right to be jealous. She had a family of her own and she had to know no one would ever replace her as Tiffany's best friend. "How do you know that's not my thing?" Tiffany asked, not hiding the annoyance in her voice.

"Because I'm your best friend and I know you better than anyone else in the world." Brooke's eyebrows furrowed and her nose scrunched up, which were the telltale signs that she was getting mad.

"Well, people change, Brooke. Maybe I'm into it now."

"Are you?" Brooke's voice softened just slightly.

Tiffany looked down toward her feet. "Maybe. Yeah. I don't know. I'm still figuring it out. It's important to the Bakers though, so I want to give it a chance. Is that really so bad?"

Now Brooke's demeanor softened completely. She reached out and grabbed hold of Tiffany's hand, which made all of her anger melt away as well. "I just don't want you to lose yourself by trying to gain the approval of someone else."

"They're family. Well, I mean, they could be. They're the closest thing I've ever had to one."

"What about me?" Even though she tried to mask it, Tiffany could see the hurt in Brooke's eyes as she asked the question.

Tiffany squeezed her hand and gave her a reassuring smile. "You're more than family to me. You're my Brooke."

Chapter 13
TJ

"I'm sorry for all the times you tried to warn me about the Bakers and I either blew you off or got mad at you. I know you were just looking out for me."

"What does that have to do with your favorite video game?" Brooke asked with a laugh.

"Well, I normally play video games with Candace and she's technically a Baker and I've been having a lot of…" TJ cut herself off from mentioning the dreams and nightmares that both haunted her every night. "I've just been thinking about it."

"You don't need to apologize. That family was a bunch of manipulative douchebags, especially Mama Baker. God, that woman was awful. It always confused me how Candace was a Baker. Even when she tried to fit in, it was always obvious how different she was."

"Yeah, makes sense why she seemed to hate me so much while I was trying to do anything to impress them." TJ chuckled but quickly let it trail off. "Seriously though. I know you were just looking out for me. I wish I had listened. Maybe if I had gotten out of that situation sooner, I wouldn't have spiraled like I did. Maybe we—"

"You can't think like that. Everything happens for a reason."

"Ugh, your positivity is one thing I haven't missed."

"Strangely enough, I did kind of miss your pessimism."

"I know." TJ smirked the way she would if Brooke was in the room saying that. She *wished* more than anything Brooke was in the same room as her right now. She loved these conversations, but after two months, she was dying to talk to Brooke in person. The knowledge that Brooke was only twenty minutes from her made it that much harder. She'd met up with girls who lived over three hours away after talking for a few days. Of course, those weren't girls whose hearts she'd broken. TJ sighed into the phone as she lay down in her bed. "Have you given any more thought to getting together in person?"

TJ was met with an even louder sigh from Brooke. "It's not that I don't want to see you. I'm trying really hard to protect my heart."

"I get it."

"Do you?"

"Of course." *Do I, though? Kind of. Kind of not.* TJ understood how much she hurt Brooke, and she couldn't blame her for not wanting to go through that again. But, if they never met in person, what did that mean for them? Were they destined to be phone-only friends forever? How long before that fizzled out? Eventually, Brooke would become busy or meet someone and stop reaching out. It was inevitable. And, honestly, it scared the shit out of TJ.

"I'm not going anywhere, you know. It might have been a while, but I was around you enough in the past to know what your silence means. I want whatever this is we have going on right now to last. And if the day comes that I think my heart can finally handle seeing you again, we'll make that happen. Okay?"

"Promise?" TJ knew she sounded like a child looking for reassurance from a parent, but she didn't care. She needed to know that Brooke meant everything she was saying.

"I promise."

TJ breathed a sigh of relief. That's all she needed to hear. "Good. Now that all that deep shit is over with… Favorite vacation spot."

"Beach. No question."

Great. Now TJ was picturing Brooke in a bikini. Not where her mind needed to be right now. *Focus.* "Which beach?"

"Any of them. I'm not picky. All I need is the sun and the sand."

"And a drink in your hand?" TJ asked with a laugh.

"The drink is optional."

"Yeah, I don't drink much anymore. I stopped with that after college. I was afraid of becoming reliant on it, like… well, you know." TJ didn't have to explain it to Brooke. Brooke was the only person who knew every detail of her past.

"Yeah, I know." Brooke didn't have to say anything else because the tone of her voice said it all. She still understood. She still cared. Even after all this time. After everything that happened. That would never cease to amaze TJ.

"So, what are you doing for Christmas?" TJ asked, desperate to change the subject.

"Just spending it at my parents' house. It's my first Christmas since things ended with my ex and my brother's first Christmas since things ended with *his* ex, so we're not in the mood to do anything crazy."

"Dude, Mateo was dating someone? Isn't he like twelve?"

Brooke laughed. "Try twenty-four."

"No way. I don't believe it. Does he have, like, facial hair and all that?"

"First off, he had facial hair the last time you saw him, since he wasn't actually twelve at that time. But he does have a lot more now. Long brown beard. He's kind of going through a mountain man phase post-breakup."

"Wow. I'd love to see that."

"If you go to my Instagram, he's in the Thanksgiving picture I posted."

Hm. Come to think of it, TJ didn't actually remember seeing him in that picture. Then again, she was pretty distracted by Brooke. "Let me take a look," she said as if she hadn't looked at that picture a million times already.

She pulled up the picture and noticed the burly man with a long brown beard that she had assumed was a distant relative. Since that was the only person who matched Brooke's description, she figured that had to be him. "No way. Mateo discovered the bench press I take it?"

Brooke snorted. "Another thing post-breakup."

"This girl must have really done a number on him."

Brooke sighed. "He thought she was the one."

"Poor guy."

"Luckily, he has his big sis who knows what he's going through to help him out."

"Yeah, I guess you guys kind of went through that at the same time, huh?"

Brooke was quiet for a minute before she finally spoke again. "This is going to sound terrible since we were engaged, but I don't think I ever really thought Priscilla was the one."

"But..." *Ah.* "Shit. I'm sorry."

"No, I'm sorry. I shouldn't have said that. I always seem to stick my foot in my mouth when I'm talking to you."

"So, does your mom still make that banging chocolate cake?"

"You're still so good at changing the subject." Brooke laughed. "Yes, she does. And it's still just as banging. She almost wasn't going to make it this year since it's only going to be our immediate family at the house, but I told her she has to since it's a tradition."

"Oh my God. I'm so jealous. Have an extra piece for me."

"Gladly." Brooke yawned dramatically, as if to make a point. "I better get to bed. The week before Christmas is always the hardest time to put up with my students. I need my rest."

"Sleep tight." A minute after TJ hung up, she realized she was still holding the phone to her chest as if she was holding Brooke there. *God, I wish.*

She kept holding the phone like this as she drifted off to sleep, afraid of what she might see in her dreams after all that Christmas talk.

Tiffany woke up on Christmas morning to the smell of bacon and eggs and figured she must be dreaming. She couldn't remember the last time she had a Christmas like this.

Probably back when she was living with the Finnegans. She rolled out of bed and strolled downstairs wearing the Christmas pajamas that matched the rest of the Baker family.

"Good morning, sweetie," Mrs. Baker said from where she was standing by the stove. "Merry Christmas."

Tiffany was happy to learn that since the Bakers went to church on Christmas Eve, they just stayed at home for Christmas. That meant she could stay in her pajamas all day and just hang out, which was perfect after a hard first semester at school. She had decided to major in computer science with a concentration in artificial intelligence, and it was no joke. She really did love it though, so it was all worth it.

"Good morning, Mrs. Baker."

Mrs. Baker turned around and placed a hand on her hip. "I hope soon you become comfortable calling me Mom, because that's exactly what I am. We're family." Her face softened and she held out her arms. When Tiffany walked over, she wrapped her in a tight hug. "You're my daughter, and I love you just the same as I would if I was the one who brought you into this world. You were chosen for me by Jesus. I have no question."

Tiffany melted into her arms. The truth was, she definitely was starting to see the Bakers as family, but it scared her to death. Family had never worked out for her in the past, so she didn't want to let her guard down too soon. "Thank you," was all she was able to say in return because she was afraid if she tried to say more, she would start to cry, and Tiffany didn't cry.

"Aw, did I miss a heartwarming moment?" Candace asked when she walked into the kitchen. She stuck her tongue out at Tiffany. Even though Candace would never admit it, Tiffany could tell she was actually starting to like her. And for as much as Candace didn't welcome her with open arms into the family, Tiffany still felt closer to her than she did to anyone else, aside from maybe Mrs. Baker. But that was only because Mrs. Baker was so warm. Tiffany felt like she had the most in common with Candace, even if Candace tried to fight her on that.

Mrs. Baker held out one arm. "Come join in."

Candace rolled her eyes but still came over and hugged both Mrs. Baker and Tiffany. "Can I have Frank over later today?" she asked once she pulled back from the hug. "His parents got divorced just a few months ago and this is his first Christmas without his dad around, so he's sad. I thought it would be nice for him to be around our family. You know, see a family who is smiling. Give him a chance to breathe and laugh."

Tiffany wondered why Candace was rambling. She was sure Mrs. Baker didn't need that much of an explanation to say yes. Except, it turned out Candace knew her mom much better than Tiffany. Go figure.

Mrs. Baker sighed and leaned against the sink. "I really don't think you should be having a boy over at your age. You know dating is off limits until you're eighteen."

Candace quickly shook her head back and forth. "We're not dating. He's just a friend."

"Well, does he attend youth group with you?"

Candace shook her head once again, this time groaning while she did. "No, Mom. He doesn't go to our church."

"Well, then what church does he go to?"

Candace seemed to shrink in on herself slightly at this question. "I don't think his family goes to church."

Mrs. Baker gasped as though she had just heard his family committed mass murder. Then she sighed and shook her head. "I just don't think it's a good idea. It sounds like that boy has a lot going on at home. I don't think he's someone you should be spending time with. But you know what? We'll say an extra prayer for him today. How does that sound?"

Mrs. Baker simply smiled as Candace growled and stomped out of the room. When she focused her attention back on Tiffany, the wide grin was still on her face. "You understand where I'm coming from, right, sweetie?"

In all honesty, Tiffany didn't at all. She had been that kid that parents didn't want their kids around just because of circumstances she couldn't control. She couldn't say that though. She didn't want to make Mrs. Baker angry. "I… I guess so."

Mrs. Baker's eyes went wide and her mouth formed an O as if she had just caught on to what Tiffany was thinking. She wrapped her up in another hug. "Oh, sweetie. It's not what you're thinking. I promise. I'm sure he's not a bad kid. I just need to look out for my family first and foremost. I love you kids so much."

No other grown-up had ever told Tiffany they loved her. Not even her own mother. Hearing Mrs. Baker say it made her forget about everything that had just happened. It just felt so good to finally feel wanted. And when she said, "I love you too, Mom," and Mrs. Baker burst into tears, she had no question she had found her forever home.

***

A few hours later, Tiffany was shocked at how many gifts she got. The small gifts that she had bought the rest of her family didn't even compare, but they had all reassured her that just having her there with them was enough of a gift. Once there was nothing else remaining under the tree, Mr. Baker announced that there was one more gift then wiggled his eyebrows at Tiffany. He stood to his feet and motioned for her to follow. As they made their way through the house, Tiffany's mind was buzzing with what it could be. Before she moved in with them, Mrs. Baker had mentioned something about getting her a car, but Tiffany was sure that was an empty promise. There was no way that's what this was.

At least, that's what she thought until she walked into the driveway and there was a blue Ford Escape sitting there with a bow on top. "Now, I know it's not exactly new—" Mr. Baker started.

"No. It's… it's perfect. It's really mine?"

"All yours," Mrs. Baker answered proudly.

"Even found it in your favorite color," Cyrus added.

Cain walked over to it and patted the hood. "And I helped Dad add a new sound system."

When Tiffany looked at Candace, she simply shrugged. "I was along for the test drive. It's pretty cool. You better give me rides in it."

Tiffany pulled Candace into a tight hug and spun her around. "Of course I'll take you for rides. Anywhere you want to go, just let me know."

Tiffany made her way to the rest of the members of the Baker family one at a time, sharing a big hug with each of them. When she hugged Mrs. Baker, she whispered that she wanted to speak to Tiffany about something later.

A few hours later, once everyone else had retreated back to their rooms, Tiffany went into the living room where Mrs. Baker was watching a movie. "What did you want to talk to me about?" she asked while taking a seat on the couch.

"Have you heard of Sacred Hearts College?"

Tiffany shook her head and furrowed her eyebrows. She had no idea where Mrs. Baker was going with this.

"It's a Christian college about thirty minutes from Bellman and twenty minutes closer to home here."

"Oh. Okay." Still not following…

"I think you should consider transferring there next year. Now that you have the car we bought you, you'll still be able to see Brooke whenever you want. You'll also be able to get home much easier. Plus, you'll be surrounded by students with the same beliefs as you."

Tiffany wasn't actually sure what her exact beliefs were still, but she didn't want to mention that to the woman who had become her mom. "I actually really like Bellman."

Mrs. Baker stood from her chair and took a seat on the couch next to Tiffany. She faced Tiffany and patted her on the knee. "I know you do, but as your mom, I really think this *is a great opportunity for you. You still get to enjoy Bellman but also make me happy. And I have no doubt that once you give it a chance, you'll be very happy there. And don't worry about the tuition. We'll be paying for everything."*

How could Tiffany say no to the woman who had given her so much? That was the thing. She couldn't.

Chapter 14

Brooke

Merry Christmas! I hope it's a great day! Brooke couldn't help but smile as she typed out her text to TJ.

She smiled even wider when TJ's reply came through a few seconds later. *Merry Christmas to you too! I hope Santa got you a ton of presents and that you eat so much chocolate cake, you burst.*

Quite the image there, Brooke typed back. *You really want me to burst?*

Your mom's chocolate cake is worth bursting over. Trust me.

"What are you smiling at?"

Brooke jumped at the sound of her mom's voice. She shoved her phone deep into her pants pocket before smiling over at her. "Nothing really."

Brooke's mom lifted an eyebrow. "It didn't seem like nothing." She pointed toward Brooke's pocket. "Who were you texting? Are you dating again?"

Her mom sounded much too excited at that prospect. Tiffany shook her head. "No, I'm not dating. I promise."

"Then who is this mystery person? You're clearly hiding something from me."

Brooke blew out a long breath. She could only imagine what her mom's response was going to be to what she was about to confess. "It's, um, Tiffany. We started talking a little bit again."

"Talking in what capacity?"

Just as Brooke predicted, her mom's voice was laced in concern. "Just talking. Catching up. As friends. Nothing more."

"Just be careful, sweetie, okay?"

Brooke could feel her blood starting to boil. She remembered this feeling of being defensive over TJ all too well. "Careful of what?"

Her mom gave her a patronizing look. "I know how much you care about Tiffany. I'm worried you'll fall right back into things with her. It took you so long to be okay after how she treated you last time."

Even though her mom's worries were the same ones Brooke had, she didn't like hearing it from someone else. "Have you ever thought that maybe she's changed, Mom? Maybe she was just going through a really shitty time after having a really shitty life, and she didn't know how to handle it?"

"Listen, Brooke, you know I love Tiffany. I always will, but—"

"Do you, Mom? Do you really? Because if you loved her, maybe you would have been there for her more. Maybe you wouldn't have completely abandoned her after things fell apart between us. Maybe you would have *actually adopted her* when things fell apart with her mom. In my opinion, you're no better than every other adult in her life that let her down."

Brooke regretted the words as soon as they were out of her mouth, but that didn't stop her from stomping out of the kitchen and up the stairs into her room without another word. She'd apologize eventually, but she needed some time to cool down. She needed to get her head on straight, so when she went back downstairs she could have a rational conversation with her mom.

After pacing back and forth across her room for at least ten minutes, Brooke was ready to have the conversation. She took a deep breath before heading back down the stairs. When she walked into the kitchen, she found that her dad and brother had come back inside from looking at something in her brother's car. None of her focus was on them though. She made a beeline straight to her mom and melted into her arms, beginning to sob as soon as her mom wrapped her arms tightly around her. "I'm sorry. I'm so sorry."

Instead of saying anything, her mom just pulled her even closer and rubbed her back. When they finally pulled apart, her mom looked at her with all the love and care in the world. "Can we talk upstairs?"

Brooke's brother and dad watched in curiosity as she and her mom left the room together. Once they were upstairs, they went to Brooke's room and her mom shut the door behind them. Her mom sat down on Brooke's bed and patted the spot next to her. "I have to tell you something."

"Okay." Brooke took a seat next to her mom.

"Remember that night everything happened with Tiffany's stepbrother?"

Brooke nodded. "Of course. How could I forget?"

"Well, I never told you what actually happened when I talked to Tiffany's mom the next day. I asked her to give up her parental rights so we could adopt Tiffany. When she said she wouldn't do that, I threatened to let social services know what happened. She threatened me right back. She said if I ever told anyone what happened or tried to get Tiffany back at any point, she would make up lies about me to get you and Mateo taken away. Looking back, I can see how dumb it was for me to think she would get away with that, but it scared me so badly, I told the agency we didn't have any interest in being foster or adoptive parents anymore. I vowed to never do anything to risk losing you kids. And you know what?"

Brooke shook her head. "What?"

"I still regret every decision I made when it comes to Tiffany. I hate everything she went through. I wish I could go back and change it. I feel like it's all my fault. If I had just stepped up, she would have a family right now."

"Yet, you don't want me to be close to her. I don't understand."

"Unfortunately, because of my decisions, Tiffany did go through a lot and it shaped her into the person she is today. That's not the person I want my daughter to end up with. You deserve better than that, sweetie. You deserve someone who can commit fully to you."

Brooke had no idea why her mom was talking as if she was going to date TJ, but that wasn't the part she wanted to focus on right now. "I never told you this, but after I cut TJ… Tiffany… off, I told her I was changing my number, but I never actually did. She texted my number every single day to let me know she was still thinking of me. How's that for commitment?"

Brooke's mom stared at her for a long time, and Brooke had no idea what she could possibly be thinking. "I trust whatever you decide. And just for the record—Tiffany is welcome here any time. I'd love to see her again."

So would I. Someday. Instead of saying anything, Brooke pulled her mom into another tight hug. As they hugged, an idea came to her head. "Could I take some of the leftover cake with me?"

***

Brooke had no idea what kind of response she would get when she messaged Candace on Instagram and asked if she could have the address to her and TJ's apartment, but she definitely didn't expect all the snark Candace had in her.

I have a few questions. What are your intentions with my roommate? Are you going to break her heart? Are you planning on using our address to kill her? Was that your plan all along? If you do kill her, will you spare me? I love TJ, but I'm not above sacrificing her to spare my own life. Answer these questions and I just *might* give you our address.

Brooke laughed as she typed back her response. ***LOL. No murder happening here. I promise. My only intention right now is to drop off some cake. I either need to come at a time when it's only you at home or come when you're both home and message to let you know when I drop it off so you can grab it once I'm gone. I'm still not ready to see TJ yet, but I want to do this for her. I would really appreciate it if you could help me out.***

The reply to Brooke's message came through before she could even close out of the app. ***That's so fucking*** *sweet. If I had any emotions, I'd probably cry. I'll give you my number. Definitely plan on just dropping it off and texting me. Trying to find a time when TJ isn't home would be almost impossible. I swear I can never get rid of her these days.*

At the end of the message was an address and phone number. The day after Christmas, once Brooke was back at her apartment, she made the drive to TJ's apartment. It was shocking to see just how close the two of them actually lived.

She walked right inside the main building, which was unlocked like Candace said it would be. Then she took the elevator up to the third floor. As she approached their apartment door, she heard laughter. Specifically, she heard TJ's laughter. Brooke got as close to the door as she possibly could and continued to listen. She couldn't believe that right on the other side of the door was *her Tiffany*. All she would have to do is knock and the two of them would be face to face once again.

She could look into those sparkling blue eyes, touch that scar right above her left eye, watch the way her lips quirk up the tiniest bit higher on the right side.

And those thoughts were exactly *why* she couldn't knock. Just hearing TJ close by already had all of those feelings she tried so hard to suppress come crashing back in on her. She put the paper plate with two slices of cake on the ground right outside the door then headed back to the elevator. She waited until she was leaving the building to let Candace know it was there, then she quickly got in her car and drove away.

As she kind of expected, less than ten minutes later, a call came through from TJ. She connected her phone to Bluetooth and picked it up.

"You brought me fucking cake," TJ said immediately. Even with the swearing, her words were soft-spoken and sincere. "I can't believe you did that. I can't believe you were just feet away from me. You don't know how much I selfishly wish I could have caught you out there."

Brooke did understand, because in a way, she wished TJ had caught her as well. "I'm just not ready yet. I'm sorry. But I really wanted you to have that."

"Just so you know, that's the nicest thing anyone has ever done for me."

"Brought you chocolate cake?" Brooke asked with a laugh.

"My standards are very low at this point. Seriously though, Brooke. You're way too good to me. I don't deserve this."

"It's cake. It's really not a big deal."

"We'll have to agree to disagree on that."

Brooke could hear TJ chewing, and then she released a long guttural moan. It was the same sound she used to make when... *No. Stop that.*

"This is even better than I remember."

Brooke could tell TJ's mouth was full as she said the words and it made her laugh once again. "I'm really glad you're enjoying it so much."

"More than you know. This is so great. I feel terrible that I didn't get you anything, but I wouldn't have even known how to get it to you. It probably would have been really weird for me to reach out to your ex-fiancée. Candace told me she gave you a hard time, by the way. I'm so sorry. She's an asshole."

TJ was talking a mile a minute, the way she only did when she was extremely excited about something. Brooke had actually only seen it a handful of times, so she was shocked this instance had her that excited. It made her even happier that she had decided to do it.

"Candace was fine. She's hilarious. I can only imagine the types of conversations you two have."

TJ laughed loudly and boldly, as if there was an exclamation point at the end of it. "You really don't want to know."

Except, Brooke did want to know. Despite her best efforts to keep herself closed off, she wanted to know every single little thing about TJ.

"Any plans for New Year's?" Brooke asked, to try to get herself to stop focusing on the sounds TJ was making as she ate.

"Nah. For once, we're just staying in. Gonna sit and watch the ball drop from the comfort of our own couch."

"That sounds glorious."

"Yeah, not gonna lie, I'm super pumped about it. What about you? Going out in the city?"

"I am, but just with my brother. He's going to come stay here for a few days."

"When is he coming?"

"He gets here on Friday and leaves Tuesday."

"Don't worry about calling me while he's there."

"Really?" *But I want to.*

"Yeah, seriously. You guys should just have that time together. We can still text and stuff."

"If you insist. I'll miss you though." *No sense not being honest at this point.*

"Brooke, I miss you from the time you hang up the phone until I hear your voice say *hello* again. Trust me, I get it."

For God's sake. How was Brooke supposed to protect her heart when everything TJ said was so fucking perfect?

***

"So, what was the deal with you and Mom on Christmas?" Mateo asked as the two of them sat and ate dinner together on Friday night.

Brooke took a long sip of her water then sat it back down on the table, staring at it for a few seconds while she thought about how to answer her brother's question. "We got in a stupid fight, and I said some hurtful things. It's all good now though."

Her brother studied her for a long time, causing Brooke to squirm in her seat. "Did I hear you mention something about Tiff?"

Brooke took a deep breath and blew it out. "I did. We've kind of been in touch again for the past few months."

Much to her surprise, her brother laughed loudly and slammed his fist down on the table as if he was excited. "No way! How the hell is she?"

Was he seriously happy about this? That surprised Brooke. He was the one threatening to kill TJ when everything was falling apart between them. "She's good. Still so much the same honestly."

His face became serious and he studied Brooke once again. "And how are you?"

"I'm good. Honestly, talking to her makes me happier than I've been in a *really* long time. It just scares the crap out of me, too."

"You're afraid she'll hurt you again?" Mateo's hand flexed around his glass of beer.

"She hasn't done anything to make me think she will, and it's not like we're trying to be anything more than friends, but—"

"You're afraid you're not able to just be her friend," her brother finished for her.

"Exactly."

"Have you ever thought about giving her another chance? You know, at being more than friends?"

Brooke laughed. What a question. "Only every single day since we started talking again. That can't happen though. She's still the same person. She's against commitment, and I want to find my forever person."

Mateo rubbed at his beard. "You tried that before though and it didn't work."

"I just don't think Priscilla was my person."

"I think that's because you already found your person... a very long time ago."

Okay. Now Brooke was *extremely* confused. She shook her head at her brother. "I don't get it. I thought you *hated* TJ."

Mateo furrowed his eyebrows. "Who's TJ?"

"Sorry. Tiffany. She goes by TJ now. It's her initials. Tiffany Jane." She waved a hand in the air. She was getting off-topic now. "Anyway, back to my point. You hated her. I believe you used those exact words once, while also mentioning that you knew where to hide a body."

"You're right. I did hate her. I hated the way she treated you at the end. But you know what I've hated even more?"

Brooke shook her head and took another sip of water while she awaited her brother's answer.

"I hate how sad you've been these past five years. You're not the same person you used to be. You lost some of your spark. And when I saw you on Christmas, that spark was suddenly back. It didn't make sense until I heard Tiffany's name. She was always the one to put that spark in you."

"She was also the one who took it away."

"I know, and that's the shitty part. I want to give you some real good brotherly advice, but honestly, I don't know what the hell you should do either. I just want you to promise me one thing."

"What's that?"

"Don't lose your spark again."

Brooke sighed and stared into her empty water glass. "I'll try my best."

Chapter 15

TJ

"I can't believe I won't be able to just walk to see you anymore," Brooke said as she sat down on Tiffany's new dorm room bed.

It was her sophomore year of college, but it felt like she was a freshman all over again since she was essentially starting over at this new school. This didn't feel like home nearly as much as Bellman did, but she was optimistic that maybe it would grow on her with time. Mrs. Baker, or Mom as she always called her now, had promised her she would love it, and Tiffany had no reason not to believe her.

"I'm just a thirty-minute drive away though. I promise I'll come see you all the time."

"And you're sure this is what you want?"

Brooke must have asked that same question at least one hundred times over the past few months and every time, Tiffany reassured her this was what she wanted. Although, she wasn't sure if she was trying harder to convince Brooke of that or herself. She loved Bellman. She didn't want to leave the campus or her friends or even her classes. This university didn't even offer the artificial intelligence concentration she was getting at Bellman.

More than anything though, she didn't want to leave Brooke. She didn't want to give up those nights when she would say she was too tired to walk back to her dorm just so she could snuggle up with Brooke in her bed. She didn't want to lose the way her heart raced when she watched Brooke's lips and wondered how it would feel to kiss her again. Sure, she was confused since the church preached that it was wrong to be attracted to the same gender, but it certainly hadn't felt wrong when Brooke had kissed her all those years ago.

"Yes, this is what I want," Tiffany answered once she remembered Brooke's question. "But I don't want this to get in the way of our friendship. Can I stay with you sometimes?"

Brooke smiled and grabbed Tiffany's hand, causing all sorts of crazy sensations to spread throughout her whole body. "You can stay with me anytime you want. There'll always be a spot right next to me that's reserved especially for you. Actually, speaking of which, I know you probably want to get settled in here tonight, but Jeff asked if we wanted to go to his frat's welcome-back mixer tomorrow night."

"Did Jeff actually ask if I wanted to come?" Tiffany tried to keep the disgust out of her tone, but it was almost impossible to mask her disdain for Jeff. He clearly wanted to get together with Brooke, and even though Brooke claimed she wasn't interested in him, Tiffany wasn't so sure.

Jeff wasn't giving up, and Tiffany worried that Brooke would give in to his natural charm. It's not like Tiffany had any sort of claim over Brooke, but also the thought of Brooke kissing anyone the way she had kissed her way too long ago at this point was heartbreaking. She couldn't even think about it without becoming irrationally angry.

"He told me to invite friends, so, naturally, that means you. Why do you hate him so much?"

"I don't," Tiffany lied. "Why do you like him so much?"

Brooke scrunched up her nose as if she was disgusted. "If you mean that the way I think you do, I don't at all. He's totally not my type."

Tiffany wanted to ask Brooke exactly what her type was, but she was scared to hear the answer. If it wasn't Tiffany, it would break her heart, but if it was, it would scare the shit out of her. "If that's what you want to do tomorrow night, I'm in."

Brooke squealed and pulled Tiffany close. "You're the best."

Tiffany rolled her eyes playfully. "I know."

***

"Can I get you ladies a drink?" *Jeff asked as soon as they walked into the party.*

Tiffany wasn't much of a drinker, especially since she knew her parents would be so disappointed if they ever found out she did it, but she needed something to loosen her up tonight. "I'll take a beer."

Brooke wrapped her arm around Tiffany. "Don't listen to her. We'll both have some of that punch you were telling me about."

"Punch?"

Brooke nodded. "Oh yeah. We're having fun tonight."

Tiffany wanted to protest, but the way Brooke was smiling at her was too damn cute and she was powerless against her. "Two punches then, I guess."

"Coming right up," *Jeff said before doing some weird twirl and walking away.*

"Can you try to be a little nice to him?" Brooke asked with a laugh.

"Can you try to be more perceptive of the fact that he's just trying to get in your pants?"

Brooke nodded to where Jeff was walking back toward them, as if to tell Tiffany to be quiet. "Let's just drink our punch and have some fun."

Two hours later, Tiffany had drunk enough punch to not have a care in the world. At least, she thought that was the case until Jeff suggested a game of Truth or Dare. Tiffany shook her head. "No, thanks. I'm gonna sit this out."

"Aw, come on. That's not fair. You can't watch everyone else and not participate." Jeff put an arm around Brooke as he spoke to Tiffany. "I'll take it easy on you. Promise. Truth or dare?"

Tiffany watched where Jeff's hand sat at the edge of Brooke's T-Shirt. "Truth."

Jeff removed his arm from Brooke's side to rub his hands together. Thank God. "Okay. Starting easy. What's your number?"

"Phone number?"

The whole room broke into laughter, making Tiffany feel like a complete idiot. Jeff took another drink of his beer then put that arm back around Brooke. "No, Miss Sacred Heart. I'm talking about your body count. How many people have you had sex with?"

Tiffany's heart rate picked up as she looked around the room to everyone waiting for her answer. "Um, I haven't. I've only ever kissed one person."

Tiffany had no idea why she said that last part. Must have been the alcohol.

Jeff looked much too amused by her confession. "Couldn't get further than that?"

Tiffany shook her head. "I don't even know if the kiss meant anything to her." Shit. Why couldn't she stop talking? She shouldn't have had that last drink.

"A girl, huh?" Jeff laughed. "Wow. Wouldn't have predicted that one."

"My turn," Brooke said from beside her.

Tiffany was sure she was doing it to help get the attention off her, but she was too embarrassed to even look at Brooke at this point.

"Alright, Sacred Heart. What've you got for her?"

Tiffany stared down at the ground. She couldn't look at anyone right now. "I… I don't know. You do it."

"Works for me."

Out of the corner of her eye, Tiffany saw Jeff pull Brooke closer to him as he leered down at her. "Truth or dare."

"Dare."

"I dare you to kiss someone in this room."

That caused Tiffany to finally look up. She looked from Brooke to Jeff, who was now licking his lips in preparation. Brooke turned toward Jeff, and it was too much for Tiffany to take. She started to walk away but was stopped by Brooke's hand on her arm.

"Where do you think you're going?" Brooke asked as she pulled her back.

Then, suddenly, Brooke's lips were on hers. Brooke was kissing her again, and it was just like the first time only a million times better than Tiffany remembered. Somehow, Tiffany had convinced herself that maybe she had played up the memory of kissing Brooke and it wasn't actually anything special. But it was. Oh my God, it was. The way Brooke's hands found their way to Tiffany's hips and squeezed. The way her tongue ran across Tiffany's lips as she asked for permission to deepen the kiss. The way absolutely everything else faded away around them as they floated away together. And then there was Brooke's hand that moved up to rest on her cheek as she pulled back to stare into Tiffany's eyes with all the love in the world. "The kiss meant everything to her."

This time, it was Tiffany who went back in for the kiss. She wasted no time slipping her tongue into Brooke's mouth. She relished in the way it slid across hers. She had no idea how long this kiss went on, but she was shocked back to reality by the sound of people cheering and clapping all around them.

When she was finally able to focus on the room, she saw one of Jeff's frat buddies elbowing him in the side. "What'd I tell you? I knew you didn't have a chance."

Jeff laughed in response and threw his hands in the air. "I don't even care. That was hot."

That's when the panic set in. Tiffany had just done that in front of a room of strangers. She didn't even have a chance to process her feelings before a whole frat house found out she was gay. That is, if she was gay. She assumed that's what this meant, especially since her eyes had always naturally lingered toward girls instead of guys. Her parents wouldn't be okay with that though. They would never accept it. She knew that for a fact.

"I... I have to go."

Except, once Tiffany was outside, she realized she had nowhere to go. She wasn't even a student at Bellman anymore. It wasn't like she could get in her car and drive back to Sacred Heart since she was completely wasted.

Luckily, she didn't have to worry about any of that because Brooke exited the house right behind her. She took Tiffany's hand and gave it a reassuring squeeze. "Let's go back to my place and talk, okay?"

Tiffany nodded and followed Brooke, her mind a complete haze as they made their way through the streets of Bellman. Once they were back at Brooke's apartment, Brooke pulled Tiffany into her room and directed her to sit on the bed.

"So," *she said as she sat down beside her.*

"So," *Tiffany repeated.*

Brooke stared at her, eyebrows furrowed and lips pursed as if she was trying to look inside Tiffany's head. "Did you really think our first kiss didn't mean anything to me?"

Tiffany shrugged. "You never said anything else about it."

Brooke chuckled. "Neither did you. I was always afraid I overstepped, so I waited to see if you ever brought it up."

"I was scared," Tiffany answered quietly. She hated to show any signs of weakness, but it was different with Brooke.

Brooke reached over and placed a hand on her knee. "And how do you feel now?"

Tiffany stared down at the skin Brooke was touching, which felt like it was on fire. But it was a fire she didn't want to put out. "Now?" Tiffany swallowed hard and chanced a look at Brooke, who was waiting wide-eyed. "I'm terrified."

"What are you terrified of?"

Tiffany chuckled to keep herself from crying. "Really gonna make me talk about my feelings, huh? I'm terrified of what this means about me because I know it's not something that parents will accept. I'm terrified of everything that kiss made me feel. I'm terrified this will change things between us and I'll mess things up and you'll leave me just like everyone else does." Tiffany's voice cracked as she said the last part.

"I'll never leave you. You're my Tiffany. Nothing could ever change that." Brooke removed the hand from Tiffany's knee and brought it to her cheek instead, pulling their two faces teasingly close together. "What can I do to help you feel better right now?"

Tiffany took a deep breath and blew it out slowly. "Can you just hold me?"

Brooke smiled and it lit up the whole room. "There's nothing I'd rather do."

Waking up from a dream about Brooke wasn't so bad when she was only a text away. Sure, it was disappointing not waking up in her arms, but knowing she would hear her voice later was a good consolation.

TJ picked up her phone and immediately opened up her chat with Brooke. Without giving it another thought, she typed out a text. **Hey! How is your morning going?**

Her (10:53am): *It's going. I like my job, but I HATE coming back after Christmas break.*

Ah, yeah. I'm sure that's no fun.

Her (10:57am): *What are your plans for today?*

Hopefully working on my book, then trying to work out a few bugs with my app.

Her (11:07am): *Are you ever going to tell me what this book is about?*

TJ cringed. Brooke had been asking her about the book a lot lately and TJ had been very hush about it. How could she ever tell Brooke that it was literally encouraging people to do one of the (many) things that led to the downfall of their relationship? When things were getting more strained between the two of them, Brooke had pointed out the fact that TJ refused to say good morning and TJ had fought with her over it. Two stupid words. Two stupid words that were important to Brooke because she thought it somehow showed TJ cared. Two stupid words that were terrifying to TJ because they made her more vulnerable.

It's really not important.

Her (11:21am): *Then just tell me.*

Maybe later.

Her (11:36am): *I'm holding you to that.*

***

"So, tell me about this book."

TJ groaned. Of course those would be the first words to leave Brooke's mouth when she called tonight. "You really don't want to know."

"I thought you were all about honesty now."

How was TJ ever going to talk her way out of this one? She wasn't. There was no way. "Trust me when I tell you that you really don't want to know."

"Why don't you let me decide that?"

TJ couldn't fight it anymore. She was going to have to tell her eventually. It's not like she could hide it from her once it was published. "It's called *Never Say Good Morning.*"

The dead silence on the other end of the phone spoke more than any words. TJ waited and waited for Brooke to respond, but she never did. "Could you please say something?" she asked when she couldn't take it any more.

"You were right. I didn't want to know."

A sick feeling churned in TJ's stomach and she could taste bile in her throat. "This is why I didn't want to tell you. The last thing I wanted to do was upset you. I'm really sorry."

More silence. Too much silence. "No, I'm sorry. I have no right to get upset about that. I guess I was just hoping… Never mind. Like I said, not my right."

"I can understand why you're mad though. I get it."

"I'm not mad. I'm… I'm just tired. I promise. I think I might actually just go to bed."

"Brooke, please." TJ wished she could tell her she would just scrap the whole idea, but then the past few months would all be a complete waste. Plus, whether Brooke agreed or not, TJ believed in what she was writing. At least, she was pretty sure she did.

"I mean it, TJ. I'm fine. I'm not mad. Just tired. Don't worry."

Even with all of Brooke's reassurance, when TJ hung up the phone, she was pretty sure she had just taken two giant leaps backward.

Chapter 16

TJ

When Tiffany awoke, she was sure the night before must have been a dream. There's no way Brooke had actually kissed her again. Except, the way she was being held in Brooke's arms right now told her everything really happened. She buried her face in Brooke's neck, happy to enjoy this moment of bliss for just a little bit longer. She wanted to soak it all in before Brooke woke up and forced them to talk about what had happened.

Unfortunately, a few seconds later, Brooke started to stir and before Tiffany knew it, she was looking into her eyes. Brooke smiled sweetly and ran a hand through Tiffany's hair. "Did last night really happen? You actually kissed me back?"

Tiffany drew circles on Brooke's arm with her fingers and nodded her head. "It happened."

"You know, I understand that you're scared, but we're going to have to talk more about it eventually."

Tiffany nodded slowly. She obviously knew this was coming. "I know."

Brooke stared at her for a long time, and Tiffany thought she might melt under that gaze. She had no idea what Brooke was thinking and it had her so nervous, she was starting to sweat.

Then, Brooke said the last thing Tiffany expected from her. "I don't wanna talk right now."

Before Tiffany could comprehend exactly what she meant by that, Brooke bent down over her and was kissing her again. This kiss was just like the night before, only so much better since it was just the two of them. Tiffany didn't waste any time slipping her tongue into Brooke's mouth. The way Brooke moaned at the contact only served to encourage her more.

Without thinking, she moved so her body was now hovering over Brooke's. As they continued to kiss, she slowly lowered herself until all of her weight was on Brooke's and their bodies were intertwined. Brooke groaned, and Tiffany thought she must have hurt her, but when she went to push away, Brooke wrapped her arms around her to stop her.

Brooke then moved her hands until they were resting right on Tiffany's ass. Sensations that Tiffany had never felt before shot through her whole body. Instinctively, she started to slowly move her body against Brooke's and those feelings only became more intense. Tiffany thought she honestly might burst if she didn't get some release soon. Being so inexperienced, she didn't know exactly what that entailed, but she knew what she was doing right now was definitely working.

Given the cute little noises Brooke was making, it seemed to be working for her as well. Brooke moved her hands up slightly and ran her fingers along the waistband of the pajamas she had given Tiffany to put on the night before.

With synapses firing from every single spot in her body, Tiffany couldn't think straight anymore. Hell, she couldn't think at all. She felt like she was watching someone else reach behind herself to grab Brooke's hand and encourage it to break the threshold.

Brooke did as silently directed and as soon as her hands met Tiffany's bare ass, they squeezed hard and Tiffany saw stars. She moved her body harder and faster against Brooke's as Brooke continued her exploration. When Brooke's hands started to wander to Tiffany's front, Tiffany thought she honestly might die. But then, as quickly as it had started, Brooke pulled her hand away and gently pushed Tiffany off her.

As Tiffany tried to make sense of everything that had just happened, Brooke wiped her mouth and scooted her back up against her pillows. "Sorry. I don't think we should do that without talking about what is happening between us. I've never done that with anyone before."

"Made out?" *Tiffany asked dumbly. She knew Brooke had made out with some stupid guy she dated in tenth grade. There were probably other people too that Tiffany just didn't know about. Brooke had gone through a whole year of college without her.*

"No. Sex. I've never had sex. I'm a virgin."

Tiffany's body heated up at the words. After completely losing her mind from just one stroke of Brooke's tongue against her own, she hadn't even been able to fathom that that's the direction they were headed in. Hearing Brooke say it caused the panic to settle in all over again.

Tiffany had never been touched by someone she actually wanted to touch her. She had only... no. Keep those memories down. She squeezed her eyes shut as if that was going to somehow push them all away. Except, that only made things worse. Her breathing was erratic and her whole body was quickly becoming drenched in sweat, and Tiffany felt like the walls were closing in on her.

She thought she was about to let the panic attack take full control of her and completely drift away into oblivion until two arms wrapped around her from the side.

"Shh." Brooke placed a kiss on her temple and pulled their bodies even closer together, slowly rocking them in the way she knew calmed Tiffany down. "Shh. It's okay. You're okay. I've got you. I got you. You're going to be alright. I promise. Shh."

Once Tiffany was finally calm, she slowly extricated her body from Brooke's, the embarrassment now taking over. She put her face, that she was sure was now beet red, in her hands. "I'm sorry."

Brooke tried to rub a hand on Tiffany's back but stopped when Tiffany instinctively flinched away. "You don't need to apologize. I'm sorry. I should have stopped us before things got more intense. I'm really sorry if I triggered those memories."

Of course Brooke knew exactly what had happened. She always just knew. "No, it's fine. Nothing like that," Tiffany lied.

"It's me you're talking to, Tiff, remember? You can be honest with me."

"Okay. I'm sorry." Tiffany wasn't able to say anything more than that right now, but she was sure Brooke would understand.

"I think we need to try to control ourselves until we talk about all of this and figure out what it means."

When Tiffany looked into Brooke's loving eyes, the last thing she wanted to do was control herself. She knew Brooke was *right though. She really had to figure out what to do with all of the feelings swirling inside of her now. Now that she had tasted paradise, she knew that she and Brooke could never go back to the way things were before, but the question was whether she was willing to take a leap and risk everything.*

When TJ opened her eyes, she was sure she could still taste Brooke on her lips. That dream was so vivid, and now all she wanted to do was kiss Brooke and never stop. Except, that was impossible for so many reasons, one of them being that Brooke still hadn't made any mention of them getting together.

Luckily, after Brooke had found out about the book TJ was working on, things had only been weird between them for a day or two. Brooke apologized for making things awkward when they were trying to be friends, a word that still cut TJ deep, and then was surprisingly able to get things back to normal. The only problem was, she was pretty sure that hadn't helped her chances of Brooke ever agreeing to see her. It was two months since that happened, and Brooke had never spoken another word about them possibly getting together.

TJ sighed as she closed her eyes, hoping she could maybe drift back to a time when Brooke actually wanted her. The loud knocking on her door wasn't going to allow that to happen though.

TJ tried to ignore it, but it wouldn't stop. She took one of the pillows off her bed and forcefully threw it at the door like that was going to make a difference. "Leave me alone, Candace. I'm sleeping."

"You're talking. You're not sleeping. Now let me in." The doorknob rattled. "I can't believe you lock your door at night."

TJ groaned. "I do it to keep you out."

"Well, let me in. I really need to talk to you."

TJ rolled her eyes but stood from her bed and walked to the door, reluctantly opening it for Candace. "What's so important that it couldn't wait for me to be fully awake?"

Candace looked at the watch on her wrist then back at TJ. "First of all, it's almost eleven. Second, I need to know what we're doing for your birthday tomorrow."

For some reason, Candace was really anxious about TJ's birthday. She must have asked her about fifty times what she wanted to do. It wasn't even like it was a big one. She was turning twenty-nine, for God's sake. "I thought we could sit on the couch and curse the day my deadbeat mom decided to have unprotected sex."

"I love the enthusiasm, but no."

"Then let's order Applebee's."

Candace scrunched up her nose. "I'll never understand your obsession with that restaurant, but if we have to eat Applebee's, we're going there."

Now, TJ scrunched up her nose. "In public? With people?"

"Gross, I know, but it's your birthday. Also, Jump Plex is in that same complex." Candace wiggled her eyebrows. "You told me you always wanted to go there."

TJ's stomach twisted at the mention of the trampoline park. "No. I told you that Brooke and I were supposed to go there, but she cut me off before we could."

"Well, I think it's time you stick it to the bitch and go back there." Candace stuck a fist in the air as if she was leading a rebellion.

"Please tell me you didn't just call Brooke a bitch."

Candace put her fist down and shook her head. "You're right. I don't know why I said that. She's much nicer than you. Much better person too."

"Could we get back to how we are celebrating *my* birthday?"

"Yep. We're going to Jump Plex, then Applebee's. Happy birthday, buddy."

Before TJ could argue anymore, Candace was out of her room. Even though that wasn't how TJ wanted to spend her day, Candace was stubborn. Now that she had made up her mind, there was no changing it.

***

"That's what you're wearing?" Candace asked when TJ came out of her room the next day, dressed in sweats to go to Jump Plex.

"Yeah. So what?"

Candace looked her up and down. "Have you given up on having sex?"

For once, TJ wasn't worried about sex. What she was really worried about was the fact that Brooke hadn't said anything to her yet today. Sure, they were on the phone past midnight the night before and Brooke had done a countdown to TJ's birthday, but it still seemed strange that it was almost 3 o'clock on her actual birthday, and it had been complete radio silence.

Since she was lost in her own thoughts, TJ didn't notice Candace leaving the room, but she was brought back to reality by the sound of Candace clearing her throat. She was now standing in front of TJ holding one of the tightest pairs of jeans TJ owned and an even tighter (and very low cut) blue T-shirt.

"What the hell is that?" TJ asked. "And since when did I say you could just go through my closet?"

Candace shoved the clothes into TJ's arms. "This is the outfit you're going to wear. Trust me, you'll thank me later."

"After I freeze to death outside?"

Candace rolled her eyes. "Wear a jacket. It's going to be hot at Jump Plex." She pointed to her watch impatiently. "Now get changed. We have places to be."

Even though TJ couldn't figure out why Candace would be acting like this, she still followed her directions, and less than ten minutes later, they were in the car heading to Jump Plex. After checking in and getting socks for jumping, Candace kept looking at her phone.

"Have somewhere else you'd rather be?" TJ asked, only the slightest bit actually annoyed.

Candace looked up from her phone and smiled sweetly. "Never. Let's go upstairs to the adults-only trampoline."

TJ followed Candace up the stairs, past the dodgeball court trampolines and the ball pit and down a long hall until they came to another set of stairs that apparently led up to a giant trampoline only open to people over eighteen.

"Oh, by the way, happy birthday," Candace said when they reached the top step.

TJ didn't understand why Candace said it that way until her eyes skipped past all the other people in the room and landed on the one person she didn't think she'd ever see again. She had to blink a few times because she figured there was no way this was real. That couldn't really be Brooke Finnegan standing on the other end of the trampoline.

But there was no denying this was the girl that she saw in her dreams every night. The auburn hair that was flowing perfectly down her back. The perfect body that looked amazing in the dark skinny jeans and Bellman baseball tee she was wearing. And those eyes. Those hazel eyes that apparently still shined when they looked at her. As Brooke got closer, TJ tried not to let her own eyes drop to Brooke's lips, but she couldn't stop herself. The smile that she was giving TJ, and the way those lips shimmered from what had to be a slight hint of lip gloss was enough to make TJ's stomach twist and turn in a way she hadn't experienced in years. TJ hadn't moved a muscle since laying eyes on Brooke. She was frozen in place, but luckily, Brooke had done the work to bring them closer together and now they were standing toe to toe. She was inches from Brooke Finnegan. How was that even possible?

Brooke tilted her head slightly and looked up at TJ. "I was finally ready to see you in person, and I thought why tell you that when I could just go ahead and surprise you on your birthday?"

TJ laughed. It was a complete belly laugh, full of more happiness than she could ever remember feeling. "Of course you would do that. Because you're Brooke and you're perfect and you're…" She let her eyes do another sweep over Brooke's body. She couldn't help herself. This still didn't feel real. "You're breathtaking."

TJ was normally much better at playing it cool, but it was no use with Brooke. Her palms were clammy, her face was red, her heart was racing. But none of that mattered because Brooke was standing right in front of her. *Her* Brooke. Her person. "Can… Can I hug you?" Her voice came out so quietly that she worried maybe Brooke couldn't hear them.

She obviously could though, because soon she was wrapped tightly in Brooke's arms. *Brooke's arms* were around her. Every worry, every bad memory, every fear seemed to float away. Her safety blanket was back. The only place she ever felt protected was right here in Brooke's arms. So, she took advantage of the moment and melted into Brooke's hug. She wrapped her arms around Brooke's back and rested her head on her shoulder. As she breathed in the scent of Brooke's perfume, so many memories flooded her mind. Brooke in her arms just like this. Brooke's smile the first time they ever met. The way Brooke stared up at her with so much wonder in her eyes the first time they made love. All of the hugs. All the kisses. Every single touch. It was all coming back to TJ.

TJ was home. With just one look and one singular touch, TJ was back in the only home she had ever known. She was afraid if she let go, this would all disappear. What if this was all a dream? What if she was about to wake up with the worst heartache yet? Except, it couldn't be a dream. No matter how real her dreams felt, they never felt like this.

When TJ finally pulled back, it was so she could look in Brooke's eyes again and make sure it was really her. Sure enough, those hazel eyes stared right back into hers, looking so deeply at her, TJ was sure they must be seeing right into her soul. "So, you're really here?" she asked softly.

"I am." Brooke took a step back but kept her hands on TJ's arms. She sighed as she let her eyes travel up and down TJ's body without shame. "And now that I am, I can't even remember why I waited so long."

"I'd be happy to remind you." Candace snickered when TJ glared over at her. "What? You're still an asshole. We can't have a sweetheart like Brooke getting the wrong idea."

Candace stuck her tongue out at TJ, and Brooke started to laugh. "Wow. You two really are like sisters."

"I never said that," TJ argued.

Candace patted her on the back and leaned in close to her. "Nope. I told her that, sis."

Then, TJ began to laugh and couldn't stop. Even though there was no reason for it, her laugh just kept growing louder and bolder. She couldn't stop herself if she tried. She was spending her birthday with her two favorite people in the whole world. She also had a crowd of onlookers staring at her while she laughed like a complete maniac, but she didn't care.

"Okay, now you're creeping me out," Candace said after this went on for much too long. "Can we go jump?"

TJ and Brooke followed Candace back onto the trampolines, and in a move completely unlike her, TJ squealed when she took her first jump. On her second jump, she laughed as she did a split in the air. "Oh my God. This is even better than I expected."

Brooke giggled as she jumped from spot to spot on the trampoline. "I know. I can't believe I went so long without coming to one of these."

TJ bounced slightly as she stopped jumping. "Wait. You've never been to one of these? You used to talk about going all the time."

Brooke stopped jumping too and stared down at her feet. "Yeah, but it never seemed right, you know, since we were supposed to do it together. I didn't want to come with anyone else."

"Me either."

Brooke smiled sweetly then went back to jumping. They spent the next two hours laughing and playing and doing everything they should have done five years ago. Except, five years ago, TJ was sure there would have been a lot more touching. Ever since their hug, Brooke hadn't even gotten within a few feet of her.

When they got to Applebee's, TJ took a seat at the booth first, and instead of sliding in beside her, Brooke sat across. Candace only faltered for a second before taking the place that TJ had reserved for Brooke in her heart. *Oh well. At least she's here.*

While looking through the menu as if she was going to get anything other than the steak she got every single time, TJ mindlessly moved her feet around under the table. When her foot accidentally hit Brooke's, her face immediately warmed from the blush that she was sure was spreading across it. "I'm sorry," she said softly.

"No worries," Brooke said without even looking up from her menu.

TJ was sure from Brooke's response and the way she was acting, that she would quickly pull her foot away, but instead she kept it resting snug against TJ's. TJ could barely follow the conversation throughout dinner because all she could focus on was their feet. She wasn't sure Brooke even noticed, since she was pretty positive Brooke would have moved her foot if she had. TJ didn't dare move hers though. She had experimented with every sexual position with more women than she could count, but Brooke's goddamn foot against hers was better than anything else. Even though she was stuffed by the time she was done with her steak, she still ordered dessert just so she had an excuse to stay in that booth longer.

Brooke giggled after TJ put in the order. "You always did love that Triple Chocolate Meltdown." She looked over at the waiter and held up her fingers. "Can we get three spoons?"

"Make that two," Candace said as she pushed herself up from the table and away from the booth. Once the waiter walked away, Candace looked between TJ and Brooke. "I'm going to the bathroom. Big shit brewing." Her eyes moved back and forth once again. "So whatever you guys want or need to talk about, have at it. I'll be gone for a while."

TJ chuckled as she watched Candace skip away. "That girl is about as subtle as a hurricane."

Brooke laughed along with her, causing her whole body to shake, but her foot remained rooted in place against TJ's. "I like that about her."

"So, now that we're, you know…" TJ cleared her throat. Why was she having such a hard time forming words? She waved her finger between the two of them like an idiot. "Hanging out… What does that mean? Is this a one-time thing or…?"

Brooke shook her head. "Now that I've seen you, I don't think I could stay away if I tried. I want to keep spending time together. I really want to try to regain that friendship we used to have. I've never had another friend like you."

That's because we were never really friends. Even before TJ could identify the feelings she was having or when she didn't want to acknowledge them, they were always there. What she felt for Brooke always went much deeper than friendship. Of course, she wasn't going to say that. Brooke wanted friendship, and TJ wanted Brooke in any capacity she could have her. "I've never had a friend like you either. I really hope we can get that back. I've missed you so much."

Before the conversation could go any further, the waiter brought out their dessert and sat it in the middle of the table. Brooke and TJ both leaned in to eat it, bringing them in the closest proximity they had been since the hug. Neither spoke, and that was fine with TJ.

Best birthday ever.

Chapter 17

Brooke

"We need to figure out what we're doing. The end of our lease is only a month away. I think I'm going to stay, but I need to figure out if I'm finding a new roommate."

Brooke had been purposely avoiding this conversation with Priscilla because she had no idea what to do. The logical choice would be to finally move back to her hometown. She could stay with her parents until she found her own place and substitute teach until a full-time position opened up. It was what she wanted since the break-up, except now there was TJ. TJ was only twenty minutes from her now, and they still hadn't seen each other since her birthday a month ago. Sure, that had to do with Brooke's hesitancy more than anything else, but her reluctance to fall back into things, *plus* a three-hour drive, was enough to keep them from ever seeing each other again.

Maybe some space wasn't the worst thing though. Ever since surprising TJ on her birthday, Brooke couldn't shake the nagging feeling of wanting more with her. The urge to jump right back into things was so strong, she worried she could lose her resolve at any minute. "I think I'm going to move back with my parents. I just need to...."

"Talk to TJ?" Priscilla finished for her.

Yes. Brooke shook her head. "No. I was going to say I have to figure out what to do about work. I need to finish out the school year, but that will go a month after our lease ends."

"If I decide to stay, it's not like I'm going to kick you out the moment the lease ends." Priscilla laughed, as if it was silly that Brooke would ever think that could be the case. "I'll tell you what. You think on it for another day or two, and I'll start putting some feelers out for a potential roommate starting in June or July. We'll reconvene in two or three days and see where we both stand with things. Deal?"

"Deal."

Now, Brooke just had to make the phone call she was suddenly dreading.

***

"Hey! This is earlier than you normally call."

The cheerfulness in TJ's voice made Brooke feel even worse about the conversation they needed to have. Rationally, she knew she shouldn't though. TJ was just a friend. As of now, they weren't even really in best friend territory. She shouldn't need TJ's blessing to move. But, for reasons Brooke definitely wasn't going to think about, she felt like she did.

"I need to talk to you about something."

"Is everything okay?"

Why is she so sweet all the time? She certainly doesn't make friendship easy. "Oh yeah, definitely. It's just… My lease with Priscilla is coming to an end, and I really shouldn't stay here. She deserves to start dating again, and I feel like I'm holding her back. The thing is, my goal has always been to move back home and with the end of the school year just two months away, the timing is really convenient. But…."

"You should go," TJ interrupted before Brooke could continue rambling.

"What?"

"You should move back home."

"Is that what you want?"

TJ laughed. "Do I want you to go from being twenty minutes from me to three hours? Of course not. But I also know that your dream is to eventually become a principal in that district. This is the first step to making that happen. You shouldn't put it off if you're ready to take the next step forward. Plus, there's really nothing for you to stay in Philly for. Things are long over between you and Priscilla, right?"

"Well, yeah, but what about us? We were trying to rebuild our friendship."

"There's no reason we can't rebuild it with you back home. That's where you want to be, so that's where you should be. I just want what's best for you."

Well, this went much easier than expected. It certainly didn't help Brooke's heart though. TJ being so sweet made it even harder to stay strong. But she couldn't let herself fall. She wouldn't. All that would do is ruin things just like it did the first time around, and that's the last thing Brooke wanted.

She was on her way to making her dreams come true, and if she was able to keep her heart in check, she would have her best friend there to support her along the way.

***

The next two months flew by. Between putting in her notice at school while also closing out the school year, helping Priscilla find a new roommate, and moving all of her stuff from their shared apartment, she barely had time to breathe.

Unfortunately, that meant she also didn't have time to see TJ. Luckily, the two of them were able to work out a time to get together the night before Brooke left. They made reservations for a restaurant in the city that neither of them had ever been to and as soon as Brooke walked in, she realized it was way too romantic for a dinner between friends.

There was nothing she could do now, so she pretended not to notice the dim room and candlelit tables. She also tried not to notice the way TJ's shorts showed off her legs or just how low her shirt dipped. Nope. She wasn't noticing that at all. Just like she didn't notice the way TJ's eyes lingered on her outfit for a little too long. Especially since she *didn't* wear this outfit with that exact hope in mind.

"This place is great, huh?" TJ asked as she looked around.

"It's awesome. Can't believe that with all my time living in the city, I never came here."

TJ looked around once again, her smile brightening up the whole room as she took it in. "I'm surprised you and Priscilla never came here. Looks like a great date spot." As if realizing what she had just said, TJ's eyes went wide and her face turned the cutest shade of red. "I mean... if you were here, you know, with someone you were dating. Not just a friend. But it is a cool place to go with a friend too. Great atmosphere. Super chill. I'll have to totally bring Candace back. Because she's a friend and it's a good spot for that."

Brooke couldn't help the smile that cracked her face at the sight of TJ sputtering over her words. This was a far cry from the smooth woman she watched doing interviews. "Hey, Tiff?"

"Yeah?" TJ's eyes were still wide and her face was becoming a darker shade of red.

"Breathe. It's just me."

With those words, TJ's features relaxed and the smile came back to her face. "Thanks. But you should know you'll never be *just* anything to me."

Brooke stared across the candlelit table at TJ, and for a moment, she thought about how easy it would be to lean forward and place a quick kiss on those lips that had been begging for attention ever since they sat down. Of course, she couldn't do that, because it would go against everything she was working toward.

Friends. You're just friends.

She repeated that over and over in her mind as her body betrayed her and leaned over the table. As her face got closer to TJ's, she saw TJ's throat move up and down as she swallowed hard. Then those wonderful lips were moving, and Brooke wasn't sure if they were preparing for a kiss or...

No. There were words coming out of them. "You... You called me Tiff. I just realized that."

TJ's voice brought Brooke back from whatever fantasy land she was previously living in and she pulled back slightly. She shook her head to try to shake away all the thoughts she shouldn't be having. "I'm sorry. I know you don't go by that anymore. I just slip up sometimes, because it was what I was used to."

Now, it was TJ who leaned forward, bringing their faces closer together once again. "I... I think I actually like when you call me Tiff. Honestly, when you say it, it makes me hate my name a little less." TJ leaned even closer...

"What can I get you two?"

Both Brooke and TJ shot back, as if they had just been caught doing something they shouldn't. And in reality, they had, because the last thing they should do was kiss. Talk about blurring lines that had no right to be blurred...

"I think we're going to start with the calamari," Brooke said as calmly as possible. She looked to TJ for reassurance, but had to look back at the table because the intensity in her eyes was too much to handle. "That's okay, right?"

"Yeah. It's... perfect."

Within a few minutes, the weirdness from their almost-kiss wore off. Even though they had talked almost every day since seeing each other last, they still filled each other in on what was new.

"Candace is still just as crazy as ever," TJ said with a laugh, before taking a sip of her water. "Different guy every week. I'm happy for her though. She deserves it after dealing with her family for so long."

Brooke didn't miss the way TJ's smile dropped and she gritted her teeth when she spoke of the family she had called her own for years. She hated the pain it obviously still caused her, so she searched for any possible way to keep their conversation light. She playfully reached across the table and stole a piece of calamari off of TJ's plate, tossing it in her mouth before speaking.

"Like you have any room to talk. You're the same way. You just happen to bat for the other team."

The plan to keep it light completely backfired since the thought of TJ hooking up with multiple women caused Brooke's stomach to churn. *Shit.* Brooke put a hand on her stomach to try to stop it from betraying her. *Just friends. Just friends.*

Much to Brooke's surprise, TJ didn't crack a smile. Her face remained serious as she shook her head. "No, actually. I haven't... been with anyone in... a while."

"Really? When was the last time you—?" Brooke cut herself off. "Never mind. That's none of my business." *Plus, I really don't want to know since I'm sure our definitions of "a while" are vastly different.*

TJ finally cracked a smile. "You're allowed to ask. *Friends* do talk about this kind of stuff. I'm pretty sure Candace keeps a fucking calendar of my sexcapades. Plus, I already told you about the last time I was with someone."

"You did?" Brooke furrowed her eyebrows as she tried to think of when they had talked about this. She was pretty sure she had done a really good job of not touching that subject.

TJ nodded. "Yeah. It was the night you called me when you were drunk."

Brooke thought her eyes might pop out of her head. Out of all the things TJ could have said to her, that was the *last* she expected. "But that was..." She quickly tried to do the math in her head. "That was over six months ago."

TJ laughed. "Even if my reputation may say otherwise, I don't *need* to have sex all the time. Plus, I've been busy."

"With your book?" Brooke tried not to grimace at the thought of the book that proved TJ really hadn't changed no matter how much it might seem like she did.

TJ shrugged. "I guess." She stared down at her plate for a moment before looking back at Brooke with more intensity than Brooke had ever seen from her before. "I really meant.... With... with you. With you back in my life, it's hard to focus on anything else."

Just friends. Brooke had to hold in a groan, because TJ really wasn't making this easy on her. "You can't talk to me like that."

TJ furrowed her eyebrows before lifting one, the serious look still on her face.

Seriously sexy.

"What do you mean?" TJ asked after a few seconds of studying Brooke.

In TJ's defense, she seemed genuinely confused, but that didn't keep Brooke from feeling frustrated that she had to reiterate the fact that she was still very much attracted to TJ after all this time. "I'm trying to be your friend."

"And I'm so happy about that." TJ reached out her hand and squeezed Brooke's, the few-second touch lingering in Brooke's body long after TJ moved her hand away. "I'm so thankful to have you back in my life. Whatever you're willing to give me, I'm going to take it."

Brooke threw her head back and groaned. *Why is she not getting this?* "You need to stop being so sweet. When you say the perfect thing, it makes me feel things I shouldn't feel. Things I *can't* feel. Not if I'm going to protect my heart." *There. I said it.*

TJ nodded then stared across the room, seemingly lost in her own thoughts. "I really am sorry about hurting you. It's my biggest regret, and trust me, I have a lot of those."

Brooke waved her hand to try to appear chill, even though that was the opposite of how she felt. Her heart was racing partially from the way TJ was saying all the right things, but partially from the reminder of just how much TJ really did hurt her. The last year before Brooke finally cut her off was the hardest year of Brooke's life, which was saying a lot from someone who spent the first eleven years of her life in and out of foster care. "Water under the bridge. No need to focus on the past. We should put our energy into the present and this *friendship* we are building."

Brooke emphasized friendship to remind TJ once again that that's all this was. It couldn't be more than that. *Who are you trying to convince?*

Luckily, TJ took the hint and they spent the rest of dinner making small talk. Once they were done, Brooke found herself searching for any reason to stay at the table. She didn't want to say goodbye. It felt like they had just said hello, and now she had no clue when she would see TJ again. *What if it was never?*

TJ must not have had the same reservations, because she stood from the table as soon as the bill was paid. She rubbed the back of her neck as she stared down at Brooke. "I know you probably have a bunch to do, but is there any chance you'd want to go for a walk? I hate the thought of saying goodbye right now."

Okay, so maybe Brooke was wrong. She quickly stood up from the table. "I'd love that."

As they walked side by side, Brooke watched TJ's hands swing back and forth, like a carrot on a string, teasing her to come closer. She shoved her hands deep in her pockets to keep herself from doing something she shouldn't.

"Any big plans for the summer?" TJ asked as they walked.

Brooke shrugged. "Just getting used to being back home. It's been so long since I've lived there that it's definitely going to be strange to be back."

"A good strange though, I'm sure," TJ said, offering Brooke a kind smile. "I hear it's great to go home." TJ shrugged and stared up at the sky. "I guess I wouldn't really know."

Her words were soft-spoken, but matter-of-fact. She wasn't saying them out of malice or jealousy. She was simply stating a fact. A fact that made Brooke's heart hurt. It didn't matter what had happened between them in the past, she still hated the thought of her not having a place she considered *home.* It was so unfair. "You've been in this area for a long time now. You don't consider it home?"

TJ shrugged once again. "Home was never really a place to me. It was...." She stopped walking and stared at Brooke for a long time.

Brooke knew what was coming, and she was dreading the words as much as she was dying to hear them. She held her breath as she waited for TJ to finish.

Instead, TJ shook her head and cleared her throat. "Never mind." She looked down at the watch on her wrist. "It's getting late. You should probably get home."

"I guess you're right." Brooke wished she wasn't though. She wanted this night to go on as long as possible.

They turned around and silently walked side by side until they were standing back outside of the restaurant.

Now, it was TJ's turn to shove her hands in her pockets. She rocked back and forth on the balls of her feet while she looked everywhere other than at Brooke. After what seemed like forever, she finally focused her attention on Brooke. "Can I...?" TJ cleared her throat. "Is it okay if I ask for a goodbye hug?"

"Of course." Brooke reached out and pulled TJ into her arms, basking in the warmth of TJ's embrace.

"I hope home is just as amazing as you remember it," TJ said as she continued to hold Brooke tight.

"I hope so too." Only the truth was, home wasn't actually back in Woodbury. It was the arms Brooke was wrapped in right now, and it was even better than she remembered.

Shit.

***

"So, how's it going? Starting to adjust?" TJ asked over the phone.

Brooke sighed as she sat down on her bed. Every day, TJ asked the same question and every day, Brooke gave her the same answer. "Getting there."

TJ chuckled. "Why do I not quite believe that?"

Brooke didn't know how to explain it. She had been home for three weeks, and while she didn't regret moving back to Woodbury, something felt off about it. It was almost as if something was missing... *or someone*... but Brooke refused to think about that. "I guess it's just weird not being in the city."

"I'm sure you'll adjust. You've always been a small-town girl at heart."

The fact that TJ realized that made Brooke's inside's churn. She had almost married Priscilla and she never even knew that. Not that Brooke was blaming her. It was her fault for never really letting her in. "You're probably right." Brooke looked over at the clock on her nightstand. *Just after noon.* "You still haven't told me why you called so early today."

"I was just reminiscing," TJ said, her voice wistful.

"Oh yeah? About what?"

They were getting into uncharted territory, but Brooke was smiling more than she had in the past few weeks, so she wasn't willing to cut off this possible walk down memory lane.

"Woodbury Middle School."

Brooke laughed. "Oh yeah? What about it?"

"Just how it was the first place that ever really felt like home to me, at least while it lasted." TJ's voice trailed off, but Brooke could tell she had more to say, so she remained quiet. "I'm glad to see it hasn't changed at all. Could definitely use a paint job though."

When her words sunk in, Brooke sat straight up. *What is she talking about? She can't possibly mean...* Her heart beat rapidly in her chest. "How do you know it hasn't changed?"

"Because I'm looking at it right now."

Brooke could tell TJ was smiling by the sound of her voice, and it made her smile too. "You're in Woodbury?"

She felt like her head was spinning, because she truly couldn't believe it. TJ hadn't been back in Woodbury since they were teenagers. It was one of the many points of contention between them, even when things were good.

"I am." TJ cleared her throat. "I wanted to surprise you, but I also don't want to force you to see me. It's completely up to you. I have a hotel for the next three nights, but I can explore on my own if you want your space."

Space was the last thing Brooke wanted right now. She wanted to run out of her house, sprint all the way to the middle school, and hold TJ in her arms until she had no choice but to let her go. Of course, she wasn't going to do all of that (not if she wanted her heart to survive), but she was going to see TJ. That was no question. "I'll be there in twenty minutes. Don't go anywhere."

"Don't worry. I'm not going to make that mistake again."

Just friends....

Chapter 18
TJ

"I'm going to miss you so much this summer. Do you think you can come visit me?" Brooke asked as she ran her hand through Tiffany's hair.

Tiffany tried not to think about how good that felt. She also tried not to think about what it meant that she craved Brooke's touch so much. They had spent the whole school year toeing the line between friends and something more. Between her religious college, visits to her home church, and the beliefs of her family, she knew it was wrong to be gay. At least, that's what everyone seemed to think. Nothing felt wrong about being with Brooke. It felt the opposite of wrong. Being in Brooke's arms felt more right than anything ever had in Tiffany's whole life. She wanted to be with her. She didn't want to be scared to touch her. She didn't want to hear her mother's voice warning of the "dangers of homosexuality" whenever they kissed. She wanted to be with Brooke without being gay, because she couldn't be gay.

"I'm not sure that's going to happen," Tiffany said quietly. She hated to hurt Brooke, but there were multiple reasons she couldn't visit her.

Brooke groaned. "But I missed you so much over Christmas break. I can't go the whole summer without you, too."

"Maybe you could visit me. I'm sure my parents would be okay with it."

Brooke pushed out her bottom lip. "But your family will be all up in our business. There's no way I'll be able to kiss you."

"Exactly. That's why you should come to me. What we're doing is wrong."

Brooke scoffed. "Says who? An old book? Some mythical man in the sky?"

Tiffany stared down at the comforter on Brooke's bed so she wouldn't have to look at her. "Says my family."

Brooke put her hand on Tiffany's chin and forced her to look up. "A family's love isn't conditional."

Now Tiffany scoffed. She'd learned time and time again just how conditional a family's love was. "Tell that to all the families who didn't want me, including yours."

"That's the real reason you won't visit, isn't it?" Brooke asked. "Because you don't want to be around my parents after everything that happened?"

Tiffany shook her head. She refused to open this can of worms. "I don't want to talk about it."

"Listen, I get it. I'm pissed at—"

"No!" Tiffany cut her off but immediately felt bad about raising her voice. She spoke softer, but still kept her voice firm so Brooke knew she meant it. "You don't get it, okay? You couldn't possibly get it."

"I know." Brooke looked away from her. "I wish I could. I really do." She looked back up and a sly grin spread across her face. "I'll visit you on one condition."

"What's that?"

"Kiss me like it's the last time."

Tiffany couldn't say no to that. For all she knew, this could be the last time, and no matter how many times she told herself this was wrong, there was nothing better than Brooke's lips on hers.

"Hello? Anyone home?"

TJ popped out of her very vivid daydream at the sound of Brooke snapping her fingers right in front of her face. "Shit. I'm sorry. I didn't see you there."

Brooke laughed. "I know. You were about a million miles away. What were you thinking about?"

You. It's always about you. TJ couldn't say that though. Brooke had made it very clear that the line of friendship couldn't be crossed. "Just how it's been way too long since I visited you here."

A small smile parted Brooke's lips. "I wasn't going to say it, but that's for sure." She tilted her head, that slight smile blossoming into the most beautiful full-toothed grin. "Can I hug you?"

And never let go, please. TJ held her arms out to Brooke. "You know you never have to ask that."

As they embraced, Brooke's warmth immediately overtook TJ. Having her close was like putting on your favorite old sweater. TJ didn't want to let go, and luckily, it appeared Brooke must have felt the same way. They clung to each other as if letting go would mean losing a piece of themselves, and that's honestly how it felt to TJ. Brooke was a part of her. She had been ever since that first time they met, and being without her was like trying to live without a part of herself.

Unfortunately, Brooke eventually pulled away, and TJ felt the loss throughout her whole body.

"So, what should we do today?" Brooke asked as her eyes darted around, focusing on everything but TJ. "We could go back to my house and hang out if you want. I'm sure my parents and brother would love to see you."

TJ's stomach twisted at the thought of seeing two of the many people who ended up not wanting her. "Can we do something else? I'm sorry. It's just hard, you know?" She stared down at the ground as she ran her foot through the dirt. "I'm really sorry. I wish I could be stronger for you."

Much to TJ's surprise, Brooke reached out and grabbed her hand, squeezing it gently before letting go much too quickly. "Hey, you're here. If you ask me, that's a step in the right direction."

Why did Brooke always have to be so sweet? It made it impossible to not fall for her all over again. Although, TJ was pretty sure she had never actually stopped loving her. Being around her again simply helped to remind her why. It also served as a reminder of how badly she had messed up all those years ago, but that wasn't worth harping on now. "Is the diner we used to go to still open?"

Brooke's eyes lit up from TJ's question. "It is. Still run by the same family. Do you remember Bri Buckholtz? She was in my grade."

TJ searched her brain but couldn't put a face to the name. She moved around so much growing up, she barely remembered anyone, aside from Brooke, of course. "Can't say I do. Sorry."

"No worries." Brooke waved her hand. "Anyway, she runs it now. From what I hear, it's even better than before. I haven't been back for a few years."

"That settles it." TJ clapped her hands together. "Want to get something to eat?"

As if on cue, Brooke's stomach growled at that very moment. She put a hand on it and laughed. "Sounds like a great idea."

"Your car or mine?"

"It's not far from here. Why don't we walk? You know, for old times' sake."

TJ agreed and as they walked side by side, she was that middle-school girl again finding her first and only home.

***

"Brooke Finnegan! I heard you were back in town, but I didn't know if the rumors were true."

TJ looked up at the tall skinny blonde standing by their table with her hands on her hips and a wide grin on her face. Since she appeared to be around their age and looked very comfortable making her way around the diner, TJ assumed she must be Bri.

Brooke stood from the table and wrapped the blonde in her arms. "Bri! It's so nice to see you. God, it's been forever." She took a step back and motioned around the diner. "Congrats on all of this, by the way!"

Bri waved her hand nonchalantly. "I'm just lucky. All I had to do was take over." Bri moved her focus to where TJ was still sitting at the booth and held out her hand. "I'm Bri Buckholtz. My family owns the diner. Technically, I guess I own it now, which still feels weird to say."

TJ accepted the handshake and stood to her feet, trying her best to make sure she wasn't rude in front of someone from Brooke's life. "I believe we met a very long time ago. I'm TJ… umm… Tiffany Edminston." She hadn't spoken her full real name in so long, that it sounded foreign rolling off her tongue. She felt like she was introducing someone who didn't actually exist anymore.

It took a moment for the realization to hit Bri, then her eyes went wide as she looked between Brooke and TJ. "Oh my God! Tiffany! You two were kind of like sisters, right?"

TJ tried not to visibly cringe at that description of her and Brooke's relationship. She had every inch of Brooke's skin memorized. That wasn't exactly sisterly. "We, um…" TJ cleared her throat, the tiny hairs on the back of her neck standing up as she struggled to figure out what to say. "Brooke's parents fostered me for a little bit, but that was a long time ago."

"Yeah. I remember we were all sad when you moved back in with your mom. Happy for you though, of course." Bri squeezed TJ's arm, her smile wide, clearly clueless to what had happened in TJ's life after she left Woodbury.

"Yeah, thanks." TJ tried to keep her voice level, but it was hard when her mind immediately flashed back to that terrible time in her life.

Brooke gave TJ a sweet, knowing smile before turning her attention to Bri. "I hate to be annoying, but we walked here, so now I'm super parched. Any chance we could get some water?"

Clearly still unaware of anything out of the ordinary, Bri winked at Brooke. "Coming right up. I'll put our best waitress on your table. I wish I could wait on you, but owner duties call." Bri rolled her eyes playfully. "Let's catch up soon though, okay?"

Brooke gave Bri another quick hug. "Definitely. I could use some friends around here. That's for sure."

"Perfect! My number is still the same from high school. Give me a call or send me a text sometime and we'll get together."

As soon as Bri whisked away from the table, TJ and Brooke sat back down. Much to TJ's surprise, a moment later a hand landed on her knee. Her whole body buzzed as that hand squeezed her knee lightly before pulling away.

"Are you okay?" Brooke asked as she studied TJ's face, her head slightly tilted the way it always did when she was deep in thought.

"I'm fine. Why wouldn't I be?" TJ wore her wide fake grin that worked with everyone else in her life.

Except, this was Brooke. Of course it wouldn't work with her. Brooke rolled her eyes. "Seriously? You should know by now that won't work on me."

TJ flashed another one of her smiles, this one her charming one that she used when she wanted to make someone forget whatever it was they were talking about. "It's been a while."

"Not long enough for me not to know you and all those stupid fake grins of yours."

You used to find my smile irresistible. That's what TJ wanted to say, but she needed to keep her promise to Brooke and not say anything that went beyond friendly banter. "I'm good. Seriously. I appreciate your concern though."

"Fine." Brooke pointed a finger at TJ as if she was a parent giving a lecture. "I'll let you get away with it this time, but this is your one free pass."

"Threat noted." TJ brought a hand to her forehead and saluted.

"So, what do you want to do while you're here?"

TJ shrugged. She really hadn't thought that far ahead. All she cared about was bringing a smile to Brooke's face and she had already accomplished that. "Reminisce on old times?"

Brooke studied TJ some more and raised an eyebrow, a wide grin coming onto her face after a few seconds. "Okay, who are you? I don't think ever in my entire life have I heard you use the word reminisce. Aren't you the person who would drive without a rearview mirror if you could so you never have to look behind you?"

TJ laughed a hearty laugh. There was nothing fake about it. She had honestly forgotten how she used to say that, and she was shocked that Brooke somehow remembered. Feeling more relaxed than she could ever remember, TJ lifted a shoulder and let it drop. "What can I say? I guess being back here has me all nostalgic and shit."

"Hmm." Brooke tapped her chin as if she was seriously contemplating what they should do. "That means we definitely have to do something that we did back in middle school. I obviously have to take advantage of the one time Tiffany Edminston feels nostalgic."

TJ decided not to correct Brooke for calling her that name, mostly because she strangely liked how it sounded coming from Brooke's lips. Unlike when TJ said it, Brooke made it sound right. There was nothing foreign about it. Instead, it was like coming home. Thinking of coming home made an idea pop into TJ's head. "What about stargazing? That used to be one of our favorite things to do together. We could get some blankets and lay in the big grassy area of the park by our… your house."

TJ's mind whirled with memories of the two of them lying together, talking about life as they stared up at the sky. Everything appeared so big and endless those nights that it actually made TJ believe that just maybe her life could be so much more than it was. She was so caught up in the memories of those nights that she almost missed the trepidation on Brooke's face. But why? They were friends when they used to stargaze together. Sure, they did it once or twice in college when there was something more between them, but when they used to go to the playground and stare up at the sky together, it was completely innocent. But then TJ remembered more memories from those nights. Her hand intertwined tightly with Brooke's. Brooke's head resting on her chest. They might not have understood what was happening at the time, but there was so much more than friendship between them even back then.

TJ was about to say never mind, when the look on Brooke's face suddenly changed. The smallest smile parted her lips and her eyes sparkled. "You know what? Let's do it."

"Really?"

"Really. I can get the blankets while you go to the store and buy some snacks."

"What's stargazing without snacks, right?" TJ asked with a laugh while even more memories of their times together flooded her mind like a much needed storm during a drought.

"Exactly." Brooke winked, and TJ knew she was completely screwed.

***

"So, what snacks did you get?" Brooke asked as she walked toward TJ carrying three blankets.

TJ held up two bags of chips. "Sour cream and onion, and jalapeño. I was banking on the fact that you still prefer salty over sweet snacks."

Brooke threw the blankets on the ground then skipped over to TJ and stole the bag of jalapeño chips out of her hand, immediately opening the bag and popping a handful of chips into her mouth. "Sure do," she said through a mouthful of food.

"I also see your manners haven't gotten any better since middle school." TJ lifted an eyebrow and tried to keep a straight face, but it was too hard when Brooke looked so damn cute. *Shit, I've missed her.*

"What can I say? Chips are my weakness."

"And here, I always thought *I* was your weakness." TJ regretted the words as soon as they were out of her mouth. That comment that was totally meant to be playful crossed multiple lines, and she hoped it wasn't enough to ruin this magic moment with Brooke. "Sorry, I shouldn't have said that."

Brooke's eyes dropped to the ground, but that didn't keep TJ from noticing the sadness that had overtaken them. "No, you shouldn't have." She stared down for a few more seconds that felt like hours before looking back at TJ, a sincere smile parting her lips once again. "But I'm excited about our *nostalgic* night together, so let's just forget you said it, okay?"

There were a lot of things TJ wished Brooke could forget, but in reality, she knew she never would. She couldn't blame her for that. TJ didn't deserve for her to forget the terrible things she did. She really didn't even deserve to be spending time with Brooke right now, which was exactly why she needed to get out of her own head and enjoy the night. She didn't know how many nights like this she would get with Brooke before Brooke realized she was still way too good for TJ. Even as friends.

"Perfect." TJ pointed to the blankets lying on the ground. "Raid all of your parents' blankets for the occasion?"

"As if. You know they have a million. I only took three. One to lay on and then one for each of us in case we get cold."

TJ couldn't remember a time when she and Brooke didn't share a blanket, but instead of letting it bother her, she walked over and picked one up off the ground. She immediately dropped it, surprised by the moisture that overtook her hand. "Did it rain here recently?"

Brooke furrowed her eyebrows and scrunched up her nose. "No. Why?"

"The blanket's wet. I figured it must have been from the grass."

Brooke's eyebrows remained furrowed for a few more seconds before her eyes went comically wide and her eyebrows went so high they practically touched her hairline. "Strange request. Could you smell your hand?"

Weird. "Smell my hand? Why the hell—?"

"Just do it, okay?"

TJ gagged as soon as she brought her hand to her nose. Her head shot up to look back at Brooke. "Why the fuck does my hand smell like piss?" TJ knew she could be dramatic at times, but there was no question what the pungent scent was. *Disgusting.* She gagged once again just thinking about it.

Brooke gritted her teeth, but at the same time, it appeared as if she was trying to hold back a smile. "So, my parents recently got a new puppy who isn't exactly house-trained yet. When I grabbed the blanket off the couch, I didn't think to check—"

"To check if the dog pissed on it? You know, before I wrapped myself up in it." Despite how disgusting it was, TJ had to bite her lip to keep from smiling.

Brooke didn't seem to have the same reservations and cackled in response to TJ's question. "I didn't think I had to!"

"And this is funny to you?" TJ laughed along with Brooke because she couldn't help it.

Brooke brought her thumb and forefinger close together. "Just a little bit."

"Ha. Ha. Laugh all you want, but you also touched it."

"But I'm not the one who smells like piss, am I?"

This damn girl. "I hate you."

Brooke smirked and shook her head. "No, you don't."

That smile. Those lips. She's right. I most certainly don't. "Whatever."

"Enough of the pouting. You can have the other blanket. I'll just suffer if it gets cold."

"Or we could share," TJ said as nonchalantly as possible, which was hard given how her body reacted to the thought of being snuggled up with Brooke underneath a blanket.

Brooke stared at TJ for a long time then swallowed hard and looked away. "I'll be fine."

She walked over to the other two blankets and laid one out on the ground then tossed the other one toward TJ.

TJ jumped out of the way, as if Brooke had just thrown a bomb instead of a blanket. "How do I know the other two don't have piss on them?"

Brooke rolled her eyes at TJ once again. "Those two are mine. They've been in my room away from the dog. Guaranteed piss-free."

"Fine. I *guess* I believe you," TJ joked.

She picked the blanket up off the ground and walked over to the one Brooke laid out. She sat down on it and laid the other blanket off to the side. There was no way she was going to use that when Brooke didn't have one. Plus, it was July. What were the chances it would even get cold enough to need it?

Not even thirty minutes later, TJ deeply regretted asking herself that question. The temperature had gone down with the sun and her short shorts and T-shirt were not sufficing anymore.

"I promise that blanket doesn't have piss on it," Brooke said from where she sat close enough for TJ to touch, but far enough for her to feel the space between them.

"I believe you. I just feel bad using it when you don't have anything."

"It's fine. I'm not even cold."

TJ pointed to Brooke's arms. "Oh yeah? Those goosebumps say otherwise."

She stared at Brooke's skin and had to stop herself from licking her lips. All she could think about was the way the goosebumps popped up anytime TJ ran her fingers over Brooke's skin and how they became even more plentiful when TJ brought her lips to Brooke's neck. *Snap out of it, shithead. She's not yours anymore. At least, not like that.*

Brooke crossed her arms in front of her chest. "Seriously. I'm fine."

"You know the whole knowing each other thing goes both ways. I can tell when you're lying."

"Just drop it," Brooke said through gritted teeth.

TJ handed the blanket to Brooke. "*You* should use it. My cold, dead heart will help keep me warm."

Brooke chuckled. "That doesn't even make sense."

"Maybe not, but I refuse to be warm if you're cold."

Brooke stared at TJ for a long time then groaned. "Fine. We can share it. It's not like sharing a blanket is sexual. We did it all the time when we were friends. I sleep with friends all the time." Brooke cleared her throat and looked up at the sky, clearly flustered. "I mean, like in the same bed, not as in sex. Just like sharing a bed. You know, things friends do."

"Brooke?"

Brooke bit her lip and finally looked over at TJ. "Yeah?"

"Let's just share the damn blanket."

She nodded then laid on her back. When TJ followed her lead, Brooke draped the blanket over the two of them. Neither of them said a word as they stared up at the sky together. In one word, it was perfect.

The warmth radiated from Brooke's body, tempting TJ to reach out and take her hand. But she couldn't. She wouldn't. It didn't matter how hard her heart was beating or how much her hands were tingling. She flexed her fingers hoping it would help, but when she did, her pinky bumped against Brooke's. She was about to move it when Brooke's moved on top of hers.

TJ's breath caught in her throat and she had to remind herself to keep breathing. Neither one of them said a word and TJ continued to stare up at the night sky, taking in a world that suddenly seemed a whole lot smaller. The only thing that existed anymore was her and Brooke. It was just this park and this one moment in time. Nothing else mattered.

Unable to control herself now that Brooke had initiated this contact between them, TJ dared to bring another finger against Brooke's. When Brooke still didn't pull away, TJ flipped her hand around in the hopes that Brooke would grab onto it. For the briefest moment, all of her wishes came true, and Brooke's fingers intertwined with hers, their hands fitting together just as perfectly as they always did.

"TJ, wait." As if it was all a dream, Brooke quickly pulled her hand away. TJ was still trying to get words to come out of her very dry mouth when Brooke spoke again. "Is that the hand you touched the other blanket with?"

"The piss hand? No."

"Thank God." Brooke laughed and put her hand back into TJ's.

TJ wanted to enjoy this moment. She didn't want to think about what it meant, and normally, she would have no problem with that. It was the way she had learned to live her life. *Don't ask questions. Don't define things. Just live.* It was different with Brooke though. It always had been and it probably always would be. "Brooke, what are we doing?" She asked the question so softly, TJ barely recognized her own voice.

"Reliving our middle school days?" Brooke asked, sounding just as unsure as TJ felt. "Is… is that okay?"

"It's perfect."

A comfortable silence settled between them once again and lasted until TJ couldn't handle listening to the sound of her own heart beating rapidly in her chest. "Any plans for your birthday next month?" she asked Brooke.

Brooke laughed. "I'm turning thirty-one. It isn't exactly a big one."

"Well, what did you do last year? Thirty is a big one."

"Honestly? Nothing really. I was reeling over the fact that I was turning thirty, still single, and living with the woman who broke off our engagement."

Brooke's voice was light, showing no signs of her still being hurt over her broken engagement, but that didn't stop TJ's heart from hurting for her. "I'm really sorry you went through that." She squeezed Brooke's hand and bumped their shoulders together. "But, hey, that's even more reason to go all out this year."

"Oh yeah? Any ideas?"

TJ thought long and hard about what she could do to make Brooke's birthday special and smiled when the perfect idea popped into her head. "We could go to the beach. We always talked about doing a beach trip together and somehow never did. Better late than never, right?"

"I don't know. It takes a few hours to get to the nearest beach. Sounds like a bit much for a day trip."

"It doesn't have to be a day trip. We could make it a long weekend or something."

"Just the two of us?"

"That's up to you. You can invite some friends if you want." TJ hadn't really thought this plan through. Of course Brooke wouldn't want to spend a weekend away just the two of them. It was idiotic of her to even suggest it, but now that she had, she really wanted Brooke to agree.

"Most of my friends were also Priscilla's friends, and as fun as a birthday trip with *both* of my exes sounds, I think I'll pass." Brooke sighed and moved even closer to TJ. "And as much as I'd love to take the trip we always talked about, I think we both know it's a terrible idea to go just the two of us."

Think, TJ, think. "I could ask Candace to come."

Brooke scoffed. "Okay, yeah, and I'll ask Mateo."

"That's a great idea," TJ said, choosing to ignore the obvious sarcasm in Brooke's voice.

"Yes. I'm sure our younger siblings would be happy to chaperone us on our beach trip."

TJ shrugged. "We'll never know if we don't ask."

"Fine. I'll make you a deal. If we can somehow convince those two to go, I'm in."

TJ smiled as she stared up at the night sky because she knew that no matter what it took, she was going to convince Candace to come along, and even if she had to hunt down Mateo and bribe him, she would make sure he agreed as well. Nothing was going to stop her from making Brooke's birthday perfect.

Chapter 19

TJ

"Can I go to the beach with Brooke and some other friends?" Tiffany asked as she bounced up and down in front of her mom, too excited to possibly stand still. Summer vacation started a month ago and she had yet to see Brooke, so when Brooke asked her to go to the beach with some of her friends from Bellman, Tiffany couldn't say no.

Now all she needed was her mom's blessing, and she would have a week away with Brooke. Even though she kept telling herself the feelings she had for Brooke were wrong, all she could think about was stealing some time alone with her and kissing her senseless. If she was being honest, she wanted to do a lot more than kiss her, and while it scared the crap out of her, it was all she had been able to think about this past month.

"Are you going with Bellman friends or Sacred Heart friends?"

Tiffany knew she should say Sacred Heart to assure her mom said yes, but she was scared to death of lying. If her parents found out, they might realize she's not who they want, and they would decide not to adopt her. She couldn't risk that. "Bellman."

Her mom let out a long sigh. "I really think you should be spending more time with your friends from your own school. That's the type of people you need in your life."

The truth was, Tiffany really didn't have any friends at Sacred Heart, since she spent most of her time at Bellman with Brooke. Plus, she didn't relate to most of the students at Sacred Heart. They were either rebelling against their parents who had forced them to go to the Christian school and were way too crazy for Tiffany, or they had grown up in the rich suburbs going to church every Sunday, which she absolutely couldn't relate to. She fit in much better with Brooke's friends at Bellman, even if she did have trouble relating to them as well. The one place she definitely fit was with Brooke, so that's who she put all of her time into.

"Can I please go?"

Tiffany didn't care if it sounded like she was begging. She needed this trip. She never knew a heart could physically hurt from missing someone, but that's how she felt being away from Brooke now.

Her mother sighed once again. "When did you say it was?"

Tiffany smiled. Maybe this was going to happen after all. "Next weekend."

"I'm afraid that's not going to happen." The smile on her mom's face and her happy tone didn't match the words she was saying. "Your father and I are traveling to that church conference, and I need you to stay home with your sister."

"You need me to watch Candace?" Candace was seventeen. She was practically an adult. Surely, she didn't need Tiffany to babysit her.

"I just need you to watch out for her."

Tiffany was pretty sure her mom had just come up with this as an excuse to say no to her beach trip, but she couldn't fight her, so she qlooked toward the ground—defeated. "Okay. Thanks anyway."

*

"So, what do you want to do tonight?" Tiffany asked Candace as they sat on the couch, flipping through the very limited amount of channels their parents were willing to have, most of which were Christian or family networks.

Candace scoffed. "I don't know what you're doing, but I'm going out with friends."

Tiffany tried not to be disappointed with Candace's response. Even though Candace didn't seem to be a big fan of hers, Tiffany still enjoyed spending time with her.

A knock at the door interrupted their conversation. "Are your friends getting ready here?" Tiffany asked as she stood to go get it.

Candace shook her head. "I have no clue who that would be."

When Tiffany opened the door, her jaw dropped to the floor. She rubbed her eyes because she figured she must be seeing things. "Brooke?"

Brooke, or this mirage of her, held out her arms. "Surprise!"

"What? How? I... is... is it really you?"

Brooke smirked and tilted her head to the side. "I'm not sure who else it would be."

"But you're supposed to be at the beach." Tiffany blinked her eyes, which were stinging from the tears that threatened to fall. The person she had been dreaming about this past month was standing right in front of her. She could barely breathe.

"Here's the thing." Brooke reached out and grabbed Tiffany's hand, causing a tingling feeling to spread throughout her body. "I'd rather be with you."

"I'm not supposed to have guests." Tiffany swallowed hard. Why did she say that? This was Brooke. She could break the rules for Brooke. What choice did she have? If Brooke left now, it would be like having all of the air sucked from her lungs.

There was no way her parents would ever find out, unless Candace told them. As if Tiffany's thoughts had summoned her, Candace walked up to the door holding a large overnight bag. She nodded at Brooke then turned her attention to Tiffany. "See you when I see you."

"Just make sure you're home by eleven."

"I'll be home when I'm home." Candace looked between Tiffany and Brooke and smirked. "You don't tell Mom and Dad that I spent most of the weekend out of the house, I won't tell them you had your girlfriend here."

Girlfriend? Tiffany's body heated up and bile rose in her throat as the panic set in. She had to mean a girl that's a friend, right? "She's not… we're not… I—"

Her rambling was cut off by Candace's boisterous cackle. "See you when I see you. Have fun."

A second later, Candace was gone and it was just Tiffany and Brooke. Brooke looked past Tiffany into the empty house. "House to ourselves, huh?"

When Tiffany nodded, her heart beating erratically for a completely different reason now, Brooke bit her bottom lip. "In that case, can I come in?"

"Please," was the only word Tiffany could push out.

Brooke walked past her into the house. When she turned toward Tiffany once again, she could barely stand it. She was so pretty. "So, what should we—?"

Tiffany couldn't take it anymore. All of the trepidation and worries about what was going on between them melted away as she watched Brooke standing in front of her. Brooke, who had chosen her over a weekend away at the beach. Brooke, who always chose her even though she was so much better than Tiffany.

Tiffany cut off Brooke's question with a searing kiss. Brooke wrapped her arms around Tiffany's neck and deepened their kiss. As they continued to kiss, right there in the hallway, hands traveled to places they hadn't dared to touch before. Tiffany's whole body was buzzing with want. Except it was stronger than that. She needed this. She didn't exactly know what it meant, but she knew she wanted all of Brooke, and she wanted her right now.

"Do you want to go to my room?" she asked once she was able to force herself to pull away from the kiss.

"Yes." Brooke's response was so soft, Tiffany almost missed it.

She took Brooke's hand and ran up the stairs and down the hall to her bedroom. As soon as they were inside, they found the bed and continued making out on top of it. Tiffany let her hand roam underneath Brooke's shirt and across her stomach, relishing in the goosebumps that popped up underneath her fingers. She had no idea what she was doing or why, but all she knew was it felt right.

"Brooke, I want—" She couldn't say the words out loud because it was too scary. If they crossed this line, there was no going back.

Brooke nodded as if she had heard all of the words Tiffany couldn't speak. "I want that, too." She ran a hand up Tiffany's stomach and stopped just below her bra. "But only if you're ready."

Was she ready? Would she ever actually be ready? Tiffany had no idea, but she wasn't going to tell Brooke that. Not when she needed her so badly. For once, she didn't want to think about the consequences of her actions. For once, she was going to do what she wanted. "I'm ready."

"Asshole."

Wait. What?

"Wake up, asshole."

TJ groaned as a hand smacked her in the stomach, waking her up from the perfect dream.

"Hey, asshole, it's your turn to drive."

TJ blinked open her eyes and focused on Candace. "Seriously, dude? You interrupted the perfect dream right before it was about to get good."

Candace wiggled her eyebrows. "Oh yeah? Was it a sex dream? Who were you with?"

TJ squeezed her eyes shut, immediately regretting bringing up the dream. This was the last thing she wanted to talk about when they were on their way to the beach to spend the weekend with Brooke and Mateo.

Candace laughed. "Oh, shit. It was totally Brooke, wasn't it? Was it just as good as you remember?"

TJ opened her eyes so she could roll them at Candace. "I wouldn't know. *Someone* woke me up."

"Sorry not sorry. I'm not doing this whole drive after I was nice enough to agree to come along and chaperone."

"Speaking of which," TJ opened her door so she could switch spots with Candace, "I'm still shocked it was so easy to convince you to come. When you said you had to think about it, I really thought you'd put up a fight and I'd be forced to bribe you."

Candace opened her door and got out of the car then took her spot in the passenger seat, smiling over at TJ once they were both settled. "Well, now that we're halfway there and *you* can't back out, I can be honest about why I said yes."

TJ cringed. *Shit. What is she up to?* "Do I even want to know?"

"Probably not, but I'm going to tell you anyway. When I said I had to think about it, what I really meant was that I had to look up this mystery guy who's coming with us, and shit. Mateo is fucking hot, dude. Have you seen that beard? I just want to pull it. I want to use it as a blanket and wrap myself up in it."

Ew. Gag. TJ shook her head. "No one is using anyone's beard as a blanket on this trip. I need you to keep an eye on me and make sure I don't do anything stupid."

"And by stupid you mean *not* getting into Brooke's pants, right?" Candace brought a hand to her chest. "Because I'm making it my personal goal to make sure you do."

TJ's body heated up at the thought of being with Brooke. Feeling her skin underneath her fingers. Sucking on her perfect neck. *No. Stop.* TJ gritted her teeth. "Not happening. I respect Brooke, and she wants friendship, so that's what I'm going to give her. I need her to know I've changed."

Candace made a sound that was between a cough and a laugh. "Have you? Miss Never-Say-Good-Morning."

"Whatever." TJ glared at Candace. She could have told her she had been struggling to write her book because the premise felt more and more stupid with each passing day. She could have mentioned that every time she sat down to write, she thought about how this attitude was exactly why Brooke left her in the first place and would never be with her. She couldn't admit any of that though. Candace would never let her hear the end of it.

Luckily, Candace didn't push the topic and they switched to a different, much lighter, subject. The rest of the drive flew by as they joked around and sang along to Taylor Swift together.

As soon as they pulled into the parking lot of the hotel, TJ spotted Brooke standing by the entrance. Her auburn hair was pulled up into a loose bun, with little pieces falling out and gathering around her bare shoulders. The tank top she was wearing made TJ's mouth water, and she had to force herself to push all the dirty thoughts out of her head. *She's just your friend. That's all she wants.*

"Where's your brother?" Candace asked as soon as they were out of the car.

Motherfucker, TJ thought to herself. Yet, she still couldn't help but laugh. She didn't know if it was actually because she found Candace's antics to be funny or just because she was so happy to be here with Brooke, but it really didn't matter. TJ was happier than she could ever remember being before. Nothing could ruin her mood.

"Did someone ask for me?" Mateo asked as he stepped outside beside Brooke.

He had gotten much bigger from the last time TJ saw him, both in height and muscles, but he still had that same soft boyish grin.

TJ's heart warmed at the sight of him. She hadn't spent a ton of time with Mateo, but being in his presence made her realize that she had missed him. Every time she visited Brooke growing up, or when Mateo visited the two of them at college, he was a total sweetheart. "Mateo Finnegan." She walked over and slapped a hand on his big beefy arm. "How the hell are you?"

Much to her surprise, Mateo wrapped his muscular arms around her and pulled her into a tight hug, lifting her slightly off the ground while he did. "Tiffany! It's great to see you."

As soon as he put her down, Candace was standing beside them. The look on her face told TJ the next thing out of her mouth was going to be something ridiculous. "Hello, you fine hunk of man."

Of course.

Mateo's smile grew as he held his hand out toward her. "You must be Candace. Brooke has told me a lot about you."

"If she told you anything positive, it was a complete lie," Candace said as she accepted his handshake. She licked her lips and smirked. "What are the chances of you letting me pull that beard of yours?"

Mateo chuckled, his face turning red from Candace's forwardness. TJ was going to step in and save him but became distracted when Brooke entered her line of sight. As usual when Brooke was around, the whole world disappeared around her. It was just the two of them.

TJ took a few steps to close the space between them. "Hey, you."

"Hello, yourself."

If TJ didn't know any better, the way Brooke was standing inches away from her with her head tilted slightly to one side and smile beaming was flirtatious. Unfortunately, that wasn't the case. That's just how their friendship had always been—teetering the line between friendship and something more. The only difference from before was there was no room to topple over that line. TJ knew that, and she respected Brooke's wishes. Hell, friendship was all TJ wanted too, because Brooke deserved the best when it came to a life partner, and that certainly wasn't TJ.

"How about we skip over the googly eyes and get our bathing suits on so we can go to the beach?"

If Candace honestly thought bathing suits were the answer to stop TJ's eyes from lingering over Brooke's body, she was completely wrong. As soon as they were checked in, they headed to their respective rooms to get changed. TJ walked out the door at the same time Brooke opened her door across the hall, and her whole body froze in place. Up top, she was only wearing her red bikini top. TJ couldn't stop herself from running her eyes over Brooke's fair skin that was splattered with freckles she wanted to trace with her fingers. As her eyes went lower, she found that there was a sheer black fabric hanging loosely over Brooke's bikini bottom that appeared to be some type of bathing suit skirt. Instead of actually covering anything up, it only served to make Brooke look even sexier. Which was a thought TJ *should not* be having.

The sound of a throat clearing stopped the path of her wandering eyes. When she moved them up to meet Brooke's, she expected to find eyes narrowed at her. Instead, Brooke's eyes were hooded as if she had been checking out TJ as well.

It wasn't Brooke's voice she heard next but instead Mateo's. "You gals ready to head to the beach?"

"Hm," Candace hummed from where she was standing beside TJ, one finger tapping her chin as if she was contemplating. "That depends. Can you point me in the right direction?"

TJ rolled her eyes. *Hopeless flirt.*

Mateo's face turned red in response to Candace's forwardness. He chuckled, and aside from the low timbre, it reminded TJ of the way he used to giggle when he was a kid. "Are you really asking what I think you are?"

Candace smirked and wiggled her eyebrows then nodded toward Mateo's arms. "What's the point of having those things if you don't use them to get the ladies?"

Mateo chuckled once again, but there was a hint of nervousness to it. Clearly, he didn't have much experience with women as outspoken as Candace. "If you insist." Mateo rubbed the back of his neck and looked to the ground then pointed down the hall, flexing his muscles as he did. "The beach is that way."

Gross. TJ pushed past Candace and began walking down the hall. "This is way too heterosexual for me. Let's get out of here."

The flirting didn't stop when they got to the beach, though. In fact, since they chose the part of the beach with a bar, with every drink, Candace became more bold and Mateo more comfortable. With all of the flirting they were doing, TJ was honestly surprised Candace didn't have her tongue shoved down his throat yet.

Since none of them were ready to leave the beach once suppertime hit, they decided to get food from the bar as well. TJ had switched to water hours ago to make sure to keep herself in check, but Candace and Mateo were still going strong.

Candace stood up on wobbly feet when a live band began to play. She held her hand out toward Mateo. "Dance with me."

Mateo only hesitated for a second before reaching out and taking Candace's hand. The two of them stumbled out to the makeshift dance floor in the middle of the sand and started doing something that somewhat resembled dancing (if you really used your imagination). TJ waited a moment too long to look away and caught a sloppy makeout between her almost-sister and Brooke's brother.

She cringed while she watched the scene like a bad car crash she couldn't look away from, no matter how much she wanted to. "Oh, shit. I'm sorry."

Brooke followed the path of TJ's eyes and laughed as soon as they landed on their siblings. She laughed loudly and shook her head. "Why are *you* sorry? They are both grown-ass adults."

TJ forced her eyes away from the scene and over to Brooke. "I just know Candace. Mateo is a nice guy. I'm afraid she's going to eat him up and spit him out."

Brooke shrugged as if she wasn't worried about it. "He's a big boy. He'll figure it out. At least, at this moment, he's not thinking about that awful ex of his."

TJ laughed. "I don't think he's thinking about much of anything right now. Well, except maybe one thing."

Now Brooke cringed. "Ew, that's definitely something I *don't* want to think about."

TJ watched Brooke while she was distracted by her brother and Candace. Her auburn hair blowing softly in the wind and the slightest smile parting her lips was breathtaking. When Brooke looked back at TJ, she crinkled her nose, which only served to make her look even cuter. "It appears we've lost our chaperones. Guess it's just you and me."

"Are you okay with that?" The last thing TJ wanted was for Brooke to feel uncomfortable on her birthday weekend.

Brooke stared at TJ for a long time, leading TJ to question what she was thinking about. "I think we should be okay." Her eyes dropped to TJ's lips, and TJ assumed she must be imagining it until Brooke licked her own lips as well. "I'm just going to have to work extra hard to control myself."

Shit. TJ took a big sip of the water that Brooke should have been the one drinking. If she was, maybe she wouldn't be looking at TJ like she wanted to devour her. *You and me both.*

***

By the last day of their beach trip, it felt more like a couple's trip than two friends and their siblings. *Just friends,* TJ reminded herself as she walked across the hall to Brooke's hotel room. Candace and Mateo had gotten up early to have breakfast together *just the two of them,* but Mateo gave TJ his key so she could wake Brooke up to be the first to wish her happy birthday. The way his eyes sparkled as he handed her the key made her believe he was up to something, but she didn't care. Room service was already ordered and would be arriving at Brooke's room in approximately ten minutes. Just enough time to greet her with a horribly off-tune rendition of happy birthday and allow her to fully wake up.

TJ slowly opened the door, trying to be as quiet as possible. Brooke was laying on her stomach and sprawled out across her whole bed. Her hair was going every which way and it reminded TJ of all the days she woke up next to her. Her heart ached for that time. She took a moment just to watch the scene in front of her, because as much as it hurt to think of everything she had lost, she was so thankful for what she had. She never thought she would have Brooke back in her life in any capacity, and she was so happy she did.

The last thing she wanted was for Brooke to wake up and find TJ creepily staring at her, so she broke into song. As soon as she started to sing, Brooke startled awake. The look of horror that originally registered on Brooke's face melted away when she noticed it was TJ singing and dancing around her hotel room.

She laughed and shook her head. "You scared the crap out of me."

TJ sat down on the edge of her bed. "Sorry about that. Mateo and Candace went to breakfast together, so he gave me his key."

"Wow. Breakfast just the two of them on *my* birthday? How dare they?" Brooke threw a hand over her chest in mock offense.

"They knew I'd take care of you. Don't worry." TJ winked, and as if she had planned it, there was a knock on the door at that very moment. "Speaking of which."

TJ went to the door and grabbed the breakfast smorgasbord she had ordered. "How would you feel about starting your birthday with some breakfast in bed?"

"I feel great about it." Brooke's smile shined brighter than the sun sneaking through the hotel windows, which caused TJ's heart to clench tightly in her chest.

Even though it was almost impossible with Brooke looking at her the way she was, TJ forced her feet to move.

She set the plates out on Brooke's bed then grabbed the one that was hers and took it over to Mateo's bed.

She could feel Brooke's eyes on her as she sat down and unwrapped her silverware. Those eyes felt like fire burning into her side as she continued to stare.

As soon as TJ looked over at her, Brooke's eyes dropped to her food that she began moving around her plate with her fork. "You can sit over here." Brooke cleared her throat. "You know, just so you don't get any food on Mateo's bed."

Instead of questioning the actual reason Brooke wanted her to move (and ignoring the voice in her head telling her it was because Brooke wanted her close), she picked her plate and silverware back up and sat down next to Brooke. Even though there was at least a foot of space separating them, the fact that she was sitting in bed with Brooke had TJ's heart beating a mile a minute.

"So, what do you want to do today?" TJ asked, trying her best to keep her cool.

"You mean you *don't* have the day all planned out for me?"

In all honesty, TJ did have some ideas, but since it was Brooke's birthday, she wanted to leave it up to her. "I thought you'd want to decide."

Brooke playfully rolled her eyes. "You know I hate making decisions."

"Oh, I do know, which is also why I came up with some ideas of my own just in case."

"As long as one of those ideas is laying out on the beach for a few hours, it sounds perfect."

That wasn't one of her ideas, but now she added it to the list of things for them to do today. "How 'bout this? Let's get our bathing suits on, and we'll start at the beach, then go from there. Sound like a plan?"

"Sounds perfect." The wide smile on Brooke's face told TJ how much she meant that.

TJ jumped from the bed. "Awesome. I'll be back in a few minutes." She walked to the door, but before opening it, she turned around one more time. "I'm going to make sure this is the best birthday of your life.

Brooke's smile grew even bigger. "I don't doubt that one bit. I can't wait."

Chapter 20
Brooke

Brooke tried to keep her eyes from roaming over TJ's body where she laid beside her on the beach, but it was hard. Impossible, really. It was so unfair that she had gotten even better looking over the past five years. What was she thinking agreeing to a beach trip where most of their time was spent barely dressed? It definitely made it hard to continue to keep her thoughts about TJ strictly *friendly*. Like right now, as she watched the sweat drip down TJ's flat stomach, all she wanted to do was lick it off. Which was actually pretty disgusting when she really thought about it, but that's how screwed she was. No matter how much she wanted to see TJ as a friend, it was proving to be pretty impossible. Luckily, her head was still able to drown out her heart and she reminded herself once again of everything TJ had put her through. She had no question that TJ truly did regret it, but that didn't change the fact that she still wasn't able to commit. She couldn't say she blamed her after everything she went through, but she also couldn't let her heart get tied up in that mess once again. No matter how tempting it was…

"A penny for your thoughts?"

Brooke was startled from her thoughts by the sound of TJ's voice. *Shit.* She couldn't tell her what she was *actually* thinking about, so she moved her eyes around the beach, searching for a lie she could tell. When her eyes landed on Candace, who was currently hanging on Mateo's back, she pointed out at them.

"Just trying to figure out what the deal is with those two. Do you think this is a beach fling or that it will actually continue once we leave here?"

TJ stared out at them and smiled, clearly unaware that Brooke wasn't actually thinking about that. "That's a great question. Given Candace's history, I'd say it's temporary, but I don't know. I know they're obviously just having fun right now, but I've never seen her look at anyone the way she looks at your brother." TJ smirked at Brooke. "But don't worry. I'll keep that to myself. If I said that to her, she'd definitely run for the hills."

"Sounds like someone else I know." The words passed her lips before Brooke could think better of them. She meant it as a joke, but she was sure it wouldn't come across that way to TJ. "Sorry. I shouldn't have said that."

TJ reached out and gently squeezed Brooke's hand. "You absolutely should have. It's true, and I deserve to be called out on my shit." One more squeeze, then much to Brooke's chagrin, TJ pulled her hand back to her side. "I know I've already said this, but I'll say it a million more times. I truly am sorry for everything I put you through. I was such a mess after what happened with the Bakers. You were the only one I had and instead of appreciating that, I dragged you along as if you weren't the only thing I was living for."

The only thing she was living for? Brooke never realized that was the case with all of the other women TJ had on the side. Women that she seemed perfectly content with, even if she did always end up back at Brooke's door. "I know you're sorry. I don't doubt that one bit." There *was* one question that Brooke had been dying to ask TJ. She figured this was as good of a time as ever to ask it, given the direction their conversation had taken. "What about now? Would you say you're at a better place?"

On the surface, TJ appeared happy, but Brooke knew better than anyone that she was good at masking her true feelings by flashing people that award-winning grin.

"I definitely like the place I'm at right now, sitting here with you." There it was. The exact grin Brooke was just thinking about.

Brooke rolled her eyes at TJ to show her that she knew exactly what she was doing. "I don't mean now. I mean overall. Have you been able to move on from everything that happened?"

"What do you mean? What happened?" TJ winked at her, clearly playing dumb.

That was an answer enough for Brooke, even if it wasn't the answer she was hoping for. "I know you're trying to blow me off so you don't have to talk about this, but for what it's worth, I hope that someday you're able to truly move past all of your pain from growing up. You deserve that."

"I really do appreciate that, but today isn't about me. Do you think we should get those two out of the water so we can start the birthday festivities I have planned for you?"

Brooke should have said yes. There was safety in numbers, and she could already feel her walls breaking down. Her brother needed this though. Even if this was a fling that wouldn't last, he deserved to have his fun for the weekend. It had been too long since that happened. Plus, she *enjoyed* her alone time with TJ, no matter how much she tried to tell herself it was a bad idea. Instead, she shook her head. "Let them have their fun. I'll text my brother and tell him we'll meet up with them later."

"Are you sure that's what you want? It's your birthday, so if you want everyone there, they can deal with it."

"I'm positive."

"In that case…" TJ stood up and reached her hand out for Brooke. "Shall we head to our first activity?"

Brooke accepted TJ's hand but dropped it as soon as they were standing. The way a pain settled in her stomach as soon as she lost TJ's touch told her it was the right decision.

TJ walked backward so she was facing Brooke. "Did you ever end up parasailing? I remember you told me how much you wanted to."

"You remember that?" Brooke was pretty sure she had only mentioned it to TJ once, so she was shocked she still remembered after all the time.

"Of course I do. It was the weekend you were supposed to go to the beach but surprised me instead. You told me the only thing you were disappointed to be missing was the parasailing that your friends were planning to do." TJ moved beside Brooke and lowered her voice, the softness expressing everything she wasn't saying. "I remember everything about that weekend. I think that was the best weekend of my life."

Brooke squeezed her eyes shut to try to push away the thoughts from that weekend. She knew why it meant so much to TJ. It was when they finally crossed the line and gave themselves completely to each other. She wouldn't say it was her best sexual experience. It was the first time for each of them, so there was a lot of fumbling around. But it was definitely the most beautiful. Back when Brooke actually believed she had found her forever and that she would spend the rest of her life wrapped in TJ's arms. *Nope. Not thinking about this.*

"I never ended up doing it. Is that what we're doing today?" Brooke asked to change the subject back to the present moment.

"It is." TJ's smile broadened. "I hope that's still something you want to do. If not, we can totally do something else instead."

The truth was, the thought of parasailing actually terrified Brooke after she read an article about a bunch of freak parasailing accidents. Yet, she still wanted to do it for some reason, so she decided to keep that from TJ. "I definitely still want to do it."

Brooke couldn't hide her fear for long. As soon as they began to float into the air after being strapped in, she was terrified. She tried her best to smile at TJ. "So, this might be a bad time to mention this, but I read an article about parasailing accidents, and now I have an irrational fear that our cable is going to snap and we'll float around for hours until we finally come to a bloody crash landing."

TJ looked over at Brooke, eyes wide and eyebrows lifted. "Well, that's fucking morbid. Why didn't you tell me that before? We didn't have to do this. I thought you wanted to."

"I did. I do. Like I said, I know the fear is irrational. I'm just having trouble laughing it off like I thought I'd be able to."

"What can I do to make you feel better?" TJ asked, the sincerity in her voice enough to quelch some of Brooke's fear.

Brooke knew what would calm her down. It was the one thing that had always worked from the time she was younger. The question was whether it was more important to feel safe right now or to continue to keep her heart safe from any future pain. When the slightest bit of wind swept across her face, the decision was made for her. *Screw my heart.* "Can you hold my hand?"

TJ seemed surprised by Brooke's request, but she still did as she was asked. Just as Brooke expected, one touch from TJ caused her whole body to relax. How crazy that she still had that effect on her after all this time. With TJ's hand in hers, she was finally able to enjoy the view, and God, was it beautiful. She could see for miles and miles, absolutely no end in sight.

"Wow. I thought the world seemed big when I looked up at the stars. This might make it look even bigger."

"Right? It makes me feel so small. Like just a small blip in this giant, ever-changing world."

TJ looked over at her for a long time, as if she was trying to decide what to say. "You're not just a blip to me. You're my whole world." TJ cleared her throat and stared straight out in front of her. "Sorry. I know I'm not supposed to say that sort of thing."

Brooke didn't know what to say to that. Even if she did, she's not sure if she could get the words out. She was too taken aback by TJ's openness. Too smitten by her honesty. *Completely tongue-tied.* When she finally found her voice, it came out in the form of a quiet question. "Do you really mean it?"

TJ squeezed her hand even tighter. "I've never meant anything more. All of the years without you in my life it was like I was just existing. I finally feel like I'm living again."

Brooke understood that feeling completely. As much as she wished she didn't understand, she couldn't deny that it was the exact same for her. "Thanks for telling me that."

"Hey, Brooke?"

"Yeah?" The word caught in her throat because Brooke could tell by the tone of TJ's voice that there was something important coming.

"Never mind. Sorry."

"Just say it." She was in so deep already—how much more damage could this really do?

TJ swallowed hard. "I just wanted to tell you that I think you're the most beautiful person in the whole world. Not just on the outside, but on the inside too. I couldn't be more proud of the woman you've become. I wish I could be half the woman you are."

"You already *are* that woman. You just need to start believing it." Brooke could still see everything TJ couldn't. The only thing holding TJ back from being all of the things Brooke knew she could be was herself.

TJ chuckled. "Maybe someday you can create a magic potion that will help me with that."

Brooke wished she could, so that TJ could be the woman they both needed her to be. This conversation had already gone too far though, so she kept that comment to herself, choosing to change the subject instead. "So, what's on the agenda for the rest of the day?"

"You'll just have to wait and see."

***

After their parasailing adventure, Brooke and TJ went back to the hotel to freshen up. Candace and Mateo were already there, so the four of them then headed to dinner together at a much-too-expensive seafood restaurant that TJ insisted on paying for. At the end of the meal, she handed Brooke her gift, which was a framed picture of them in middle school. It was their first *ever* picture together to be exact. TJ seemed embarrassed about giving something that she claimed to be "lame," but the truth was, it was Brooke's favorite gift of all time. She had to hold back tears for the rest of dinner because she was overcome with emotions since the gesture was so sweet.

Full of some of the greatest fish Brooke had ever eaten in her entire life (and way too many feelings she shouldn't be having), TJ led them to the next surprise. After a few minutes of walking along the beach, they stopped in an area filled with a bunch of small fire pits. TJ pointed to one of the only ones that didn't have people around it. "It's ours for the night."

"You rented us our own fire pit?" Brooke's heart thudded in her chest. There was no way this could have been cheap, but TJ did it all for her.

"Is that okay?" TJ's smile dropped as she rubbed the back of her neck, suddenly looking very unsure. "Because we can do something else if you prefer."

Brooke reached out and grabbed TJ's hand then gave it a reassuring squeeze. "There's nothing I'd rather do. This is perfect."

TJ's eyes dropped to where Brooke was still holding her hand. The smile returned to her face, but this time it was even more childlike as she beamed at Brooke. "Yeah. Perfect."

Brooke should have let go, but the pull was too strong between them. It was like TJ's hand was the only thing holding her together and if she let go, she would completely fall apart. Just like she had done when they stargazed a month prior, she didn't let herself think into it. She just wanted to enjoy the moment for once and not get caught up in the bigger picture. She deserved that. It was her birthday, after all.

She held TJ's hand as she figured out how to start the fire and continued to hold it as they sat down next to each other, their bodies pressed together as if they needed each other for warmth. Between the fire, the heat from TJ's body, and the still-warm summer air, Brooke was practically sweating, but she didn't care. She felt completely whole for the first time in forever, and she didn't want to do anything to ruin that.

Just in case her loss of inhibitions had anything to do with the two strong drinks she had with dinner, she decided she wouldn't have anymore, even though she was positive it actually had nothing to do with that.

Apparently, Mateo and Candace didn't have the same reservations. They spotted a beach bar way past the end of the fire pits area and stumbled toward it to get more drinks. Her brother giggled like an idiot as his body bumped up against Candace's as they walked. She kept watching them until they were too far away to see anymore. It was nice to finally see her brother so happy after the heartbreak he went through, even if it was just for the weekend.

She sighed and naturally leaned her head on TJ's shoulder. "I really hope she doesn't break his heart all over again."

TJ rested her head against Brooke's. "Candace might be crazy, but she's also honest to a fault. Whatever this is that is going on between them, I guarantee your brother knows the score."

Her words were reassuring and actually helped Brooke to relax. *What is going on with us?* was what she wanted to ask TJ in response, but she couldn't. They were already crossing into a territory they shouldn't. Brooke worried if she asked that question, it would only encourage them to fall in even deeper.

"The stars are beautiful tonight," she said to keep herself from saying all the words that were on the tip of her tongue.

TJ was quiet for a moment, before she spoke, her voice coming out barely above a whisper. "Second most beautiful thing out here tonight."

Normally, this was when Brooke would tell her she shouldn't say that sort of thing, but she couldn't. She was at a loss for words. Her heart leaped, her mouth dried, and just like a vivid dream, she could feel herself free-falling even as she sat on solid ground. Instead of saying anything, she let herself soak up this moment beside TJ. She could worry about the consequences tomorrow. For now, she was going to enjoy the best birthday she'd had in years.

The air was quiet around them for what felt like forever. The only sounds being the people in the distance and mother nature. That was, until Mateo and Candace showed back up, crashing into the area like a boom of thunder on an otherwise clear day.

Candace smirked as she stared at TJ and Brooke then dropped Mateo's arm and fell down next to where they were sitting. "How are *you* doing?" Candace asked as she bumped her shoulder against Brooke's. "Having a good birthday?"

The tone of her voice told Brooke she already knew the answer to that, but she decided to humor her anyway. "One of the best."

Candace leaned even closer to her but didn't say anything for a long time. When she finally spoke, it was in the form of a whisper into Brooke's ear. "I don't know how to word this in a way that won't disgust you, so I'm just going to say it. I really want your brother to dick me down tonight. I know it's your birthday and all, but any chance you'd switch rooms with me?"

Yuck. If Brooke wasn't so distracted by the woman on the other side of her, she probably would have thrown up from that imagery. "As long as you don't say the words *dicked down* in reference to my brother *ever again,* you can do whatever you want."

That seemed to be exactly the answer Candace was looking for because she kissed Brooke's cheek then jumped up. She reached into her purse, pulled out a key, and held it in Brooke's direction. "We'll be fine with just one, but here's the key to my room in case you two need a second one."

You two. Of course. Because now she and TJ were sharing a room. She was so worried about trying to shut Candace up, she hadn't even thought about that.

"What was that all about?" TJ asked after Mateo and Candace said their goodbyes and practically ran from the beach.

"It turns out you have a new roommate for the night."

"Oh? Oh!" TJ chuckled. "Well, good for them, but are you okay with that?"

"Of course. We're friends. We can obviously handle a night sharing a hotel room. It's just like being back in middle school." *Back before I knew exactly what you look like when you come.* Brooke shook these thoughts from her head. Nope, she absolutely *wouldn't* go there.

"Definitely. Just like middle school." TJ didn't do as well at masking the uncertainty in her voice, but Brooke chose to ignore it.

No matter what TJ might think, they could *definitely* handle this. They weren't animals. They were two grown adults who knew how to make adult decisions. No problem at all.

***

We have a problem. They hadn't even been back in the hotel room for five minutes and Brooke was already having impure thoughts. It didn't help that TJ had given her shorts and a T-shirt to put on and they smelled just like her. It also didn't help that TJ simply turned around to change into her pajamas, rather than going into the bathroom. She didn't blame TJ. She didn't ask Brooke to watch her as she slipped out of her summer dress and into a pair of boxers and an old T-shirt. Brooke knew she shouldn't watch, but she couldn't force herself to look away. No matter how hard she tried, her eyes kept returning to TJ. That perfect skin. Her muscular back. Those arms that Brooke used to spend hours wrapped in.

"Everything okay?" TJ asked when she turned back around.

Suddenly, it was easy for Brooke to look away. She moved her eyes around the room to focus on *anything* other than TJ. "Everything is great." She held up the clothing she had yet to change into. "I'm just going to go to the bathroom and change."

TJ's eyes narrowed and her lips pursed as she stared at Brooke, clearly concerned about how strange she was suddenly acting. "Okay. If you need anything just give me a shout, okay?"

I need you to stop being so sweet. Maybe get a new face and a different body. Instead of saying any of this, Brooke simply nodded before jumping from the bed and going into the bathroom.

Once inside, Brooke turned the faucet to the coldest setting and splashed water on her face. This whole day was perfect, and now they were in a hotel room together… no one else around… with TJ looking like *that.* All Brooke could think about was finally putting her hands back on that body she had gone years without touching. All she wanted to do was bury herself deep inside of TJ and watch her as she came. She wanted to be the one to make her come. Not just tonight, but every night for the rest of their lives. But she also wanted so much more than that. She wanted *good nights* and *good mornings* and everything in between, and no matter how much she wished she could, TJ couldn't give that to her.

"Brooke? I'm really sorry if you're uncomfortable right now. I'll go tell Candace she needs to come back here if you want your room back. Or, if you don't want to interrupt them, I'll go to the front desk and see if they have another room that I can book for the night. It's your birthday. I want it to be perfect for you."

That's it. Brooke couldn't take it anymore. She pushed the door open with such force, TJ had to jump away to avoid getting hit. TJ's eyes were wide as Brooke closed in on her like a ravenous animal. Her eyes became even wider when Brooke grabbed her by the collar of her T-shirt and pulled her close, only stopping when their lips were inches apart because, even with all of the adrenaline pumping through her veins, she wasn't going to kiss TJ without her consent. "Is this okay?"

TJ swallowed hard, her eyes now staring right at Brooke's lips. "On-only if it's what... what you want."

"It is."

Brooke wasn't sure who closed the remaining distance between them, but soon, their lips were on each other, and it was exactly as Brooke remembered. Scratch that. It was better. It was as if TJ's mouth was made for hers, and they quickly found their rhythm.

Before she could fully comprehend what she was doing, her hands were moving inside the shirt TJ just put on. *God. That skin. Always hot to the touch.* Brooke had missed it so much. Now that she had a taste, she craved more. She needed to touch TJ everywhere. She needed TJ to touch her too. Luckily, TJ must have felt the same way because her fingers played with the waistband of Brooke's shorts.

Brooke nodded her head and put her hand on top of TJ's, encouraging her to break the plane and *finally* touch her. And when she did... *holy shit.* Just one swipe of TJ's fingers had Brooke seeing stars. She moved her hips against TJ's hand, desperate to feel her even more. As if sensing her need, TJ pushed a finger deep inside of her. Brooke moaned as one finger became two and they both moved in and out of her.

Shit. I'm not going to last long.

Right when she thought she might topple over the edge, TJ abruptly removed both fingers and took a step back. "Wait."

No. Now is not the time to be chivalrous. Brooke was way too turned on to stop now. She was ready to beg and grovel if that's what it took. She was about to say that when TJ spoke instead.

"This isn't right. I've waited way too long to touch you to treat you like some bathroom quickie." She nodded toward the bed. "Lay down."

Brooke let out a sigh of relief. *Thank God.* She followed TJ's instructions and lay flat on the bed. TJ got on the bed as well, but instead of laying on the mattress, positioned herself on top of Brooke. Brooke could barely breathe, and it had nothing to do with the weight of TJ's body. It had everything to do with how good that body felt on top of hers. She and TJ were like two puzzle pieces. They were made for each other, and the way their bodies connected perfectly proved that.

TJ leaned down and took Brooke's bottom lip between her teeth, causing chills to spread through her whole body. *Holy shit.* Their lips connected in another scorching kiss that lasted for a few minutes before TJ pulled away, leaving Brooke gasping for air.

Before she was able to fully catch her breath, TJ brought her hands to the bottom of Brooke's shirt and slowly pulled it over her head. Brooke did the same, and her breath caught in her throat when TJ's body was on display for her. She looked even better from the front. Brooke's hand shook as she ran it across TJ's rock-hard stomach, not because she was nervous, but rather because she couldn't stay still with the electric pulses surging through her body. She ran her hands over TJ's breasts and purred. *Why is everything about this woman so perfect?*

TJ's hands began to touch Brooke's body as well, moving slowly over her as if they were exploring an uncharted land for the first time. When TJ brought her mouth to Brooke's breast, Brooke thought she might lose it. She used one hand to hold TJ tight up against her, while using the other to touch anywhere she could.

TJ moved from one breast to the other then sat back and wiggled out of her boxer shorts. She licked her lips as she moved her eyes to Brooke's shorts. She didn't have to say a word. Brooke knew exactly what she wanted. She wanted it too. She *needed* to feel TJ's naked body against hers.

She slid her shorts off as well and gasped when their bodies came together. TJ brought her hand down to Brooke's center once again, but it was so much more intimate this time. TJ stared into Brooke's eyes as she touched her, looking at her as if she could see right into her soul. Honestly, she probably could. This was TJ, the woman who knew her better than anyone else ever had and probably ever would.

She moved her hand down so she could touch TJ as well and moaned when she felt how wet she was. She was dripping. Brooke had done that to her by barely touching her. *So fucking sexy. Shit.*

Brooke moved a finger inside of TJ at the same time TJ did the same to her. As if no time had passed since the last time they had sex, their bodies immediately found a rhythm. They moved against each other while their fingers moved in and out.

Brooke's breathing became labored as she came closer to the edge. She pushed against TJ, desperate for release. TJ removed her fingers then pulled Brooke tight up against her. "I've got you. You can let go now."

As if her body had been waiting for permission, the orgasm shot through her at that very moment. If the noises TJ was making were anything to go by, she was coming as well.

TJ rolled off Brooke and onto her side. Brooke did the same, and they stared into each other's eyes as they both struggled to catch their breath.

"Wow. That was… wow." TJ gazed into Brooke's eyes for a long time, and Brooke could feel it in her core. Something big was coming. When the words slipped into the silent room, they didn't come as a surprise. The look in her eyes said it all. "I love you, Brooke."

The way TJ looked at her as she said those words was everything Brooke ever wished for. Back when Brooke was clinging onto a ghost of what she thought could be all she wanted was for TJ to tell her she loved her. She constantly searched for any sign of the sincerely adoring way TJ was staring at her right now. All it would have taken to keep her around was one minuscule piece of hope, but she never got it.

Now TJ was giving her all of that and more, but it was too late. Instead of answering, Brooke burrowed herself into TJ's side and shut her eyes. TJ kissed her head and pulled her even closer as they both drifted off to sleep. It would have been the perfect moment if she wasn't thinking about how she had to break both of their hearts in the morning.

Chapter 21

TJ

Tiffany stared up at Brooke moments after giving herself completely to her. She always assumed the first time she had sex would leave her feeling vulnerable and scared, but this was the opposite. For the first time in her life, she actually felt alive. Brooke was so gentle and caring and touching her felt more natural than anything ever had.

"Are you okay?" Brooke asked, slipping off her and burrowing into her side instead. "I hope that was all right."

Tiffany smiled at Brooke's concern. No matter what, Brooke always put her first, which was more than she could say for anyone else in her life. "It was more than all right."

"So..." Brooke stretched out the word. "What does this mean for us?"

For the first time since Brooke showed up at her front door, fear crept in. Tiffany didn't know what this meant. Brooke's question sobered her, and there was so much to consider now that she wasn't only running on emotions and hormones. "I'm... I'm not sure. I'm not ready to define things." Tiffany knew the truth. Saying the words... embracing her true self... would put a lot at risk.

The disappointment on Brooke's face was heartbreaking though. TJ pulled her closer. "Don't get me wrong, I love what just happened. I want to be with you more than anything. Being with you like that didn't feel wrong. It felt like everything I've always been looking for but never able to find. I don't want to lose that." She squeezed her eyes shut to try to keep from crying. "I'm scared though, Brooke. I'm so *scared. I'm not ready to be this person. I can't be this person."*

"Shh." Brooke placed the softest kiss on Tiffany's temple, but she felt it throughout her whole body. "It's okay. I understand. We can move as fast or slow as you need to, okay?"

Brooke was unlike anyone Tiffany had ever met and suddenly all of those feelings, every bodily reaction she had when Brooke was around, the way all of her problems melted away with just one touch from her… it all made sense. "Brooke, I love you."

Brooke smiled because she understood. She knew this wasn't the same as all the other times Tiffany had said those words. "I love you too, Tiff."

When TJ startled awake, she was happy to find that Brooke was wrapped tightly in her arms. Last night wasn't just a dream. Their naked bodies made that very obvious.

She watched Brooke, hoping to soak in everything about this moment. Much too soon, Brooke's eyes blinked open. "Good morning," she said through a big yawn.

"Hey, you." TJ couldn't stop the wide grin that spread across her face. This was everything she had wished for ever since losing Brooke. Normally, she wasn't one to talk about what a hookup meant, but that's because most hookups didn't mean anything to her. This was different. This was *her* Brooke. "So, about last night…" The way Brooke's smile dropped cut off the words TJ wanted to say. "You regret it, don't you?"

Brooke placed a chaste kiss on TJ's temple. "Last night was everything I dreamed of and I could never regret it. But that's exactly why it can't ever happen again."

TJ's heart clenched. *No.* This couldn't be happening. Not again. She couldn't lose Brooke. She had barely survived the first time. *Shit. How the hell did I mess this up?* "It's different now. I don't only want sex. I promise." It was hard to push out the next words after seeing Brooke's trepidation and feeling the impending rejection, but she had to. She needed Brooke to know that she meant them. "I love you, Brooke. I'm in love with you. I have been for as long as I can remember. It never stopped for me. I know I did a really shitty job of showing it most of the time, but I'll make it up to you. I'll be better this time. I promise."

"I want to believe you. I really do." Brooke squeezed her eyes shut and TJ feared she was going to cry. "But, TJ, you hurt me so bad before. I almost didn't survive the pain you caused me. You made so many promises every single time we had sex, and you never kept them."

"I've changed." Did she really though? Her whole brand was based around not getting attached to people. Even this morning, she hadn't been able to bring herself to say good morning to Brooke because of the fear that gripped her over those two stupid fucking words. TJ was still the same mess she had always been. *Fuck.*

"Have you?"

Shit. She couldn't lie to Brooke. She couldn't continue to be the woman who made promises she couldn't keep. "I will. For you. I'll get help. I'll finally face my fucking past. I'll do anything."

Brooke smiled sweetly, her eyes filled with so much love. Even if she wasn't speaking the words out loud, TJ could see it there, and it was the one thing helping her to hold on to hope. "I want *all* of that, but I don't want you to do it for me. I want you to do it for yourself."

"What if I do it for both of us?" TJ was desperate. She couldn't let Brooke slip away once again.

Brooke was eerily quiet as if she was strongly considering TJ's question. "That's fine... I just don't want you to think that, even if you get help moving past everything that happened to you, that it means we can be together. I'm always going to be your friend, and I'll be your biggest cheerleader, but I can't guarantee that I'll ever be able to fully open my heart to you again. I wish I could, but I don't know. I'm scared."

TJ understood fear all too well. She spent her whole life in fear, but instead of facing it, had pushed it into the deepest depths of her soul, never truly dealing with it. "I understand that completely." She grabbed Brooke's hand and took a deep breath, looking fear straight in the face since what she was about to say was probably the most honest she had ever been in her entire life. "You're it for me, Brooke. I'm sorry it took me this long to realize it and that I caused you so much pain along the way. No matter what happens between us, whether we're friends or something more, I'll spend the rest of my life making it up to you. I don't want anyone else. I don't want to pretend that another woman's touch comes close to comparing to yours. If that means a life of celibacy, so be it."

The way the word *celibacy* stung made TJ wonder if maybe she shouldn't have gone so far. Sex was the one thing that she let herself feel. Could she really go without it? Yes, she could, because those were empty feelings. After experiencing Brooke's touch once again, she knew it would never be the same with anyone else.

Much to TJ's surprise, Brooke leaned in and placed a lingering kiss right on her lips. "I love you, TJ. I need you to know that no matter what happens, that won't ever change." She sighed and pulled away, causing the empty feeling that TJ knew way too well to return. "I need to go, though. I might talk a big game, but I'm still human. I won't be able to control myself if I stay wrapped up in your naked body."

"Can I see you soon?" TJ asked, her voice like one of a scared child.

Brooke smiled the sweet smile that never ceased to put TJ at ease. "Of course. I would love that. Thanks for the greatest birthday of my life."

And just like that, Brooke was gone as if everything from the night before was just an illusion. Except, it wasn't at all, and TJ knew exactly what she needed to do.

***

"I think I'm going to start seeing a therapist."

Candace whipped her head toward TJ so fast that it was a wonder it didn't fly off. "*You* want to see a therapist?"

Not exactly the reaction I was expecting. TJ rubbed the back of her neck. "Yeah. Is... is that bad?"

"Not at all. I've been seeing a therapist for years. You don't go through the shit that we've both been through and *not* see a therapist. At least, not if you want to be a functioning adult. No offense."

How did TJ never know that Candace saw a therapist? "Why would I be offended?" TJ asked, deciding to ask one question at a time.

Candace chuckled. "Because I pretty much just insinuated that you're not a functioning adult."

TJ laughed along with her, because how could she be mad about something that was true? "Hence why I'm going into therapy."

"And why the sudden change, huh?" Even though TJ was watching the road as she drove them home from the beach, she noticed out of the corner of her eye that Candace was looking at her with a raised eyebrow. "Does this have anything to do with the time you spent with your dream woman last night? Something you've been very hush-hush about this whole drive."

"And what about you?" TJ asked in hopes of changing the subject. "While I appreciate not getting all of the gory details, it's weird for you not to tell me anything after you've had sex."

Candace shrugged. "That's because we didn't have sex."

"What?" Now it was TJ's head that was on a swivel. She had to have heard that wrong.

"We stayed up most of the night talking. Mateo isn't like anyone I've ever met. I'm sure we'll have sex at some point, and I have no doubt that it will be amazing, but last night wasn't that time."

TJ shook her head. There was no way any of this was true. "So, instead of having sex like you planned, you spent the night talking?"

"*Technically*, we never planned to have sex. I don't want to speak too soon, but I think this might actually be the real thing for once. I don't want to ruin it by jumping in too fast."

"But you said—"

Candace put up a hand to cut her off. "All lies to give you and Brooke the alone time you never would have taken on your own. And if this sudden self-awareness has anything to do with last night, then I'd say it turned out well."

TJ cringed. "Depends how you define *turning out well*." The night was perfect. The morning… not so much. Still, she wasn't going to let herself get frustrated. She meant everything she said to Brooke and she was ready to make the changes she needed to.

"Did *you* have sex?"

TJ tried her best to bite back her smile at the thought of Brooke underneath her, nails digging into her back just like the old days. "Kind of."

"Kind of?" Candace scoffed. "How do you *kind of* have sex? That sounds like something a straight girl says when a guy comes too quickly and doesn't get her off. Did Brooke not make you come? Did *you* not make her come? If so, I'm very disappointed in you."

TJ laughed at her ridiculous friend. "No need to be disappointed. We both came. All I meant was that it's not just sex when it's with Brooke. It's so much more than that. Comparing it to what I've done with so many other women doesn't seem right."

"Oh, wow. You've got it bad. So, what does this mean? Are you two dating now? Friends with benefits? Fuck buddies?"

TJ's head was spinning from all of Candace's questions. *Is she going to even let me talk?* "Just friends. Nothing more. According to Brooke, last night was a one-time thing."

"Ouch. Sorry, dude."

"It's okay. It's what I deserve. Brooke thinks I need to work to move on from everything that happened in my past before I'll fully be able to commit to someone."

"She's not wrong there."

"I know, which is exactly why I'm finally going to face my demons."

"Aw, my little girl is growing up." Candace took out her phone and immediately started to type. "I'm sending you the name of my therapist and links to all of my favorite self-help books. You're welcome."

***

"We need to talk."

Tiffany watched Brooke with wide eyes, worried about what she was going to say to her. It was most likely that whatever this was that was happening between them couldn't happen anymore. Brooke probably realized that Tiffany wasn't good enough for her. As much as it hurt, she knew it was only a matter of time until that happened. She had never been good enough for anyone.

Tiffany swallowed hard and wiped her sweaty hands on her jeans. "Yeah?"

Brooke put a hand on Tiffany's chin and forced their eyes to meet. "Please don't look at me like that."

"Like what?"

"Like I'm about to break your heart."

"Well, are you?" Tiffany chuckled, but it was completely forced, which she was sure Brooke noticed.

"If anyone is going to be breaking hearts, it's you."

Tiffany furrowed her eyebrows and wiped her hand on her pants once more before intertwining her fingers with Brooke's. "I would never break your heart."

"I know I told you we didn't have to put a label on this, but it's been months of spending weekends in bed together, late nights on the phone, and expressing how we feel about each other."

"And you don't want that?" Tiffany wasn't trying to play dumb. She just honestly didn't know where Brooke was going with this.

"Of course I want that, but I also want to know that this is more than just a fling. I'm going to graduate in a few months, and I need to make some big decisions. There's nothing I want more than to stay around here with you, but I need to know what this is before I do that."

"So, what do you want from me?" Tiffany asked softly, still worried that this was all leading down a road to where Brooke left her.

"I don't know." Brooke rubbed her face as if she was frustrated. "I don't want to give you an ultimatum, but I also want a commitment from you before I decide to stick around."

"Meaning?"

Brooke laughed and threw her head back. "Come on, Tiff. You're not dumb. Do I really have to spell it out for you? I want you to be my girlfriend."

"You want me to be your girlfriend?" Tiffany pointed to herself, as if there was someone else in the room Brooke could be talking about.

"Yes, you. The girl I haven't been able to keep my hands off of. The one I say 'I love you' to every night before bed. You, Tiffany Edminston. I want you to be my girlfriend."

The word Tiffany assumed would terrify her did the exact opposite. That one word made her happier than she had ever been before. "I want to be your girlfriend."

"Really?" The way Brooke's voice went up two octaves was too adorable for words.

"Really." Some of TJ's initial excitement was drowned out by thoughts of her parents. "I'm not ready to tell my family yet. Is that okay?"

"We don't have to tell anyone you don't want to. All I care about is that both of us understand what this is." Brooke squeezed Tiffany's hand. "And now that we have that sorted out, I have one more question for you. If I can find a job close to your school, will you move in with me next fall?"

TJ jumped up at the sound of her name being called. *Shit.* Did she really just doze off waiting for her therapist to take her back? *How embarrassing.* It was most likely due to the fact that she rolled around all night instead of actually sleeping since she was so worried about her first therapy session.

She followed the therapist back to the room then sat silently, her hands sweating as she waited for the therapist to speak.

After what felt like hours, the therapist finally did just that. "I'm Noelle Trixie. It's very nice to meet you TJ. I wanted to start out this first session by asking you what you are hoping to get out of therapy."

What a loaded question. How the hell am I supposed to answer that? "I'm not going to lie. I'm not really sure what I'm doing here. Don't you have a magic wand or something that you can wave to magically make my shitty past and all my issues just go away?"

The therapist laughed as she shook her head. "I wish I did."

"Do you really, though? Wouldn't that kind of put you out of a job?"

The therapist raised an eyebrow and smirked. "I guess it would make this job useless, but think of how much money I could charge if I could wave a wand and make someone's every trouble go away?"

"Very true." Without even realizing it, this back and forth had helped TJ to relax. This wasn't like the therapy she saw on TV where the therapist simply nodded, jotted down notes, and asked "How do you feel about that?" At least, not yet. "So, where do we start? Do you at least have some magic words to save me from myself?"

"I want to start by hearing about you, from the beginning. I got a little bit from your intake form, but it wasn't very detailed."

TJ flashed her the grin she used to win people over. "Sorry about that. I'm not a big fan of talking about myself."

"Well, the first step of therapy is going to be to help you get more comfortable with that. Once we get past the details of your past, we'll focus on how to keep them from affecting your future. At least, in a negative sense."

"A little late for that," TJ said with a laugh, since the only way she knew how to get through awkward situations like this was to make jokes. And talking about her past was *definitely* awkward.

Instead of laughing, her therapist studied her, eyes laser-focused as if she was taking in everything down to each breath TJ took. "Let's start with your childhood. I know you said you were in and out of foster care. Can you tell me a little bit about how you ended up there?"

TJ shrugged. "No dad. Deadbeat mom. You know, the usual."

"I'm going to need a little more than that."

TJ took a deep breath and pictured Brooke's face. She had to take this seriously for her. She knew Brooke said she should do it for herself, but it was much more motivating to do it for the woman of her dreams, so that's exactly what she would do. "The first time I went into foster care was when I was…" *And we're off.*

***

"So, how is therapy going?" Brooke asked during one of her and TJ's nightly phone calls.

"It's going." TJ still wasn't sure how she felt about it. After a month of two sessions a week, they were still struggling to get through her life story. She knew that was no one's fault but her own, since she wasted half of the session trying to avoid talking about the hard stuff. The worst was yet to come since they were going to start talking about college in her next session, which meant not only talking about the Bakers but also the rise and fall of her romantic relationship with Brooke. Even though she would never admit it to anyone, even Brooke, she spent a few hours after each therapy session crying on her couch. Thank God she still had money coming in from her app and first book because she certainly wasn't doing anything else. "How is substitute teaching?" she asked to change the subject.

Brooke let out a long sigh. "It's going."

"Not what you want to be doing, I take it?"

"No, but I know it's a step in the right direction. I just have to keep reminding myself of that." Brooke was silent for a minute before she spoke again, her voice softer now. "When can I see you? I miss you."

TJ missed Brooke too. God, she missed her so much. "Tell me when and where, and I'll be there."

"Well, as we learned at the beach, we probably shouldn't be sleeping in the same quarters. I can get a hotel by you and—"

"Nonsense." TJ knew Brooke had taken a pay cut going down to substitute teaching, and even though she didn't have to pay for rent, she was paying off her master's classes. "I'll come to you. I don't mind getting a hotel. You're busier than me right now, so that way you don't have to travel."

"Are you sure? I know you don't like coming—"

"Positive. If I can survive another week of therapy, I'll definitely be able to survive a weekend in Woodbury."

***

"I'm so excited you're here!" Tiffany said as she skipped down the sidewalk to greet Brooke before pulling her into a tight hug.

It was two days after Christmas and Brooke was visiting Tiffany at her parents' house. Thank God. After living together the past semester, Tiffany had gotten so used to waking up next to Brooke that the past two weeks apart were awful. She wanted to stay at their place until Brooke was on Christmas break, but her parents insisted she come home, since they didn't understand why she would want to stay after school ended just to be with a friend.

Which was exactly why Tiffany had decided to come out to them. Brooke was sweet enough to be there while she did, which was part of the reason she was visiting (that and the fact that neither one of them could stand to be apart).

"How are you feeling?" Brooke asked as soon as they split apart.

"I'm good. It's going to be fine. I mean, they're my parents. They chose me. Even if it's not legal yet, they've still treated me better than anyone before. They have to accept this. It might be hard at first, but they'll get there. Yeah. They'll get there." Tiffany wasn't sure if she was more so trying to convince Brooke or herself.

"That's great, sweetie." Brooke quickly squeezed her hand before dropping it again, making Tiffany long for the day they could hold hands in pride. "Do you want to tell them now or…?"

"I do want to do it soon, but let's spend a few good hours together before I do. You know, just in case it doesn't go well."

The hours flew by and when dinner time rolled around, Tiffany figured that was as good of time as any to come out. Since her brothers weren't there, she'd have to come out to them later, but at least her parents and Candace would know.

"So, there's something I need to tell all of you." TJ had barely gotten the words out when Brooke's hand was holding hers underneath the table. She squeezed gently as Tiffany took a deep breath and prepared herself to continue. "I know this may come as a surprise, and although our church says it's wrong, there are more and more churches that are starting to say that God doesn't actually have a problem with it. What I'm trying to say is, I'm gay."

A deadly silence took over the room with her announcement. Both of her parents stared at her with wide eyes and mouths agape. Candace smirked, but Tiffany couldn't tell if that was because she was happy for her or excited for the possible impending blow-up.

She wasn't going to have to question it for long, because Candace was the first to speak up. "Wow, that's really—"

Tiffany's mom put up her hand to stop Candace. "An abomination. That's what it is." Her face slowly turned more red than Tiffany had ever seen it, but what was even more unnerving than the glare accompanying her ever-reddening face was when she suddenly smiled. She linked her hands on top of the table while her smile grew bigger. "Don't worry. We will figure this out as a family." She averted her gaze from Tiffany to Brooke. "Brooke, you need to go home."

Brooke moved her eyes between Tiffany and her mom a few times before letting them stay on Tiffany, who was having trouble even looking at her. It was too much to handle. She had no idea what to do. Brooke squeezed her hand just as she had done before. "I'm not going to leave you, don't worry."

Brooke's words should have been comforting, but they hurt so bad. It hurt knowing whatever happened was going to end up affecting Brooke in one way or another. Brooke… the only person who had been there for her for what felt like her entire life. Brooke… the girl she was head over heels in love with. But, what was she going to do? This was her family. The only family that ever wanted her. She couldn't handle a huge blow-up between her person and her family.

She forced her eyes over to Brooke's and blinked back the tears. "I think you should go."

Brooke forcefully shook her head back and forth. "No, I'm not leaving you. Not now."

Tiffany squeezed her hand and forced a smile to try to reassure her. "It will be okay. I promise. I'll call you later, okay?"

Brooke waited another moment before she dropped Tiffany's hand and stood from the table. "Are you sure?"

Of course Tiffany wasn't sure, but she didn't really think she had much of a choice. "Yeah, um, let me walk you out."

The two of them walked to Brooke's car in silence. When Brooke went to open the door, Tiffany pulled her into her arms. All of her emotions overtook her and she sobbed against Brooke's shoulder. "I'm sorry. I'm so, so sorry."

Brooke held her for a moment before pulling back and swiping her thumb over the tears on Tiffany's cheek. "You don't need to be sorry. We'll get through this together. No matter what happens, I'm here for you."

"I feel so bad you drove all this way and now—"

"Don't give that a second thought. If you need me at any point I'll be here in an instant."

"I... I didn't even get to kiss you."

A small smile came to Brooke's face. "I can fix that." She pulled Tiffany tight up against her and kissed her like nothing could ever touch them. It was the kind of kiss that made Tiffany feel like she was right where she was meant to be. Like no matter what happened with her parents, it was going to be okay because she had Brooke, and nothing else mattered.

After a few seconds, she pulled away from the kiss. If only she had known that would be their last kiss as a couple, maybe she would have held Brooke close just a little bit longer.

The sound of her phone ringing woke TJ up from her restless sleep. A cold sweat engulfed her whole body as she thought back on her latest nightmare. That didn't stop the smile from spreading across her face when she saw who was calling her.

"Hey there," she said sleepily.

"I didn't wake you, did I?" Brooke asked.

TJ pulled her phone away and looked at the time. "You may have, but it's a good thing you did. I need to be at therapy in less than an hour."

"Well, in that case, you're welcome. I'm just driving to work and wanted to say good morning."

Good morning. Two simple words that TJ still couldn't get out. Speaking them would be like drinking poison. Even though she couldn't explain her logic, saying them was sure to hurt her. "I'm excited to see you later." Not exactly a *good morning*, but that still seemed like a reasonable consolation.

"Me either." Brooke's voice was soft and loving and pulled at TJ's heart. "I don't want to keep you when you need to get ready for therapy. I hope your session goes well. See you later."

Once they hung up, TJ hopped out of bed, showered, then headed to therapy. As usual, as soon as she was seated in her therapist's office, they jumped into things.

"So, tell me, TJ, how have you been doing since starting therapy? Do you feel as though anything has changed for you?"

"I'm having even more nightmares, so there's that." TJ laughed as if they weren't completely crippling.

Her therapist furrowed her eyebrows and jotted down a note. "And when was the last time you had a nightmare?"

"Last night."

Her therapist nodded slowly, giving nothing away about what she was thinking. "What was it about?"

"Do I really need to talk about it?" Another laugh, but this time she couldn't hide the strain behind it.

"If you could."

TJ recounted the nightmare, stopping right at the point where Brooke called and woke her up. *Thank God.* At least that saved her from the worst part. Or so she thought...

"We haven't talked about this yet. Tell me what happened after Brooke left."

TJ swallowed hard. This was near the top of her list of worst memories, which was saying a lot since there were so many of them. "When I went inside, the people I called my parents sat me down and told me I needed help."

"Did you think you needed help?"

TJ's eyes burned as the tears threatened to fall. *No. Not here. Not right now.* "I didn't know what to think. I was so confused."

"Did you accept the help?"

TJ scoffed. "You mean therapy, AKA conversion therapy with someone from my church. I'm sure you'd be shocked to learn that didn't work."

"When you talked about kissing Brooke goodbye, you said that was the last time you kissed as a couple. Can you elaborate on that?"

Please. No. Please don't do this. Even though she tried to push them away, flashbacks came of her so-called parents giving her the worst ultimatum of all time—she was to break things off with Brooke or they would have no other choice than to not move forward with the adoption. Now that she was old enough to understand what gaslighting was, she saw the situation in a whole new light. Everything they said about looking out for her, all of the blame placed on her shoulders, the fucking shit about *what was best for the family. The only family she ever had. The only family she ever would have.* A sob escaped from her throat and the dam was broken. Her tears fell like never before.

"That was when I made the biggest mistake of my life. I broke up with the only person whoever truly loved me—at least, the real me. The worst part is, even though it broke her heart, breaking up with her was the least horrible thing I did to her at that time."

"I really want to get into this more. I hate to say it, but we're actually running out of time, and I want to talk about one other thing with you before we finish. But before I do, is there anything else you really want to talk to me about? I don't want to leave you feeling unfulfilled."

TJ laughed through her tears. *Why the hell would I want to talk about this more? No thank you.* "I'm good."

"I kind of figured that." The therapist winked. "Now, I want to talk to you about an assignment I have for you. It's all about forgiveness. For others, but especially for yourself. I can tell you hold a lot of guilt over the pain you caused Brooke."

TJ scoffed. That was an understatement. "I've caused a lot of people pain. Brooke is just the only one I've let myself feel bad about." She looked down at the floor. That sounded so much douchier when she said it out loud. "It's not something I'm proud of."

"I don't think that's the case. The fact that you're even saying that tells me you actually do feel bad, even if you don't realize it. What I want you to do as you feel comfortable is ask for forgiveness and give forgiveness. Write letters to those you have hurt and also those who have hurt you. You don't actually have to send any of these letters, unless you feel inclined. They are for you. Do you think you can do that at some point?"

"Believe it or not, I think I can." And for once, TJ actually did believe it. Maybe forgiveness and a clean slate was exactly what she needed. The only question now was where did she start?

Chapter 22

TJ

"You know you don't always have to come to me, right?" Brooke asked. She was sitting across from TJ at a picnic table at a playground they used to play on as kids. "You've been here the past four weekends. I feel bad."

TJ shrugged. "It's no big deal. I don't mind. Plus, it's the least I can do. For way too long, you were the only one putting in any effort. It's my turn now."

It turned out, TJ had been putting in a lot of effort lately, and it wasn't just with Brooke. Since her therapist gave her the forgiveness assignment a month ago, TJ had apologized to the majority of people in her life she felt she had hurt, most of them being women she had hooked up with. It had gone surprisingly well. Most of them didn't seem to care, the majority pointed out that they got what they signed up for, and some even asked her to meet up again (which she obviously declined).

Two of the people she hadn't apologized to yet were the ones that were still in her life—Candace and Brooke. She owed them so much so she had been putting off their apologies. Plus, between TJ visiting Brooke, and Mateo and Candace spending practically every weekend together here, there, and everywhere, she didn't see Candace nearly as much as before. She made a mental note to change that. She couldn't just put all of her attention on Brooke. Candace deserved it too. She had plans to sit down with her soon anyway and read her list of apologies, so she would make sure to make a whole day of it. Aside from those two, there were two other people she needed to apologize to, but that was a little more complicated, so she would face that when she finally felt strong enough to forgive those who hurt her.

For now, her focus was on Brooke. There was a five-page note (which was the edited and condensed version) burning a hole in her pocket, and if she didn't address it soon, she was afraid she would chicken out.

"Remember how I told you my therapist gave me the assignment on forgiveness?"

Brooke nodded knowingly. She had spent endless hours listening to TJ talk about what was happening in therapy. "Yeah, how's that going? Did you get through all of your girls yet?" Brooke chuckled.

"All of the ones I don't talk to anymore."

"And how many do you still talk to?" Brooke tilted her head. There was nothing accusatory about her question, just sincere interest and maybe a little bit of hurt.

TJ definitely couldn't have that. She needed Brooke to know the truth. "Just one. The only one I ever really wanted to stick around—you."

Brooke's eyes went wide, and she dropped the sandwich she was about to take a bite of back onto her plate. She shook her head. "You don't have to do that. You've apologized to me enough. I know you regret everything that happened. There's no need to harp on it."

"Could I do this though? Please?" TJ cleared her throat and pulled the long note from her pocket. "Even if you don't need it, I do."

Brooke smiled, then reached across the table to put a hand on top of TJ's. "Whatever you need to do. But before you start, I want you to know I forgive you for everything. Truly. I know it might not seem like that given—"

"The fact that I've been friendzoned?" TJ asked with a chuckle. "You don't need to explain it. I completely understand. Just because you forgive me for the things I've done in the past doesn't mean you have to open yourself up to more possible pain in the future." She turned her hand and intertwined her fingers with Brooke's. "Not that I'd ever hurt you." *Don't make promises you might not be able to keep.* "At least, not intentionally."

"I don't doubt that one bit ,TJ."

TJ let go of Brooke's hand only because she needed two to hold the note since her hands were shaking so bad.

"I'm sorry for all of the times I expected more from you than I should have. I'm sorry about all the times you had to rescue me, not just from my biological mom, but also from myself. I'm sorry I waited so long to say how much that first kiss meant to me. I'm sorry I was scared to define our relationship. I'm sorry I refused to come to Woodbury and visit you. I'm sorry that when I came out and the Bakers reacted so terribly that I chose them over you. I'm sorry I broke up with you because I was scared. I'm sorry I ran away. I'm sorry about the year I strung you along." The list went on and on and TJ made sure to read out every single apology, most of them from that last year they had before Brooke finally cut her off. She cleared her throat once more when she got to the last paragraph, blinking through the tears that were now clouding her vision. "Most of all, I'm sorry about all of the times I should have said I love you and didn't. You deserved to hear that every day from the moment we met. I've loved you ever since you took my hand and walked into the middle school with me. I didn't know what it was at that point. All I knew was I finally understood what it felt like to be home. I'm sorry I couldn't be your home in the same way you were to me."

"TJ." Brooke sucked in a long breath. Tears stained her cheeks as well. "You've always been home to me, even when I wished you weren't. That never changed."

TJ nodded. She knew Brooke meant it because she didn't say things she didn't mean. If this was a list of things she loved about her, that would have been one of the top things she mentioned. "In that case, I'm sorry I wasn't the home you deserved."

"You did the best you could," Brooke answered quietly.

"I can do better. I *will* do better. I promise."

Brooke smiled sweetly at her in a way that put TJ completely at ease. "I know you will. I don't doubt that one bit. And even though I didn't need you to apologize again, I want you to know how much it means to me that you did. I know that wasn't easy for you."

TJ chuckled and took a long, shaky sip of her water, spilling some as she sat it back on the table. "I don't know what could have possibly given you that idea." TJ took the last bite of her sandwich then put all of her trash back into the bag. "Want to go for a walk before I head back to my hotel for the night? It's getting kind of cold." *Fall is definitely here.*

"I would love that."

The two walked side by side through the streets of Woodbury, both of them quiet throughout most of the walk. She wasn't sure who initiated it, but at one point, their hands found each other and their fingers remained interlocked for the rest of their walk.

"So, were you able to write any of the letters to the people who hurt you?" Brooke asked when they were approaching the playground once again.

"Not yet. It's hard to forgive people who aren't sorry."

"I know." Brooke looked toward the ground. "I'm sorry your life has been filled with so many shitty people."

TJ turned to face Brooke and put the hand that wasn't holding hers onto her chin to force their eyes to meet once again. "I'm just sorry I became one of them."

"You didn't. Trust me."

As Brooke… her Brooke… looked at her with those loving eyes, TJ actually believed her. Brooke not only made her want to be a better person—she helped her to see the good in herself. No matter what happened between them in the future, she'd never be able to thank her enough for that.

That night, with Brooke's words running through her head, TJ sat down at the desk in her hotel room to write the first letter. She wasn't sure who this one was going to be for until her hand decided for her and wrote, "Dear, Mr. and Mrs. Baker…" After that, the words (and tears) flowed freely.

***

Four and a half months. After four and a half grueling months of living with her parents and commuting to school, it was finally graduation day. Tiffany had no idea where she was going from here, but she knew she needed to get out of the house. Who knew, maybe a little space would be good for them. Maybe it would help her family realize that no matter how many therapy sessions she sat through, her feelings weren't going to change.

Even though she hadn't admitted it to anyone, even Brooke, she was still madly in love with her. How couldn't she be? Even after the breakup, Brooke had stayed by her side as her friend, which was so much more than Tiffany deserved. Not only had she ended their relationship, but she had also been forced to move out of the apartment they shared together. Luckily, she was still able to sneak over there sometimes while her parents thought she was in class. Unfortunately, those times didn't involve her lips on Brooke's and her hands in Brooke's hair like she wished they did. She had an irrational fear that if she crossed the line of friendship with Brooke, an alarm would sound and her parents would automatically know. If they did, there was no way the adoption would ever go through. It had already been pushed back as they tried to "fix" Tiffany's "problem."

As soon as the graduation ceremony ended, Brooke met Tiffany at the edge of the football field and wrapped her in a tight hug. "I'm so proud of you, Summa Cum Laude college grad."

"Thanks, Brooke. Thank you so much for being here."

"Where else would I be?"

Tiffany's gut reaction was to point out that Brooke could be spending time with someone who wasn't too much of a coward to be with her, but she feared if she did that, Brooke would finally leave her.

"Brooke, what are you doing here?"

Tiffany turned at the sound of her father's voice. Instead of finding him with a proud smile on his face, she found him glaring at Brooke.

Brooke didn't cower to the flames he was shooting in her direction. She stood taller instead. "I'm here to support my friend."

Even though that's exactly what they were, the word friend still sounded so wrong coming from Brooke's mouth. That's because Tiffany knew the truth. No matter how hard they tried to be friends, it would always go deeper than that.

Instead of responding to Brooke, Tiffany's dad turned to her. "Do what you need to do here then head home immediately. We have a lot to discuss."

Tiffany looked from her mom to her dad, hoping she would have something else to say. Maybe "Congratulations" or "We're so proud of you." Instead, she simply nodded in agreement.

They turned and walked away with Cyrus, Cain, and Candace following closely behind them. The only one who even gave her a second glance was Candace, who had a look in her eyes that Tiffany couldn't read. It almost seemed apologetic, but that was so different from the sister she had grown to know these past few years.

"What the hell was that about?" Brooke asked once they were out of earshot. "You're not seriously going to go home now, are you? You deserve to celebrate, not be put through whatever they have planned for you."

If fire could truly shoot out of someone's ears, Tiffany was sure that would have happened to Brooke at that moment. Tiffany had never seen her this mad, which was saying a lot since Brooke had expressed her anger toward Tiffany's family many times over the past few months.

Tiffany looked at the sky then down at the ground. Pretty much anywhere to avoid looking at Brooke since she knew she was about to disappoint her once again. "I have to. They're my family."

Brooke scoffed. "Well, then maybe they should start acting like it."

"Please, Brooke, let me do this. I'll call you later, okay?"

"Okay."

Tiffany ignored the disappointment in Brooke's eyes because she couldn't handle disappointing yet another person in her life. She turned around without another word and walked right to her car. She didn't stop to take pictures with the few friends she had made at Sacred Heart. She didn't take a moment to bask in her accomplishment. Instead, she headed home to what was about to be one of the biggest shit storms of her life.

"We're in here," Tiffany's mom called as soon as she opened the front door.

Tiffany followed the voice and walked into the kitchen to find her whole family sitting at the kitchen table. It was far from a warm welcome. They were all glowering at her, aside from Candace, who couldn't look at her at all.

Tiffany's mom pointed to the one empty seat. "Sit down." Tiffany followed her directions and as soon as she did, her mom's eye bore into her, completely devoid of the love that was once very present in them. "We've discussed this as a family, and we don't believe this arrangement is working anymore."

"What arrangement?" Tiffany choked on her words. Her mom couldn't possibly mean what she thought she did.

Her mom motioned around the room. "This. You staying here with us. It's run its course."

"But…" Tiffany shook her head, which was already developing a splitting headache. "You're my family. You're supposed to be adopting me soon."

Her father cleared his throat. "That was before you decided to make certain decisions. The devil is alive in you, and you are allowing it. We will not stand for that sort of deviance in this family."

Tiffany became dizzy as the world spun around her. "But I did everything you asked. I saw the therapist. I broke up with Brooke."

"Brooke is still in your life," her father pointed out.

"That's because she's my friend. She has been forever."

"So, you made your choice." The man sitting across from her, who Tiffany didn't even recognize anymore, pointed toward the stairs. "The devil isn't ugly. We gave you multiple chances to reject your sins. Now you need to leave. You're not wanted here anymore."

Not wanted. Tiffany understood that feeling much too well. Her breathing became labored and her heart raced as she tried to take it all in. This couldn't be real. She finally found a family. There's no way this was being ripped away from her. "Are... is this a joke?"

Her mother furrowed her eyebrows. "Why would we joke about this? You clearly need help that we can't provide you, but I strongly suggest finding it unless you want to be alone forever."

Alone forever. Tiffany squeezed her eyes shut in the hopes that it would somehow make those words stop ringing in her head. Alone forever. Alone forever. "Please, no. Please don't do this."

"You have an hour to get out of here before we call the police and have you arrested for trespassing. It shouldn't be too hard to pack up since we don't want you to take anything that we gave you. Cyrus has offered to drive you to the bus station. We will give you money to get wherever you want to go."

It was all a blur as Tiffany went to what used to be her room and packed one lone bag. She could barely comprehend what was happening as she shoved clothes and the phone she had luckily bought on her own inside of it. At one point, Candace stopped by her room, and Tiffany was pretty sure she apologized for what her family was doing to her, but she couldn't focus on her words enough to know for sure. She was stuck within a heavy fog.

Cyrus was silent as he drove her to the bus station, only speaking when he dropped her off to emotionlessly tell her he would pray for her, which was the same thing the other Bakers had told her right before she left the house. As he drove away, leaving her there all alone, she felt herself snap. The innocent girl she once was now completely gone. No hope left for the future. She didn't know who she was anymore, but she certainly wasn't Tiffany Jane Edminston, *and she needed to leave everything behind that reminded her of that person. Well, almost everything…*

TJ awoke to find herself draped over the hotel room desk, drool running out of her mouth and pooling on the note she wrote to the Bakers. When she looked at her phone, she found it was 2:30 AM, so she dragged herself over to the bed. As much as she didn't want to sleep, scared to death of what she might dream of next, she was too exhausted to keep her eyes open. Just as she feared, she drifted away into the next nightmare.

"What happened?" Brooke asked after picking up her phone after two rings.

"They kicked me out." Tiffany was deadpan. All of the emotions had been swept from her body at this point.

"Oh my God, where are you? I'm coming to get you."

Tiffany looked around the bare room she was sitting in. "That's not necessary. I'm in Philadelphia. I found a shelter to stay at."

"What? Why didn't you come to me? This is our place. You're always welcome here, especially now."

"I couldn't. I can't be there anymore. The thought of being anywhere associated with the Bakers makes me sick."

"I understand. I'll come to you. And while I'm there, we can talk about where we want to go next and I can start job hunting and we'll—"

"No."

"No?" Brooke sounded genuinely confused. *"We can be together now. There's nothing holding us back. I still love you, Tiff."*

For now. Not wanted. Alone forever. No matter how hard she tried, she couldn't stop the voice in her head reminding her that nothing was permanent. Not even Brooke. She would leave eventually, just like everyone else. Tiffany couldn't let herself believe this would be different. All that would do is break her heart even more when Brooke inevitably left her.

"We're not together. We never will be again. I'm meant to be alone."

"You're not thinking straight. Your judgment is clouded."

Tiffany shook her head. *"No, it's the opposite. I'm seeing clearly for the first time."* She hung up the phone without another word.

Chapter 23
TJ

"I wrote your parents a letter forgiving them for everything they did to me."

Candace dropped the piece of pizza she was holding as her eyes widened at TJ. "You did *what*? Did you send it?"

"Fuck no. I'd never give them the pleasure of actually reading it. It was for me... for therapy. I actually wrote it a few weeks ago, but I've been afraid to tell you."

"Why?"

"I didn't know if you'd get mad at me for it."

Candace shrugged. "You gotta do what you gotta do. Whatever works for you. I hope you don't think I'm ever wasting a piece of paper on those assholes though."

TJ laughed. "Never." She reached in her pocket and pulled out the apology letter she had written to Candace. "Speaking of letters, though, this one's for you."

She threw the letter at Candace, who only hesitated for a moment before opening it up to read it. TJ didn't mean to watch her read it, but she was too nervous to look away. As Candace read, tears came to her eyes. The more she read, the more tears gathered on her cheeks. When Candace chuckled, TJ figured that meant she had gotten to the part where she apologized for not telling her Brooke had a good-looking brother. It only took another minute before Candace looked over at her.

She stood up and held open her arms. "Get over here, you big asshole."

TJ walked over and accepted the tightest hug Candace had ever given her. "I love the shit out of you, dude," Candace said with a laugh.

"I love you, too."

"There is something I need to talk to you about," Candace said as soon as they pulled apart.

"Sounds ominous." TJ was joking, but the tone of Candace's voice did have her a bit concerned.

Candace sat down on their couch and patted the spot next to her. "Mateo invited me to spend Thanksgiving with his family."

That definitely was *not* what TJ expected to hear. "Wow. That's huge. Have you guys even had sex yet?"

Candace snorted. "I didn't know sex was a prerequisite for holidays."

"Normally, for you, it's a prerequisite for everything."

"True, but I'm a changed woman." She playfully elbowed TJ in the side. "I'd say we both are, Miss Celibate-for-anyone-but-Brooke."

TJ shrugged. "There must be something about those Finnegans."

"You're telling me. Don't worry, the sex is coming soon. I just want to make sure this time is different, so I'm taking it slow."

"Molasses pace, apparently."

"Whatever." Candace rolled her eyes. "Anyway, since you're my family and we always spend holidays together, I want you to come with me. I know there's a lot of history with Brooke's family, but this would be a good chance for everyone to move on."

TJ knew Candace meant well, but that sounded like a terrible idea. "I agree that I need to face what happened with Brooke's family, but I don't think Thanksgiving is the right time to do that."

"I kind of figured that. I'll tell Mateo I can't come." Even though she tried to mask it, TJ could hear the disappointment in Candace's voice.

"Don't do that. You should go. I could use some alone time to do some self-reflection anyway."

"Self-reflection? Who the hell are you?"

TJ laughed along with Candace. "I know, right? It's ridiculous."

Candace gave her a long look. "Only if you're sure."

"I am. Have fun with your future in-laws."

***

With Candace out of the house, TJ set herself up in their family room with a turkey sandwich and her computer. She pulled up the document entitled, "Never Say Good Morning" and cringed as she read it. It felt like she was reading a book written by a completely different person. In a way, she was. TJ had grown so much in the past few months, she wasn't the same girl who wrote the words in front of her.

She opened a new document and without overthinking it, started typing away. After two hours of working on her new book idea, she shut her computer and pulled out a piece of paper and a pen.

Now was as good a time as ever to write the note she had been putting off so far.

Dear birth-giver,

I forgive you. It couldn't have been easy trying to raise a child all by yourself, especially one you never planned on having. Even though most memories I have are bad, I want to thank you for the few good ones you gave me. At one point, I adored you more than anything in the world. I know something kept you from feeling the same way about me, and that's okay. All of your shortfalls helped shape me into the woman I am today. I'm far from perfect, but I'm slowly becoming proud of the woman I've grown into. I have no idea where you are now or what your life has become, but I truly hope you have also grown into someone to be proud of. Even if it was for completely selfish reasons (I'd like to think that very deep down maybe it wasn't), thank you for giving me up. I don't know what my life would look like if I had stayed with you, but I know it wouldn't be good.

Take care.

TJ figured she would want to tear this note up right after writing it, but instead, she took it into her bedroom and placed it in her nightstand right next to one of the only pictures she had of herself as a little girl. It would serve as a reminder of how far she had come and the possibility of how far she could go.

TJ allowed herself to relax and watch the Thanksgiving Day parade on TV then went back to writing. She went to bed early, since the next day she was going to see her therapist before taking a very special trip to Woodbury.

***

A proud smile spread across her therapist's face as TJ told her everything she had accomplished with her forgiveness assignment. "You've certainly come a long way. I've learned a lot about you, but there's one missing part to your story. You haven't told me what happened during that first year of living in Philadelphia. Do you feel comfortable doing that now?"

"I think I can do that." For once, TJ let her mind wander to the place it only went in the midst of her worst nightmares.

"Brooke! Bestie! I'm so drunk."

Tiffany had barely talked to Brooke in the month since moving away, but now that she was drinking, Brooke was all she could think about.

"Are you okay? Are you by yourself?"

Tiffany shook her head as if Brooke could see her. "No, I'm with my friends Angel and Demi. Shit, Brooke. You should see them. They're both so hot. And fucking amazing in bed. Not as good as you, of course, but I don't think anyone is."

"You're… umm… you're hooking up with other people?"

Shit. This wasn't the way Tiffany had meant to tell her. It's not like she was cheating on Brooke since they weren't a couple anymore, but it still didn't feel right that she was exploring this side of herself and hadn't mentioned it to the girl who showed her who she was. The girl who was supposed to be her best friend.

"Yeah. I'm finally fucking free. I'm making the most of it."

"I have to go."

Tiffany couldn't be positive since she was so intoxicated, but she was pretty sure Brooke was crying. Instead of dealing with it, she took another shot and tried to erase her trembling voice from her mind.

When she woke up the next day with a killer hangover, that voice still played in her head. She didn't think twice before hopping in her car and driving to Brooke.

When Tiffany knocked on the door to the apartment that used to be hers, Brooke opened the door, and the first thing that Tiffany noticed were her bloodshot puffy eyes that she was sure she had caused.

"Can I come in?" she asked timidly.

She wouldn't have blamed Brooke if she slammed the door in her face, but of course, she stepped off to the side and motioned for Tiffany to come inside.

They were both silent as they walked to the couch and sat down on separate ends, the foot that separated them feeling more like a mile.

Tiffany rubbed her sweaty palms on her pants. She couldn't remember a time when she was ever this nervous around Brooke. "I'm really sorry about last night. I was so drunk."

"It's okay." *Brooke's eyes darted around the room.* "I guess it just surprised me to hear you were hooking up with other people. I know you said we were done, but I dumbly thought I still had a chance."

Tiffany had no idea what to say to that. "I'm sorry I hurt you."

"It's okay. You can't help how you feel. If I'm not the one you want, there's nothing I can do about that."

Tiffany scooted a little closer to Brooke, her heartbeat speeding up from their close proximity. "There's no one I want more than you. There never will be. But I don't want a relationship."

"How many girls have you... you know, been with?"

Tiffany swallowed hard. It had been a busy month for her. Something she didn't regret until she was sitting here with the only person she ever loved. "Six."

"Wow." *Brooke picked at a fray on the couch.* "Did you mean what you said?"

"What did I say?"

"That they aren't as good as me."

"No one could ever be as good as you, Brooke." Tiffany reached out and touched her cheek, happy when Brooke leaned into her touch. "It's just sex with the other women. It's so much more with you."

The way Brooke was staring at her with a mixture of sadness, hope, and love in her eyes, was too much for Tiffany to handle. Even though she knew she shouldn't, she leaned in and kissed her, the feelings she had tried so hard to forget immediately returning. She made love to Brooke on the couch before following her back to the room they used to share and making love to her there too. For the next week, Tiffany stayed with Brooke, and they spent every free moment they had together making love.

"I love you," Tiffany said one night as she lay wrapped in Brooke's arms.

"I love you too." Brooke squeezed Tiffany even tighter up against her. "Don't go back to Philly."

Tiffany's whole body tensed. "I can't stay here."

"Then let me go with you. We love each other. We should be together."

Not wanted. Alone forever. No one will ever want you. All of the voices from her past came back to haunt her. "No. We're not together. That's not what I want. I want to live my own life."

Brooke dropped the subject and didn't try to stop Tiffany a few minutes later when she said was leaving.

TJ took a tissue from the side table and wiped her eyes. "I wish I could say that was the last time I did something like that, but it was only the beginning. I flitted in and out of Brooke's life for the next year, coming back to her every time I needed the comfort I knew only she could give me. Sometimes, I showed up in the middle of night. Other times, I called her in tears and begged her to come hold me. Every time, I spent at least a day, if not more, treating her as if she was my girlfriend. Then I would remind myself that no one stays and I'd push her away. I pushed her away until I gave her no choice but to do what I feared most and cut me off for good."

"And that's when she told you she was changing her number?"

TJ nodded. "I gave it a few days, then I reached out and heard nothing back, so I figured she had done it. I sent multiple texts with no response, so I figured the phone number just didn't belong to anyone. That's when I started to use it to talk to her even when I couldn't." TJ chuckled. "Little did I know, I was actually talking to her the whole time."

The next hour flew by as they talked about her relationship with Brooke, the letter she wrote to her biological mom, and the new book she started working on.

Her therapist looked at her watch then back at TJ. "Technically, our time is up, but most of my clients for today canceled because of the holiday, so if you have anything else you want to talk about, I'm all yours."

TJ looked up at the clock on the wall and shook her head. The session had already gone longer than she wanted. "That's okay. I actually have somewhere to be, so I need to go."

After leaving the office, TJ got in her car and drove directly to Woodbury. She drove until she got to the house she spent so much time in while growing up. The house she had at one time called her own. She took a deep breath to steady herself before knocking on the door.

Even though she expected Mr. or Mrs. Finnegan to open the door, her heart still sped up when she saw Mrs. Finnegan standing in front of her. She looked the same as TJ remembered, only older. The soft features and the loving way she has always carried herself were still very present.

Just like Brooke, she had the power to make someone feel right at home with just one smile.

When she didn't say anything at first, TJ assumed she didn't recognize her. How could she expect her to? It'd been years.

"Tiffany." Mrs. Finnegan flashed her a big white smile. "Wow. It's so great to see you." She looked past TJ, as if she was searching for someone. "Did Brooke tell you she'd be here? She's Black Friday shopping with Mateo and Candace right now."

"I know that." Another deep breath. "I'm not here to see Brooke. I'm here to see you. Well, and Mr. Finnegan, if he's home."

"He ran out to buy groceries for dinner later." She waved a hand. "But come in. Come in. It's freezing out there."

As soon as she was through the door, Mrs. Finnegan took her coat and led her to the kitchen. "Can I get you a coffee or hot chocolate or anything?"

"No, thank you." TJ's stomach already hurt from the impending conversation, so the thought of adding a hot liquid only made it worse.

"Sit down. Please." Once they were both sitting, Mrs. Finnegan looked at her the same way as she always did growing up, with a mixture of care and concern. "What do you need, sweetie?"

TJ stared at her hands that were fidgeting on top of the table. "I have a lot to say to you. I'm not really sure where to start, but I guess the best place is with an apology."

Mrs. Finnegan waved her hand. "You don't have to apologize to me."

"I do. For so many things. I'm sorry I never came around when Brooke and I were together. I'm sorry I never once thanked you for everything you did for me. I'm also so sorry that I hurt Brooke. I'll never forgive myself for the way I treated her."

Mrs. Finnegan put her hand on top of TJ's. "It's okay. Really. I've never had hard feelings toward you. Even when things fell apart for you and Brooke, I always wanted the best for you."

"That's the other thing. You might not have had hard feelings for *me*, but for years, I held a grudge against you and Mr. Finnegan. I blamed you for the fact that I didn't have a family because I had hoped you would've taken me back in when things blew up with my mom. I know you don't actually have anything to be sorry about, but I want you to know I forgive you. I've been working through a lot and I don't blame you anymore."

Mrs. Finnegan didn't say anything, but instead, picked up a napkin and dabbed at her eyes.

She wasn't crying, was she? *Shit.* "I'm sorry. I didn't mean to upset you."

"I'm not upset at you, dear. I'm upset with myself. I'm going to share something with you that I kept to myself up until a year or so ago when I shared it with Brooke. I wanted to adopt you, but your birth mother threatened me. I should have known she couldn't do anything to me, but I let fear win in the end. I still haven't forgiven myself for that."

A raging heat traveled from TJ's feet up to her face. *Damn her. Damn the woman who couldn't be her mother, yet wouldn't let someone else do it.* Shit, she was going to have to write another letter after this. This opened a whole new list of things TJ had to try to forgive her birth mother for.

Right now isn't about that, she reminded herself. She forced herself to cool down then smiled at Mrs. Finnegan. "None of that is your fault. I still forgive you."

Really, she should be thanking both her mom and Mrs. Finnegan. If she had been adopted by the Finnegans, she and Brooke would have been sisters. *Ew.*

"Thank you for that." Mrs. Finnegan stood from the table and held out her arms. "Do you think I could get a hug?"

TJ accepted and walked around the table to allow Mrs. Finnegan to wrap her up in her warm embrace. She might not have talked to her for years, but even after all this time, this woman was still the closest thing she had to a mom. TJ imagined this warm feeling in her heart must be what it feels like to be welcomed home again.

When they pulled apart, Mrs. Finnegan turned and looked at the kitchen clock. "The kids should be home anytime now. Do you want to stick around until they get here?"

TJ wanted to say yes, but that would ruin what she had planned. "I would love to, but I actually need to go. I'll be back tomorrow morning though. Could you do me a favor and not tell Brooke I was here?"

Mrs. Finnegan tapped her finger against her nose. "Your secret's safe with me. I'll see you tomorrow."

TJ gave Mrs. Finnegan one more hug then drove to the hotel that had become her second home. *Thank God for unused hotel points.* For the next few hours, she stood in front of the mirror practicing speaking out loud the two words that scared her more than most: *good morning.*

Chapter 24

Brooke

Brooke thought she was dreaming when she awoke from her sleep to the sound of a knock on her bedroom door. Since it was still dark out, she knew it was early and had no idea why someone would wake her up. Unless the house was on fire... and in that case, she hoped they would break down the door.

"Who is it?" Brooke called. She didn't try to hide her groggy voice because honestly, whoever was knocking at this ungodly hour *deserved* to feel bad.

She had to blink her eyes when the person causing all the ruckus walked through the door. There was no way TJ was standing at her door... inside her house... with her parents here. Brooke quickly sat up because if TJ was here, there had to be some type of emergency. "Are... are you okay?"

TJ nodded and took a few steps closer to Brooke, an eerily wide grin on her face. "I'm fine. I'm sorry to wake you, and I promise I'll leave soon so you can go back to sleep." She closed the space between them even more and stopped when she was standing beside Brooke's bed. "I just wanted to come here so I could say...." She took a deep breath and closed her eyes as she blew it out.

When she opened them back up, her smile returned. "Good morning, Brooke Finnegan. I'm sorry it took me so long to say the words that are so easy for everyone else, but I promise to say them to you every day for the rest of our lives." TJ chuckled and rubbed the back of her neck as she looked toward the floor. "Or at least until you tell me to stop. I'm sure if you start dating someone, they probably wouldn't be too happy about another woman texting you every morning."

Brooke was in such a state of shock that she had no idea what to say. Her mouth was dry and her tongue felt like cotton, making it impossible to form any words.

TJ knelt down beside Brooke's bed. "I got myself a hotel for the weekend. Once you get up and around, give me a call. I'd love to see you."

And just like that, TJ stood back up and walked out of the room. Brooke closed her eyes and opened them back up, sure it must have been a dream. When that didn't seem to do anything, she pinched herself. *Ouch.* If she had been dreaming just a few seconds ago, she certainly wasn't anymore. She jumped out of bed, ran to the window, and found TJ's car sitting in her driveway.

This was real. TJ had come into her room, said *good morning*, then left without anything from Brooke in return. Not only that, but she had also promised to say good morning to Brooke for the rest of their lives… or until Brooke met someone else.

Her heart tugged inside of her chest. There was nobody else. There never would be anyone else, no matter how hard she tried.

She ran from her room, down the stairs, and grabbed the first coat she saw before running out of the house. She wasn't wearing shoes or socks, but she didn't care. Just as she had done all of those years ago, she caught up to TJ and grabbed onto her wrist.

When TJ turned around and looked at her with wide eyes, Brooke pulled their bodies close together. "I still want you. Just like I told you after our first kiss, I want you, and I always will."

"Brooke, are you saying—?"

Before TJ could finish her question, Brooke pulled her close and kissed her as if it was the first and last time all at once. As TJ's lips moved against hers, she knew it wouldn't be the last. This was just the beginning for them.

They broke apart when they heard the sound of clapping coming from the direction of the front door. Brooke looked over to find Candace and Mateo walking toward them, both clapping and both with shit-eating grins on their faces.

"It's about damn time," Candace said when she reached them. She pointed back toward the front door. "Want us to find an excuse to get Mama and Papa out of the house so you two can have some alone time?"

TJ slipped her arm around Brooke's waist and pulled her close then looked over at her as she spoke. "That won't be necessary. I'm going to do things right this time. Speaking of which, Brooke Finnegan, will you go on a date with me tonight?"

Brooke's heart swelled. Even when things were good between them, TJ had never asked her out on an official date, mostly because she was scared to put a label on them. "I would love to."

"Should we make it a double?" Mateo asked, wrapping his arm around Candace in the same way TJ had her arm around Brooke.

TJ took the hand that wasn't around Brooke and patted Mateo's shoulder. "Let's save the double date for tomorrow. I don't need anyone else to witness me fumbling around as I try to impress your sister."

Brooke was so distracted by the idea of TJ being nervous about impressing her, that she almost missed the fact that she had just promised to take her on not just one, but *two* dates this weekend. "Did you just commit to two date nights in a row?"

"Two of many. I have a lot to make up for."

Candace went up on her toes to give Mateo a kiss on the cheek. "Sorry, babe, but I'll have to ditch you later today. I need to help my *sister* get ready for her big date."

***

Brooke was standing in front of her bedroom mirror, checking her outfit for the millionth time, when the doorbell rang. TJ told her to dress casually, but she wasn't sure if she had gone too casual with her jeans and low-cut red sweater.

"Are you sure this outfit is okay?" she asked her brother, who was sitting on her bed tossing a tennis ball into the air. He was clearly bored without Candace around. That, or he was just over her asking him so many questions.

"You look fine."

"Fine?" *Ugh.* "I don't want to look fine. I want to look great. I want to look sexy."

Mateo scrunched up his nose. "You're my sister, so I'm *never* going to say you look sexy. That's just weird. Also, I told you I'm not the right person to ask."

Brooke groaned. She loved her brother, but he was useless in this situation. "Just humor me, *please.*"

Her brother stood from the bed and dropped the tennis ball then walked up behind her and put his hands on her shoulders. "You could wear a paper bag and TJ would still look at you like there's a rainbow coming out of your ass." He squeezed her shoulders. "But this outfit is much better than a paper bag. I promise."

Brooke took a deep breath and nodded. She really had no choice but to believe him. "I guess we should go get the door, huh?"

"Yeah. Kind of rude of us to leave our girls waiting out in the cold."

Our girls. Brooke liked the sound of that. "Did you ever think we'd be the type of siblings to date other siblings?"

"No." Mateo chuckled. "Especially not crazy ones like Candace and TJ."

"Who's crazy?" Candace asked when Mateo opened the door.

"Um, no one, sweetie. Definitely not you."

Their voices faded out as Brooke took in TJ's outfit. She was wearing black jeans, a white T-shirt, and a black leather jacket. Brooke casually ran a hand over her mouth just in case she was drooling. Who could blame her? TJ was sexy as hell.

"TJ… you look… wow."

"You like it?" TJ asked shyly.

"Like it? I love it."

"Thank God," Candace cut in. "She changed her outfit about five hundred times, which is saying a lot since she only has three outfits with her." Candace elbowed TJ in the side. "Now is when you tell your girl how good she looks."

"Oh shit. Fuck. I'm sorry. Of course. You look gorgeous as always, Brooke." She made a move that somewhat resembled a plié, and even though Brooke tried to hold it in, she couldn't help but giggle at the sight. TJ shook her head but didn't break a smile. "I'm sorry. I'm really fucking nervous right now."

Brooke reached out and grabbed TJ's hand, happy that she could finally let herself enjoy the tingles that touch sent through her whole body. "It's just me. There's nothing to be nervous about."

"I'm nervous *because* it's you. You're not *just* anything to me. You're Brooke. My Brooke."

Brooke felt a goofy grin spread across her face at the same time an equally goofy grin appeared on TJ's. This was the best date she had ever been on and it hadn't even started yet.

"Gag." Candace looked between Brooke and TJ and rolled her eyes. "You two need to leave before you make me throw up." She pushed both of them toward the sidewalk. "Have fun. Don't get her home before eleven." She winked before turning around and smacking Mateo on the ass. Now Brooke was the one who might throw up.

"So, where are we going?" she asked as they walked to the car.

"You really think I'm going to tell you that? You'll find out soon enough."

It didn't take long after TJ started to drive for Brooke to figure out where they were headed, since it was the only thing she knew of on this side of town. "Are you taking me to the skating rink?" she asked, bouncing up and down in her seat since she was so excited.

"Aw, man. How'd you know?"

"Where else would you be taking me in this direction?"

TJ shrugged. "The prison?"

"I figured that was more of a second date location."

"Very true."

They made comfortable small talk the rest of the way to the skating rink. When they got there, TJ hopped out and ran to Brooke's side of the car. Before Brook even had time to figure out what she was up to, TJ opened the door for her.

They walked side by side through the parking lot, their hands swinging close together but never touching.

"Remember when we used to come here in middle school and we were the only two people from our class who *weren't* on a date?" TJ asked. When Brooke nodded, she continued. "I was always jealous of our classmates who had someone to hold hands with while they skated, but at the same time, I never wanted to be there with anyone else but you. That makes a lot more sense to me now than it did at age thirteen."

"So, what you're saying is you wanted to hold *my* hand?"

TJ walked even closer to her. "I guess I did."

Brooke wiggled her fingers so they lightly brushed TJ's. "Well, now's your chance. What are you waiting for?"

TJ squeezed her hand, but much to Brooke's disappointment, let it drop. "I'm waiting until we get our skates on, because once I take your hand, I'm never going to want to let go."

Swoon. Thank God Brooke wasn't trying to hold in her feelings anymore because TJ's sweetness probably would have made her explode.

TJ stuck to her promise and from the time they had their skates on, she never once let go of Brooke's hand. "If only little Tiffany could see me now," TJ said as she skated backward during the couple's skate.

Brooke giggled as if she was back in middle school. "What do you think she'd say?"

TJ pursed her lips and stared up at the ceiling as if she was really considering the question. "Once she gets past the fact that it's okay for two girls to be together, she'd probably say *it's about time.*"

"She's right about that." Brooke leaned forward and placed a quick kiss on TJ's lips. Now that she decided it was safe to fall, how could she resist?

Once they could barely stand from being on their skates for so long, they went to the food stand and split nachos and chicken fingers just like they did as kids.

"There's one more part to the date," TJ said as they walked out of the skating rink, still hand in hand.

TJ didn't drop Brooke's hand until she opened the car door for her, but once they were both in the car, she grabbed it once again. TJ drove for about ten minutes before pulling into the parking lot of her hotel.

Brooke raised an eyebrow at her. "Your hotel? I don't know what you've heard, but I'm not the type of girl who puts out on the first date." *Thank God this isn't actually our first date.*

"I didn't bring you here to have sex, don't worry. I want to spoil you and prove myself trustworthy before we jump back into bed together. Like I said, I'm doing it right this time."

Shit. Damn her for being so respectful. "If that's not what we're doing here, what *are* we doing?"

TJ smiled a malicious smile. "You'll see."

She turned off the car and ran over to open Brooke's door again then held her hand as they walked into the hotel and took the elevator up to her room.

TJ stopped in front of the door to her room and turned toward Brooke. "Since stargazing has kind of always been our thing, I thought it was only right to do it on our first date. But since I didn't want to make you freeze by taking you to the stars," she swiped her key and opened the door then pointed to the ceiling that was covered with glowing stars, "I decided to bring the stars to you."

Brooke wrapped her arms around TJ and lay her head against her chest. She listened to TJ's heartbeat that sounded as erratic as hers felt. "I think this is the sweetest thing anyone has ever done for me."

"Get used to it, babe." TJ pointed to the blanket laid out across the bed. "Shall we?"

Brooke was about to sit down on the bed when she caught sight of a big cage across the room. When she looked more closely, she realized there was a furry black creature inside. "Oh my gosh! Is that the infamous Mr. Hobbles?" Brooke had heard a lot about him and had gotten countless pictures from TJ, but she had yet to meet the most important man in TJ's life. From what TJ told her, Mr. Hobbles was the one constant in her life for years.

"It is. That's my little boy." TJ opened the cage and pulled out the bunny, snuggling him close to her. If Brooke hadn't been a complete goner before, TJ completely stole her heart at that moment. "Do you want to hold him?"

Brooke squealed in excitement. "Can I?"

"Of course." TJ carefully handed him over and as soon as she did, he snuggled up against Brooke.

"I think he likes me," she said with a giggle.

"Of course he does. He's my son. Runs in the family."

They spent the next few minutes taking turns snuggling Mr. Hobbles before putting him back into his cage.

Brooke laid down and stared up at the plastic stars sprinkled across the ceiling. As soon as TJ was laying next to her, their hands found each other once again.

How did I go years without this touch?

It was a few minutes before TJ broke the comfortable silence between them. "I'd love for this to be a tradition, even after we have kids. I can picture our whole family stargazing together."

Brooke had to look beside her to make sure it was really TJ who was talking. The woman who was afraid of commitment was really talking about kids right now? Brooke didn't know talking about the future could be an aphrodisiac until TJ Edmonds did it. Now, all she could think about was how easy it would be to roll on top of her and touch every spot of that perfect body.

Brooke needed to respect the fact that TJ was being respectful so she forced herself to stay rooted in place. "So, let me get this straight. You don't have sex on the first date but you *do* talk about your future children?"

TJ squeezed her hand. "Only with you."

"I never even knew you wanted kids."

"I did but also didn't. I always loved the idea of kids, but I knew I wasn't at a good enough place to give them the life they deserve. The last thing I want is to completely fail like my mom."

Brooke studied TJ's face, which somehow seemed to have gotten even more beautiful. The woman that she always knew TJ was hiding deep inside was finally coming to the surface, and Brooke couldn't be more proud of her. "You could never be like her. You never have been. You're a really good person, even if you try to hide it." She stuck her tongue out so TJ would know she was only kidding. After they got their fit of giggles out, Brooke became serious again. "I like that, even after all this time, I'm still learning new things about you."

"Promise me something?" TJ asked, the sincerity written all over her face enough to make Brooke squirm with delight.

"Anything."

"Let's never stop learning about each other. Even when we're eighty-five, I still want to learn new things about you."

Amazed. Stunned. Flabbergasted. Those were just a few of the words coming to Brooke's mind in response to TJ's capacity to plan and talk about the future. The very distant future… with the two of them. "Wow. Therapy must be working really well. I don't know if I've ever heard you plan more than a few weeks ahead." Brooke snuggled in close to TJ. "I'm really happy for you, and I couldn't agree more. I want to spend the rest of my life learning about you."

"And I want to spend the rest of my life making you feel like the most important person in the world, because you are."

The two of them lay side by side for hours. Aside from holding hands and cuddling, nothing physical happened, but it was still the most intimate night of Brooke's life.

She felt like she was floating as TJ walked her to the front door and gave her one lone goodnight kiss.

"Thanks for such a great night," Brooke said. She had her hand on the doorknob but wasn't ready for the night to end. She worried if she went inside, she would find out this was all a dream.

As if sensing her hesitance, TJ stepped closer to her and placed a hand on her waist. "This is just the beginning. I promise."

***

The next few months were proof that Brooke wasn't dreaming, and TJ meant everything she said. She called to say good morning everyday, traveled to Woodbury, had family dinners with Brooke's family, and even spent Christmas and New Year's with them. With a new year starting, Brooke had high hopes of what was to come for them. The only subject they hadn't broached was TJ's career. All of the money she made (and was still making) was based on an image of not getting attached. Brooke wanted to ask her about the book she had been working tirelessly on whenever they weren't together, but she was scared to know the truth. She knew the TJ she'd been around recently was the real her, but how was she going to balance that with the image she created for herself?

Chapter 25
TJ

TJ sighed as she looked through all of her emails. Apparently disappearing for the past year had piqued a lot of interest. The old TJ would have loved that. If she had done it on purpose, it would have been the perfect plan. Disappear and get people talking, then come back with a bang. While the ideas she had been tossing around in her mind these past few months would cause a bang, she definitely didn't plan it that way.

She carefully read through each email, trying to decide who she wanted to reach out to about an interview for the book she had been working tirelessly on. She had kept the topic of the book so under wraps that even Brooke didn't know what it was about. The only person who knew, funny enough, was her therapist. TJ laughed to herself as she thought about this. *My, how times have changed.*

When she came across an email from Elon Drumheiser, she deleted it without even reading it. There was no way she was giving that asshole the chance to berate her again. Although, in a way, maybe she should be thanking him. It was that podcast that led to her and Brooke talking again. She shook her head at herself. *Still an asshole.*

Her head started to hurt from staring at her computer, so she grabbed Mr. Hobbles from his cage and laid on the bed with him, trying to think of which interview made her feel the most comfortable. Since this was going to be a *coming out* of sorts, she wanted someone who wouldn't attack or question her. Well, not any more than someone doing an interview is supposed to *question* you.

An idea popped into her head and she clicked on the contact in her phone before she could overthink it. After just two rings, the recipient picked up.

"Are you finally taking me up on my offer to show you around LA? I was about to give up on you," the late-night talk show host said. *Still a hopeless flirt.* "Does this mean you're single?"

"Quite the opposite, actually." TJ couldn't stop the smile that came to her face at the thought of Brooke. *Brooke. My Brooke.* It felt so good to finally be able to say that. There was no way TJ was ever going to mess it up again.

"Oh, do tell. Was someone able to tame *The* TJ Edmonds?"

TJ smiled even wider. "You could say that."

"Always so mysterious. You're really not going to give me more than that?"

"I'd love to, but I was hoping we could do it on air."

"Very sly. It seems you haven't completely changed."

TJ cringed. She hoped that wasn't the case. Looking back, she wasn't very fond of the person she was back when she did that interview over a year ago. "I guess we'll have to see. That is, if you're interested."

"I'm very interested. If I'm going to do this, though, I need a little something. I don't like going into interviews completely blind."

"I have a book that I'm going to release after the show." TJ took a deep breath. This next part was hard, but if she was putting this book out for the world to see, she needed to start somewhere. "I'll send you a copy. That will tell you everything you need to know." *And more.*

"I can't wait. I'll email you a contract and we'll work out the details."

Perfect. Now that she had that taken care of, TJ had to focus on the next order of business. She put Mr. Hobbles back in his cage then sat back down at her computer. She opened a folder in her email entitled "Potential Buyers," where she had saved every email she received through the years offering to buy her app from her. In the past, TJ didn't have any interest in selling the rights and losing that control, but it wasn't as important to her now that she had lost the passion for it that she once had.

After sending a few emails, she went out to the living room where Candace was waiting for her to have dinner. "So, what did you make me?" TJ asked as she threw herself onto the couch.

As soon as the question was out of her mouth, there was a knock at the door. Candace pointed to it. "I *made* a call to get us pizza. You're welcome."

She went to the door and grabbed the pizza then sat the box on the coffee table and opened it up. TJ shut her eyes and breathed in the glorious smell of cheesy goodness. This was exactly what she needed after a long day.

Candace took out a slice and sat down next to her. "So, I was thinking."

Her voice was uncharacteristically serious, which made TJ laugh. "Uh-oh. That's never good."

Candace threw her pizza back onto the coffee table and punched TJ's arm. "Shut the fuck up. I'm trying to be serious for once."

TJ put her hand on her chest in mock offense. "Ouch. What would Jesus think of this behavior, young lady?"

Candace playfully rolled her eyes. "I repeat. Shut the fuck up. Let me talk."

TJ reached out and grabbed a slice of pizza then used her hand that wasn't holding pizza to motion at Candace. "Go on."

"So, our lease is ending in a few months…"

"It is…." *Why the hell is she being so dramatic about this?*

"I don't want to be one of those crazy girls, but I really think Mateo is the one. I've never felt this way before. And, shit, the sex… I don't know why I waited so long. His fingers and tongue are magical, and I love the way his beard feels against—"

Ew. TJ put up a hand to stop Candace. This was getting way too heterosexual for her liking. "Could you just get to your point?"

"I really like living with you, but—"

Oh, now I can see where this is going. "You're going to ditch me to be with your man candy?"

Candace rolled her eyes once again. "You know, it'd be much easier to get to the point if you stopped interrupting me. No, I'm not ditching you. I want us to move together... to Woodbury."

TJ choked on the piece of pizza she had just taken a bite of. Out of all the things she expected Candace to say, that wasn't one of them. "You *what*?"

Candace shrugged. "I'm not married to my job. Hell, I'm still trying to figure out what I want to do with my life. And you work from home... well, when you *actually* work. Mateo and Brooke are both established there. Plus, that's where their family is. You weren't really going to ask Brooke to leave, were you?"

TJ glared at Candace. "Of course not." She might not be perfect, but she would never stand in the way of Brooke's dreams. Plus, she liked Woodbury. She knew she would move there, eventually. She just wasn't planning on it being so soon. "But I haven't even officially asked Brooke to be my girlfriend yet. Won't I look like a crazy person if I ask and then say, *oh, by the way, I'm moving to you*?"

"The only thing making you look like a crazy person is the fact that you haven't asked her to be your girlfriend yet. What the hell are you waiting for?"

"I don't know. I just want it to be perfect."

"You're such a closet romantic." Candace stuck her tongue out at TJ. "Whatever you do, though, don't ask her in some big public way, like doing some TV interview about how you've changed and sealing the deal by calling her up on stage and asking. That's so gross and cliche."

Well, there goes that idea. TJ scoffed to try to hide the fact that Candace had totally just called her out. "Obviously, I won't do that. I just want it to be done in a way that proves I've changed."

"Have your therapist ask her for you." Candace laugh-snorted, as if she thought she was the funniest person in the world. "Seriously, though, what do you say?"

Moving to Woodbury. To be with the love of her life. With Candace. It was more than TJ ever could have dreamed of. Just thinking about it, made her heart feel like it might burst. If this could really work out, her life would be as close to perfect as it possibly could be. "Can I have a little time? I just need to ask Brooke to be my girlfriend, and *then* I'll ask her how she feels about us moving there. Is that cool?"

"Perfect. I'll start looking at apartments."

"Did you listen to anything I just said?"

"Of course I did. You said you need to talk to Brooke. Do you really think she's going to say she *doesn't* want you to move closer to her?"

Touché.

***

After a few emails back and forth with Veronica, they set up a time for the interview. Veronica was excited to get TJ back to her studio as soon as possible, but they needed time for her to read the book after it was shipped to her, so they chose a date that was a month away. That gave TJ plenty of time to put the finishing touches on the book so she could publish it soon after the interview aired. *The joys of self-publishing.*

Now, all she needed to do was convince Brooke to come, and she had the perfect idea how to make that happen. Since Candace was visiting Mateo this weekend, she asked Brooke if she wanted to come to her. Normally, she traveled to Woodbury, but this was the perfect chance for them to have some alone time together, which was important if TJ was finally going to ask her to officially be her girlfriend.

When Brooke arrived late Friday evening, TJ had everything set up and ready for her. The living room was lined with candles, and she had chicken parmesan ready on the dining room table, along with two glasses of wine. In the middle of the table was a gift that TJ had spent way too much time wrapping meticulously to make sure it looked perfect. Now, her only hope was that *Brooke* would think the contents were perfect. She hadn't run her idea past Candace, mostly because she worried Candace would tell her it was a bad idea, which would have just pissed TJ off.

"What is all of this?" Brooke asked as soon as she was in the apartment. She took TJ into her arms and kissed her long and hard.

TJ's heart rate picked up and a tingling sensation started in her hands and feet before spreading throughout her whole body. *I hope I never get used to this.* She loved the feeling of loving Brooke. She hadn't said that word again after things took a turn for the worse when they had sex at the beach hotel, but she was sure Brooke knew. Just like she knew Brooke loved her even though she hadn't said it yet. At least, since getting back together.

"I wanted to do something nice for you, since you deserve all the best."

Brooke pulled TJ closer to her once again, so their noses were touching. Only, this time, she didn't kiss her. "You need to stop saying such sweet things, or I'm not going to be able to control myself anymore."

TJ's breath caught in her throat. Brooke's words, along with the way she was staring at her with hungry eyes, had TJ suddenly so turned on. The two of them still hadn't had sex, mostly due to TJ's insistence that they take it slow. But this had been slow enough. She couldn't take it anymore either.

She bit her lip and smiled at Brooke. "We *do* have the place to ourselves, and it's well past our first date now."

Brooke smirked and rubbed her nose against TJ's. "It certainly is."

TJ felt like her brain was short-circuiting. She knew there were other things she should be considering right now, but all she could think about was getting Brooke naked. *Dinner. Gift. Duh.* "Should we wait until after dinner? I'm sure you don't want to eat cold food."

"Fuck the food."

TJ burst into laughter. That was *not* what she expected Brooke to say. "You almost never swear."

"Yeah, well, desperate times..." Brooke pointed over toward the table. "Sorry for saying that about the food when you clearly worked hard to prepare it, though. It's really sweet, and I'm sure it tastes amazing. I would just rather taste you right now."

Holy mother fucking shit. TJ's mouth was somehow dry, yet watering at the same time. She knew that wasn't possible, but her brain wasn't functioning enough to figure out what was actually happening to her body. Aside from the fact that she was very turned on. "No, you're exactly right. Fuck the food. Let's go back to my room."

She blew out the candles because the last thing she needed was for a fire to interrupt what she had waited so long for. Once they were safe from any erupting flames, she took Brooke's hand and led her back to the bedroom.

Once inside, they continued the kiss they had started in the living room. It was slow and sensual, which was surprising since TJ really wanted to rip Brooke's clothes off. But what she wanted even more was to worship her, so that's exactly what she was going to do.

After making out with Brooke until she could barely feel her lips, she moved her lips to her chin and then onto her neck. She sucked at Brooke's pulse point long enough that she was sure it would leave a mark. *Oops.* She'd definitely have to cover that up before going to school on Monday.

She moved her hands to the bottom of Brooke's shirt and slowly lifted it over her head. She ran her eyes and her fingers over the skin she had been denying herself for way too long. She traced the freckles across her stomach and smiled when goosebumps popped up everywhere her fingers brushed.

"I don't know how I ever convinced myself I could live without this," Brooke said

"My amazing sexual prowess?" TJ joked.

"*You.*"

The word was barely above a whisper, but TJ heard it loud and clear. "I love you, Brooke. I love you more than anything in the world. I always have and I always will."

"I love you too, TJ. I'm so in love with you."

"Hey, Brooke?"

Brooke looked at her with more love than TJ had ever seen from another person. "Yeah?"

"Call me Tiffany from now on, okay?"

Brooke's smile lit up the whole room. "Hey, Tiff?"

"Yeah?"

"Make love to me."

So, that's exactly what she did. She removed the rest of Brooke's clothes, and following her lead, Brooke did the same to her. TJ took her hand and led her to the bed, where she let Brooke lay down first so she could go on top of her. When their naked bodies touched, TJ groaned in pleasure. Being connected to Brooke in this way was better than anything else in the world.

As they continued their kiss from before, TJ ran a hand down Brooke's body and slipped it between her legs. TJ pulled back from their kiss so she could stare into Brooke's eyes as she ran her fingers through her folds. Brooke bit her bottom lip and pushed her hips up. TJ watched every single reaction as she touched her, making sure to give extra attention to the spots that elicited the biggest reaction from Brooke.

When Brooke brought a hand between TJ's legs as well, it was almost too much to take. Her heart swelled with love, her body pulsed, and her skin tingled. Brooke knew just where to touch her. She understood what every sound meant that came from TJ's mouth.

It didn't take long before they lost all control. What started out slow and sensual became needy and rushed. Their bodies thrashed against each other as they searched for release, which came just a few seconds later.

TJ rolled off Brooke and stared up at the ceiling as she struggled to catch her breath. "Ready to eat?" she asked once she could get the words out.

"I am." Brooke slithered away from her and TJ assumed she was going to stand from the bed, until she positioned herself between TJ's legs instead. "The real question is, are you ready?"

Chapter 26
Brooke

By the time they left the bedroom, Brooke was completely satisfied, but also ridiculously starving. She didn't mean to ravage TJ for hours upon her arrival, but once she started, she couldn't stop. Sex had never been the same with anyone else, most likely because her feelings for other people never reached the level she was at with TJ.

She took a seat at the table as TJ lit the candles and reheated the food. Once she was done, she placed the food on the table and took a seat across from Brooke. She picked up her glass of wine, then nodded at Brooke's, which Brooke took as a sign to do the same.

"To you," TJ said. "The greatest woman I've ever known. The one and only love of my life."

Brooke clinked her glass against TJ's. "To us and everything yet to come. This is just the beginning."

TJ took a big sip of her wine, but not even the glass could hide the wide smile on her face. That smile was contagious, and Brooke could feel her own growing as well.

"Speaking of new beginnings." TJ put her wine glass down and picked up the object that was perfectly wrapped in brown paper. She held the wrapped object, which appeared to be a book if the shape was anything to go by, out toward Brooke. "This is for you."

"A gift? For me?"

TJ's face turned the slightest bit red and she bit her lip, her demeanor changing from sincere happiness to extreme anxiety in a matter of seconds. "It's not a gift, exactly. More of a surprise than anything else." She brought her hands on top of the table and nervously fidgeted with them. "It's my new book."

Her book? Shit. Now Brooke was nervous too. She had no idea what TJ would have written that could possibly stick with her brand *and* also be true to the woman she had become. Brooke took a deep breath. She knew the woman sitting across from her. She knew her better than anyone else ever would, and she loved everything about her. No matter what this book was about, that wouldn't change. She wouldn't let it taint how she felt. They had come way too far to go backward again.

Just open the damn book. Her hands shook as she took the paper off. She watched TJ as she did it, and TJ's bulging eyes only made her shakiness worse. As soon as she saw the front cover, her trembling fingers stilled. She ran them over the title. *Taking Back Tiffany.* She immediately turned the book around so she could read the description, more and more tears coming to her eyes with each word she read.

TJ Edmonds—you probably know her as the overly confident, often cocky, player who became famous for her best-selling novel, 11:59, and her app of the same name. In this tell-all from her own point of view, the woman who made a whole brand based around not getting attached brings you the heart-wrenching story of what brought her to this point.

From spending her early years with a drug-addicted mother and in and out of foster care, to the family who almost was, and the woman who should have been (and now is), learn what led her to believe that no one stays.

Follow her journey to taking back the life she lost and showing that scared little girl that there could be true happiness on the other side.

This book is for anyone who wants to believe their past does not define their future. By telling her story, Tiffany (aka TJ) shows readers they can defeat the demons holding them back and create a future to be proud of.

     Brooke had to take a few deep breaths before she could speak. Her heart and head were whirling with emotions. Brooke understood how much TJ had grown in the past year, but this went beyond the confines of that. Even Brooke, who had been in touch with her emotions from a young age and very open about them didn't think that she could write the type of book that this appeared to be.
     "Tiff, this…" Brooke blew out a breath. "You definitely want to put this out there? I mean, you're not doing it because you think it's what I want, right? Because it sounds like you're going to let people into the darkest parts of your life, and if that's only to make me happy, please don't do it."
     "It's not about you." There wasn't even the slightest hint of snark to TJ's words, but she still cringed as if she had said something wrong. "What I mean is that I did this for me. I decided to make my life public when I wrote my first book and created the app. *I* was the one who chose to do a ton of interviews where I showed off my fake persona, mostly because I hoped if I faked happiness long enough, that maybe someday I would be. That's the side that I showed the world, and I did a disservice by presenting myself that way. This is my way of making up for that. It's my way of *Taking Back Tiffany* and regaining power over the life that I let other people rip away from me. But I'll also obviously have you read it and let you tell me anything you want out, because obviously you play a big part in it. I changed the names of everyone I wrote about, but it won't be too hard to put the pieces together that you're Bethany Fitz."
     Brooke laughed, mostly because the name was so ridiculous but also because she had so many emotions bubbling up inside of her and had to let them out in some

way or another. "Especially since you literally used my initials."

TJ smirked. "Touché. That will be the first thing on my list of changes." She reached out and tapped the book. "Obviously, I'm not going to have you read it now, but can you do me a favor and look at the dedication?"

Brooke opened the book and her tears immediately returned as she read the words written. *To Brooke, my person and the love of my life. I'm sorry it took me so long to get here. Thanks for never giving up on me. I'm so lucky to call you my girlfriend.*

Her eyes lingered on that last word for a long time, her heart beating faster the longer she stared at it. When she finally looked up at TJ, she couldn't stop herself from smiling. "Girlfriend, huh?"

TJ nodded and bit her lip once again. "That's another thing I can change if you're not ready for that title, but it does bring me to the next question I wanted to ask you. Brooke Emerald Finnegan, will you be my girlfriend?"

Oh God. Not that middle name. She held up one finger. "I'll be your girlfriend on one condition."

"Name it. I'll do anything."

"Never mention my middle name ever again."

"Consider it done." TJ jumped from her chair and pulled Brooke tightly into her arms. "I do have one other question," she said, her breath hitting Brooke's neck in a way that made her want to drag TJ back to the bedroom again.

"Oh yeah? What's that?"

"I have an interview about my book in LA in a few weeks. Will you go with me?"

"Of course. I haven't missed an interview of yours yet. Now that I'm your girlfriend, I definitely think it makes sense for me to be there in person."

TJ pulled back and looked at Brooke with furrowed eyebrows. "You haven't missed an interview yet? You mean—"

Brooke cut TJ off by placing a kiss on her lips and pulling her tight up against her once again. "It was always you, Tiff. Even when I didn't want it to be, deep down, I always knew you were it for me."

TJ laughed a full belly laugh while tears ran down her face. "Thank God for that."

**

A few weeks later, Brooke sat in the front row for TJ's late-night interview with Veronica Carlson. She watched as the host did her normal introductions and talked about the *very special guest* she had coming on tonight. TJ had told her this host was a hopeless flirt, so it didn't surprise her when she gave TJ a very appraising look as soon as she walked out onto the stage. *You can look all you want, honey. You'll never be able to touch.*

Even as TJ shook Veronica's hand, her eyes still searched the crowd and landed right on Brooke. She winked at her as she took her spot in the hot seat.

"I'm not even sure where to start," Veronica said with a shake of her head. "I feel like I'm interviewing a completely different person than the last time you were here."

TJ laughed her real laugh, unlike the one Brooke had become used to hearing during her interviews. "I mean, you kind of are."

"I guess we need to fill everyone else in on what we're talking about, huh?" She held up a copy of TJ's book. "Let me tell you, when I read this, I was shocked. I knew you were in foster care, but I had nowhere near any idea about everything you went through growing up."

"That's because I didn't want anyone to know." TJ winked in the direction of the camera.

Flirt. Brooke smiled as she playfully rolled her eyes. Some things never changed.

"Without giving away the whole plot of the book, could you give everyone a little insight?"

TJ took a deep breath that was so quick, Brooke was most likely the only one who noticed. "My mom never really wanted to be a parent, and that became apparent to me at a very young age. At the same time, she was too proud to have me taken away, so that led to a life of going in and out of foster care. In my late teens, things blew up for good and she gave me up once and for all, which now, I'm actually very thankful for. Back then, it made me feel like there was something wrong with me."

"According to your book, she was just one of the many people who hurt you by walking out of your life, and that's what led you to decide it was better to not allow yourself to get attached. Is that right?"

TJ nodded. "In a nutshell, yes."

Veronica smirked and very quickly let her eyes drift to Brooke before going back to TJ. "But you're very attached now, aren't you? People have been wondering why they haven't seen pictures of you with a new girl each week. Wanna tell us why that is?"

TJ looked at Brooke once again, and the smile that lit up her face said it all. The love written all over it was something Brooke could only dream about for way too many years. "I reconnected with my first love. My *only* love. The truth is, I never stopped loving her. People who speculated I was a cold bitch because I had my heart broken were absolutely right. Although, that's all on me. I won't go into detail here. You can read my book for that. But I brought that heartbreak on myself. I'm just lucky I happened to fall in love with the most amazing woman in the world, who saw something in me even when I couldn't see it in myself."

Brooke's face heated up because she was pretty sure everyone in the audience was now staring at her since TJ hadn't taken her eyes off her the whole time she spoke. *Let them stare.* Nothing could possibly ruin the happiness she felt from TJ's words.

Veronica's stage laugh pulled Brooke's attention back to her. "So, the woman who created an app about not getting attached is very attached. What now? Are you going to change the app?"

TJ wiped her hands together and held them in the air. "Whatever happens to the app isn't up to me anymore. It's been sold."

This wasn't a surprise to Brooke. TJ had discussed this with her and they both agreed it was for the best. Plus, the amount of money she was receiving for it was more than Brooke could even fathom, which wasn't a terrible thing.

"So, what *is* next for you?"

"Since I sold the app, I have some time to figure that out, but I definitely want to put my time and money into our foster care system in one way or another."

Brooke's mind drifted as the interview continued. TJ already had so many ideas of ways she wanted to help kids that were growing up in situations very similar to hers, and every time she spoke about it, Brooke fell even more in love with her. The way her eyes lit up when talking about it was the most beautiful sight in the whole world, and Brooke would do anything she could to help make all of TJ's dreams come true.

After a few more minutes, TJ's segment of the show ended, and Brooke anxiously bounced up and down in her seat until she was finally able to get up and go see her. As soon as she made her way over to TJ, she hugged her tightly and lifted her off her feet. "I'm so proud of you."

"I couldn't have done any of it without you, babe. Thanks to you, I'm finally excited about the future."

"Speaking of which. I have something to tell you." Brooke had gotten big news right before they left on their trip and had been holding it in because she didn't want to cause TJ any distractions before the biggest interview of her life. "I was offered the Woodbury Middle School Principal job. I didn't accept it yet because I wanted to talk to you first, but it's mine if I want it."

TJ pointed to Brooke's purse. "Call them now and tell them of course you want it. That shouldn't even be a question."

"I just wanted to see how you felt about it. This is going to root me to Woodbury. That means more long distance."

A smirk came onto TJ's face. "I've been wanting to talk to you about that actually. Candace and I were talking and we want to continue living together… in Woodbury. That is, if that's something you'd want."

Brooke leaped into TJ's arms. She couldn't stop herself. For as happy as she had been since TJ came back into her life, this was by far her happiest moment. Her heart burst with love and gratitude for the woman holding her. "There's nothing I want more."

"That's good, because I really wasn't going to take no for an answer. I love you so much, Brooke."

"I love you too, Tiffany Jane Edminston."

Epilogue

Tiffany
Ten years later

"Am I the only person in this house who has any respect for time?"

Tiffany ran out of her bedroom. Brooke's tone was teasing, but she knew it was only a matter of time before she actually got annoyed that the rest of them were moving so slowly.

When she got to the top of the steps, her three-year-old twin daughters with bouncy blonde curls were just about to walk down. She scooped them each under an arm and ran down the stairs with them. "We need to hurry. Mommy is getting impatient."

They both giggled as they wiggled around in her arms. After fostering them for a year, their adoption had just gone through a few months ago, but Tiffany was their mom from the first time they were brought into the house. The same way she was with every child they fostered over the past six years.

Brooke stood at the bottom of the steps, tapping her high heel on the ground, as if she was actually annoyed at them. The wide smile on her face told a completely different story though.

She shook her head at Tiffany. "Cutting it close, don't you think, sweetie?"

Tiffany allowed her daughters to jump out of her arms, and she leaned in to kiss Brooke. "Oh, stop. You love me and my tardiness. It's why you married me."

Even after seven years of marriage, Tiffany still had to pinch herself every time she remembered that Brooke was her wife. It was still so unreal to her.

"Correction. I married you in spite of your imperfections."

Thank God for that. Tiffany certainly had a lot of them. That's why she only waited a year after asking Brooke to be her girlfriend to propose to her. The last thing she needed was for Brooke to finally realize she could do so much better than her. "And I'm so lucky you did," Tiffany said, before giving her another kiss.

Brooke looked down at the watch on her wrist. "Where is Harrison? It's his special day, and he's nowhere to be found."

"I'm right here, Mom," Harrison said as he walked around the corner, his shaggy brown hair only somewhat covering his eyes today and his usual sweatpants and T-shirt replaced with a suit and tie.

Harrison was the first boy they fostered. He was placed with them when he was seven years old and after six years of struggling to gain parental rights, it was finally happening. Tiffany had watched him grow from a scared little boy to a moody teenager, and the amount of love she felt for him was incomprehensible.

Brooke pushed out a long sigh. "And your brother? Where is he?"

"Right here!" a squeaky voice called from the top of the stairs.

Instead of walking down the stairs, their newest foster child, Nolan, slid down the long banister. At five years old, he was definitely their wild child. He had only been with them for six months so far, but he had made himself at home from the moment he arrived.

He was the perfect fit for their family, which gave Tiffany an extra sense of pride, since she had helped to create the new program that aided in the family-matching process.

Tiffany shook her head at Nolan, but she chose to ignore his blatant disregard for house rules and ruffled his wild red hair. "Let's get out of here before we all have to endure a lecture from Mom."

Brooke rolled her eyes at Tiffany and pinched her in the side. "That's Principal Mom to you."

Tiffany reached her hand out toward Brooke. "Well, what are we waiting for, Principal Mom? Let's get out of here."

Brooke took her hand and squeezed it, then the two of them walked out of the door together, with all four kids following close behind. Tiffany unlocked their minivan and ushered everyone inside.

If someone had told twenty-something Tiffany that she would one day be a minivan-driving-soccer-mom, she would have laughed in their face, but here she was living that exact life. As she got into the car and listened to the loud chatter of her family all around her, she took a moment to breathe it all in. This might have been the last thing she expected, but it was everything she had ever dreamed about.

Made in the USA
Middletown, DE
06 May 2024